BASTIAN FAULKS'S b‌...
Possible Life, A Week in December, ...
...*phin Street, Charlotte Gray* and *Birdsong*.

In his acclaimed 2011 book *Faulks on Fiction*, which ...ompanied his series for BBC Two, he wrote, 'If I were ...be quite honest, I suppose I would have to admit that a...cene in *The Mating Season* is probably my favourite in t... whole canon of English literature.' As a lifelong fan o... P.G. Wodehouse, he was delighted to be asked by the W...dehouse Estate to write a new novel using the immortal cl...acters of Jeeves and Wooster.

P. ... WODEHOUSE wrote more than ninety novels and s...e three hundred short stories over seventy-three years. P...aps best known for the escapades of Bertie Wooster a... Jeeves, Wodehouse also created the world of Blandings C...tle, home to Lord Emsworth and his cherished pig, the E...press of Blandings. His stories include gems concern-i...g the irrepressible and disreputable Ukridge; Psmith, the ...egant socialist; the ever-so-slightly unscrupulous Fifth ...arl of Ickenham, better known as Uncle Fred; and those ...elated by Mr Mulliner, the charming raconteur of The ...ngler's Rest, and the Oldest Member at the Golf Club.

In 1936 he was awarded the Mark Twain Medal for ...aving made an outstanding and lasting contribution to ...e happiness of the world'. He was made a Doctor of Letters by Oxford University in 1939, and in 1975, aged ni... ...zabeth II. He di... ...y.

'The voice of the novel is **recognisably and pleasurably Wodehousian** . . . It is surefooted and diverting. The plot is just as twisty and absurd as you'd want . . . Credit to old Faulks. I'd like to see someone try to do this better.' **OBSERVER**

'This light-hearted romp is **delightfully witty**, packed with puns and boasts a few phrases that Wodehouse himself would have deemed top-hole. **Splendid stuff.**' **SUNDAY MIRROR**

'Happily this authorised "homage" shows respectful affection for Wodehouse . . . Faulks introduces a brilliant variation on old themes, with Jeeves forced to impersonate a member of the peerage while Bertie acts as his valet . . . I was soon **laughing out loud** and occasionally forgetting this wasn't the real thing . . . this is a top-hole treat.' **MAIL ON SUNDAY**

'He catches the Wodehousean idiom, periphrasis, **surreal similes and bally silliness** to a T, all done with love.' **LITERARY REVIEW**

'The plot is satisfyingly convoluted **in the best Wodehouse tradition** . . . A genuine addition to my growing Wodehouse collection and there is no higher tribute.'
DAILY EXPRESS

Also by Sebastian Faulks

SEBASTIAN FAULKS

JEEVES

and the WEDDING BELLS

A homage to **P.G. WODEHOUSE**

arrow books

Published by Arrow Books 2014

2 4 6 8 10 9 7 5 3 1

Copyright © Sebastian Faulks 2013

Sebastian Faulks has asserted his right under the Copyright, Designs
and Patents Act 1988 to be identified as the author of this work.

This work is published with the permission of the Estate of P.G. Wodehouse.
The rights of the Estate and its copyright in the works and characters of
P.G. Wodehouse are reserved throughout the world.
First published in Great Britain in 2013 by Hutchinson

Arrow Books
Random House, 20 Vauxhall Bridge Road,
London SW1V 2SA

www.randomhouse.co.uk

Addresses for companies within The Random House Group Limited can be found at:
www.randomhouse.co.uk/offices.htm

The Random House Group Limited Reg. No. 954009

A CIP catalogue record for this book
is available from the British Library

ISBN 9780099588979

The Random House Group Limited supports the Forest Stewardship
Council® (FSC®), the leading international forest-certification organisation.
Our books carrying the FSC label are printed on FSC®-certified
paper. FSC is the only forest-certification scheme supported by
the leading environmental organisations, including Greenpeace.
Our paper procurement policy can be found at:
www.randomhouse.co.uk/environment

Typeset by SX Composing DTP Ltd, Rayleigh, Essex
Printed and bound by CPI Group (UK) Ltd, Croydon, CR0 4YY

To the memory of P. G. Wodehouse – and for all those who have laughed at and treasured his books.

AUTHOR'S NOTE

This book is intended as a tribute – from me, and on behalf of any others who don't think it falls too lamentably short of the mark – to P.G. Wodehouse: a thank you for all the pleasure his work has given. I have been reading him with joy and admiration for almost half a century. I am no expert or mastermind on things Wodehousean; I am just a fan.

The great man's descendants hope, I know, that a new novel may help to bring the characters of Jeeves and Bertie to a younger readership – that lucky group of people who have yet to open *The Mating Season* or *Right*

Ho, Jeeves. I hope so too, and I envy them the joys that lie in store.

To the old hands, meanwhile, I would say only this: that yes, I did understand the size of what I had taken on; and yes it was as hard as I expected. Wodehouse's prose is a glorious thing; and there's the rub. I didn't want to write too close an imitation of that distinctive music for fear of sounding flat or sharp. Nor did I want to drift into parody. What I therefore tried to do was give people who haven't read the Jeeves books a sense of what they sound like; while for those who know them well I tried to provide a nostalgic variation – in which a memory of the real thing provides the tune and these pages perhaps a line of harmony.

I would like to thank Gillon Aitken, Peter Straus, Jocasta Hamilton, Keith Kahla, and Gail Rebuck for easing it all into print, and Edward Cazalet, P.G. Wodehouse's step-grandson, for his encouragement.

I hope that readers of this story will be encouraged to go back to the peerless originals, and thence to a brighter world.

Sebastian Faulks

CHAPTER ONE

I was woken in the middle of the night by what sounded like a dozen metal dustbins being chucked down a flight of steps. After a moment of floundering in the darkness I put my hand on the source of the infernal noise: the twin copper bells on top of a large alarm clock. There followed a brief no-holds-barred wrestling bout before I was able to shove the wretched thing beneath the mattress.

It was a panting and lightly perspiring B. Wooster who then consulted his wristwatch to find that it was in fact six o'clock – the appointed hour at which I was to throw off the bonds of slumber and rise to tackle my new duties.

This was a dashed sight harder than it sounds. Easing the person to an even semi-recumbent position caused pains to shoot across the small of the back. Whoever had designed the palliasse on which I had lain these seven hours had clearly been of the opinion that nature's sweet restorer, as I have heard Jeeves call it, can get the job done in five-minute bursts. It required a steadying grip on the bedstead before I could cross the bare boards and don the dressing gown. It's possible that a sharp-eared observer might have heard a few groans as, sponge bag in hand, I headed down the passageway towards the servants' bathroom.

Mercifully, I seemed to be the first to the ablutions. Hot water came from a geyser in a boiling trickle over the bath, but in the basin the H and C taps might more accurately have been labelled 'Cold' and 'Frozen'. It was a haggard Bertram who stared back from the glass as he plied the morning steel and sponged the outlying portions. I dried off with a strip of material less like a towel than a yard of well-used sandpaper.

It's funny how quickly one gets used to certain things in life. At school we had been compelled, on pain of six of the juiciest, to keep a keen eye on our kit and know at all times where the socks (grey, six pairs) and footer bags (navy blue, two pairs) were to be found. The services of Tucker, my accommodating scout at Oxford, however, and several years of Jeeves's care had left me rather vague in such matters. To say it was something of a trial to dress myself in the uniform of a gentleman's personal gentleman would be an under-statement. Eventually, after several attempts and some pretty fruity language, the shirt, collar stud and tie achieved some sort of coming-together, after which the outer garments were a breeze. Pausing only to rub the shoe on the back of the trouser, I went gingerly out on to the landing and down the back staircase, which gave off a powerful whiff of lime wood.

There was a lengthy passageway that led to the kitchens. I pushed at the double doors and entered the cook's domain with as near as I could manage to a spring in the step. To fill the kettle and bung it on the range was the work of an instant; the problems began with an attempt to locate pot, tea leaves, milk and so forth. I had never previously paused to think just how many items go into the making of the morning cupful. I opened a hopeful-looking cupboard to be confronted by a variety of what may have been fish kettles.

I pushed off into the scullery, where I spied a bottle of milk with a paper twist. A quick sniff established that it was not of recent origin and I was beginning to feel that I was not cut out for this sort of thing when I heard footsteps outside.

Fearing the cook, Mrs Padgett, would not take kindly to an intruder, I made as if to exit towards the dining room, but to my surprise it was the housekeeper, Mrs Tilman.

'Mr Wilberforce! Goodness, you are the early bird!'

'Yes, what ho! A lot of worms to catch, don't you know. I was just looking for the tea leaves.'

'Are you taking up tea for Lord Etringham? Isn't it a bit early?'

'Seven o'clock was what he told me.'

'I think seven-thirty's quite soon enough. Why don't you get on with some shoe-cleaning and let me make the tea in a moment. Goodness me, you've put enough water in the kettle for a regiment of soldiers. Off you go down to the butler's pantry. You'll find polish in the cupboard. And you brought down Lord Etringham's shoes last night, didn't you?'

'I did indeed. Two pairs of them.'

I left the tea-making in the hands of this excellent woman and got down to some spit and polish work on the black Oxfords and the brown brogues, size eight, that I had scooped up the night before. In my experience, the butler's pantry, in addition to corkscrews, candles and other odd bits of chandlery, often holds a bottle or two of the right stuff, but it was too early in the morning even for a constitution as strong as mine. The thought, however, bucked me up a little. I wouldn't say that a song rose to the Wooster lips as I worked, but I went about the buffing and shining with a certain gusto.

When I returned to the kitchen, I found that Mrs Tilman had laid a tray with all the fixings.

'Oh dear, look at you, Mr Wilberforce. You didn't put on your apron, did you? You've got polish on your shirt. Here. Let me.'

With a cloth, she removed most of a black smear from the affected area; and, with the coat re-buttoned, she seemed to think I was ready for action.

I turned to the waiting tray and attempted to raise it to a carrying position.

'You're all fingers and thumbs, aren't you, dear? Nothing to be nervous of. Come on now, this way.'

So saying, the housekeeper waved me down the corridor towards the green baize door, which I was obliged to open with an undignified nudge from the rear end.

Things stayed on a fairly even keel as I crossed the main hall to the oak staircase and began my ascent. There was a square half-landing before a shorter flight to the first floor. My destination was a corner room of dual aspect that overlooked the rose garden and the deer park. Most of the tea was still in the pot when I lowered the tray to the floor and knocked.

'Come in,' said a familiar voice.

I've seen the insides of a few country house bedrooms in my time, but I must say Lord Etringham had really landed seat-first in the butter. I found him sitting up in bed in a burgundy dressing gown with a light paisley pattern that I recognised as one of my own and reading a book whose title, if I remember right, was *The Critique of Pure Reason* by one Immanuel Kant.

'Your tea, Lord Etringham,' I said.

'Thank you. Please be so good as to leave it by the bed,' replied Jeeves – for it was he and no bona fide member of the aristocracy who reclined among the crisp linens of the four-poster.

'I trust you slept well,' I said, with a fair bit of topspin.

'Exceedingly well, thank you, sir.'

But hold on a minute. I see I've done it again: set off like the electric hare at the local dog track while the paying customers have only the foggiest idea of what's going on. Steady on, Wooster, they're saying: no prize for finishing first. What's this buttling business, and why the assumed names? Are we at some fancy-dress ball? Put us in the picture, pray, murky though it be ...

Very well. Let me marshal my facts.

In the month of May, about four weeks before this hard kitchen labour, I had taken a spring break in the south of France. You know how it is. It seemed an age since the ten days in January I had spent at the Grand Hotel des Bains up in the Alps and the pace of life in the old metrop had become a trifle wearing. So I instructed Jeeves to book two rooms in a modest hotel or *pension* on the Promenade des Anglais and off we went one Friday night from Paris on the Train Bleu.

I envisaged a spartan regime of walking in the hills, a dip in the sea if warm enough, some good books and early nights with plenty of Vichy water for good measure. And so it was for a couple of days, until a misunderstanding of swing-door etiquette as I re-entered my hotel early one evening caused a fellow guest to go sprawling across the marble floor of the lobby. When I had helped her to reassemble her belongings, I found myself staring into the eyes of perhaps the most beautiful girl I had ever seen. It seemed only gallant to invite her into the Bar Croisette for something to restore the bruised tissues while I continued my apologising.

Georgiana Meadowes was the poor girl's name. She worked for a publisher in London and had come south for a few days to labour away on the latest typescript from their best-selling performer. I had only the faintest idea of what this entailed, but held my end up with a few 'indeed's and 'well I never's.

'Do you do a lot of this editing stuff on the Côte d'Azur?' I asked.

She laughed – and it made the sound of a frisky brook going over the strings of a particularly well-tuned harp. 'No, no, not at all. I usually sit in the corner of a small office in Bedford Square working by electric light. But my boss is very understanding and he thought it would do me good – help clear my mind or something.'

We Woosters are pretty quick on the uptake, and from this short speech I deduced two things, viz.: one, that this G. Meadowes had a dilemma of a personal nature and, two, that her employer prized her services pretty highly. But one doesn't pry – at least not on first acquaintance with a girl one has just sent an absolute purler on a marble surface, so I moved the subject on to that of dinner.

And so it was that a couple of hours later, bathed and changed, we found ourselves in a seaside restaurant ten minutes' drive down the Croisette tête à tête over a pile of crustacea. After two nights of Vichy water, I thought it right to continue the restorative theme of the evening with a cocktail followed by a bottle of something chilled and white.

Those familiar with what I have heard Jeeves refer to as my *oeuvre* will know that over the years I have been fortunate enough to have hobnobbed with some prize specimens of the opposite sex – and to have been engaged to more of them than was probably wise. One does not bandy a woman's name, though since the facts are in the public domain I fear the bandying has been done and it may therefore be permissible to mention Cora 'Corky' Pirbright and Zenobia 'Nobby' Hopwood as strong contenders for the podium in the race for most attractive prospect ever to pitch over the Wooster horizon. I should also mention Pauline Stoker, whose beauty so maddened me that I proposed to her in the Oak Room of the Plaza Hotel in New York. Even Madeline Bassett was no slouch as far as looks were concerned, though her admirers tended to dwindle in number pretty rapidly once she gave voice.

I can honestly say that where these paragons of their sex left off, Georgiana Meadowes began. One rather wondered whether she should be allowed out at all, such a hazard did she pose to male shipping. She was on the tall side, slim, with darkish hair in waves and eyes about as deep as the Bermuda Triangle. Her skin was pale, though frequent laughter caused variations of colour to play across it. The poor old wine waiter sloshed a good glass and a half on to the tablecloth and I noticed other fellows gathering and whispering behind their hands at the door to the kitchen. The girl herself seemed quite unaware of the havoc she was wreaking.

My task was to keep this vision entertained, and I pushed on manfully, even when it became clear that I was well out of my class — a selling-plater panting along upsides a Guineas winner. But the odd thing was that, although I hadn't a clue what she was talking about half the time, it didn't seem to matter. Perhaps this is what they mean by a light touch, but the long and short of it is by the time the coffee came we were the firmest of friends and had agreed to meet for luncheon the following day in the garden of the hotel, where she could take an hour off from her editing labours. It was a pretty elated Bertram who, twenty minutes later, went for a stroll on the seafront, looking up at a bucketful of stars and hearing the natter of tree frogs in the pines.

Jeeves, once I had put him in the picture, made himself scarce in the days that followed, taking off in the hired car with rod, net and line, a picnic lunch packed by the hotel and doubtless a bracing volume or two of Kant. This left the coast clear, as it were, for the young master, and I found myself reluctant to stray too far from the vicinity of our hotel. There was hardly anyone to be found in town, the French having, it seemed, very little interest in the beach or in bathing or in lawn tennis — or in anything at all very much beyond the preparation of a series of exquisite *plats*, beginning with the strong coffee and fresh croissant at nine-ish and giving the system small respite till roughly ten at night.

Once Jeeves had returned from his fishing, Georgiana and I set off in the car. On the second evening, she persuaded me to let her drive. 'Go on, it can't be that difficult. Please, Bertie. I've driven hundreds of cars before.'

To say she drove in the French fashion would be to cast a slur on that fine people. The pedestrians leapt like lemmings over the sea wall; the roadsters swerved into the dust; the goods lorries blew their claxons. But in all their evasive actions, you felt, there was a measure of respect: they recognised one of their own. The fifteen-minute journey was achieved in half that time, with only a minor scrape along the passenger door as we swept into the restaurant car park.

Despite being put together in the most streamlined fashion, Georgiana took a keen interest in matters of the table. 'Perhaps we could just *share* a few langoustines, Bertie,' she'd suggest after the main order had been bunged in. The days and the evenings passed in a sort of rush, with the air blowing through the old open-top as we drove home, Wooster now firmly at the wheel, and the sound of Georgiana's laughter playing over the drone of six cylinders in top gear.

On the night before her departure, she confided in me the nature of her problem. Meadowes *père* had been a surgeon of some repute, working in London but with a base in the Vale of Evesham, where Georgiana had passed a sunny childhood, mostly on the back of a pony or horse. A German U-boat had deprived her of both parents at the age of fourteen when it sank the RMS *Lusitania*, and though they had left her considerable means, it was held in a trust until she reached the age of thirty – a point still some years distant. Her uncle-cum-guardian, who had taken in the orphan girl and to whom she consequently felt an enormous debt, was now so strapped for cash that he was on the point of having to sell his family house, complete with substantial acreage. The one daughter had fallen for some handsome but penniless fellow, so the only solution was for Georgiana to marry a man with readily available means – and such a suitor had been found.

A proper tact had made her tell this story without actually naming any of the dramatis personae.

'The problem is, Bertie, that I don't love him,' she said, spooning up the last of a strawberry meringue.

She was looking deep into my eyes as she spoke, which made it difficult for me to think of anything sensible to say.

'Rather,' I said.

'But I owe my uncle so much. It would seem so ungrateful, so ... churlish not to help, when the house means everything to him. And how many married couples go on really loving one another anyway? Why not start off on a low flame?'

There was a wistful silence as I gazed into those fathomless eyes, glinting now with moisture.

I coughed and pulled myself together. 'Do you think you could grow to love this fellow?' I said.

'I think so,' she said, but with a sigh that came up from the soles of her evening pumps.

I took a deepish breath. 'I lost my parents at a fairly young age, too, but happily the coffers were unlocked when I was twenty-one and still at Oxford.'

'You were at Oxford?'

I thought there was an edge of surprise in her voice, but I let it pass.

'Absolutely,' I said.

Another pall, if that's the word I want, seemed to descend. Then Georgiana stood up suddenly and said, 'Come on, Bertie. Let's not be gloomy. Let's go to that café with the gypsy trio.'

I felt her take my hand in hers and, pausing only to bung a note on the bill, trotted off with her to the car.

Back at the hotel an hour or so later, we said good-night, exchanged addresses and I wished her bon voyage. She kissed me lightly on the cheek and made off across the lobby, this time without being sent sprawling, and from outside I watched her disappear into the lift. A faint scent of lily of the valley hung in the air behind her.

Then I went across the road to the beach for a bedtime gasper. It was another pleasant evening, but I had the strangest feeling – something I had never known before, viz.: that someone had gone to the lighting fuse-box, found the one marked 'Wooster, B.' and yanked it from the wall.

Unused as I was to this sensation, I found it a relief when life in the metropolis resumed its merry course. May turned to June; Royal Ascot and Pongo Twistleton's birthday do at the Drones were both within hailing distance, and I had little time to think of Bedford Square.

I was in bed one morning, easing myself into the day with a blend of Indian teas and turning over a tricky choice or two – Walton Heath or West Hill for the invigorating nine holes; the lemon-coloured socks or the maroon – when my eye fell on a notice in the Announcements page of *The Times*, and it was only a finely tuned instinct for self-preservation that prevented a cupful of boiling fluid making its way into the Wooster bedding.

'Jeeves!' I called – though I fancy 'squawked' may have been more the *mot juste*.

'Sir?' he said, materialising in the doorway.

'Georgiana Meadowes is engaged.'

'Indeed, sir?'

'Yes, in-bally-deed, sir.'

'A notable development, sir, though perhaps not entirely unforeseen.'

'Come again.'

'One feared the young lady might ultimately be unable to resist the pressure exerted by a persistent suitor and a forceful guardian.'

I scratched the old bean with more than usual intent. 'Sort of a pincer movement, you mean.'

'I fear the military metaphor is an apt one, sir.'

I scratched again. 'I'm not sure. I think it's . . . What's it called when you make someone feel a pill if they don't do what you want them to do even if you know it's not what they want to do?'

'Moral blackmail, sir?'

'That's the chap. Moral blackmail. And this Venables. His surname seems to ring a bell. What do you know about him?'

'He is an author of travel books, I believe, sir.'

'I thought Baedeker had pretty well cornered that market.'

'Mr Venables's books are by way of a personal narrative, sir. The "By" series has enjoyed something of a *succès d'estime*.'

'Did you say the "By" series, Jeeves?'

'Yes, sir. *By Train to Timbuctoo* and *By Horse to the Hellespont* are among the more recent.'

'And have you read these wretched tomes?'

'I have not had occasion to do so, sir. Though I was able to send a copy of *By Sled to Siberia* to my aunt for her birthday.'

'And did she like it?'

'She has yet to vouchsafe an opinion, sir.'

I cast a moody eye back to the paper. A second reading seemed to make the news, if possible, more final. 'The engagement is announced between Georgiana, only daughter of the late Mr and Mrs Philip Meadowes of Pershore, Worcestershire and Rupert, elder son of Mr and Mrs Sidney Venables, of Burghclere, Hampshire, late of Chanamasala, Uttar Pradesh.'

'Will there be anything else, sir? Shall I put out your golfing clothes?'

The prospect of hacking through the Surrey heather looking vainly for the stray white pill had suddenly lost its allure.

'This is no time for the plus-fours.'

'As you wish, sir. A gentleman called an hour ago to see you, but I told him you were not to be disturbed. A Mr Beeching, sir. He said he would return at eleven.'

'Good God, not "Woody" Beeching?'

'He did not confide his first name, sir.'

'Tallish chap, eyes like a hawk?'

'There was a suggestion of the accipitrine, sir.'

From infancy, Peregrine 'Woody' Beeching and I had been pretty much blood brothers – from the first day at private school to the last commem ball at Oxford. Our parents had been the best of friends, and as a youthful partnership Woody and I had seen more scrapes than a barber's strop. I have been lucky with my pals over the years, but I doubt that any had been more like a brother to me than this Beeching.

'Good old Woody,' I said. 'Is he still a bundle of nerves?'

'The gentleman did appear a trifle agitated, sir.'

I laughed – a merry but a brief one, as I glanced back to the tea-stained copy of the morning newspaper. 'What brought him here?'

'He came to seek my advice, sir.'

This struck me as odd, since Woody, while prone to fretting, is not short of the grey matter. Since coming down from university he had made himself a considerable living at the Chancery Bar and was not the sort of man to be found short of an answer – and often more than one, I gathered, when faced by their lordships' fire from the bench.

'You intrigue me, Jeeves.'

'I believe the issue is a sensitive one, sir. As you know, Mr Beeching is engaged to be married to Miss

Amelia Hackwood and one suspects that the path of true love has encountered some anfractuosity. However, Mr Beeching felt it improper to say more until he had properly renewed his acquaintance with yourself, sir.'

'Quite right, too.' I consulted the bedside clock. I had time enough to wash, shave and ready myself for the day before Woody returned. Pausing only to stipulate the eggs poached and the bacon well done, I sprang from the place of slumber and headed sluicewards with all speed.

It was a fragrant if pensive Bertram who at the appointed hour opened the door to his old friend Peregrine 'Woody' Beeching.

'Ah, good afternoon, Bertie. Bit of an adventure for you being up at this hour,' said Woody, sending his hat with a carefree toss in Jeeves's general direction.

'I've been up for some time,' I informed him coolly. 'I have something on my mind.'

Woody raised an eyebrow and made a visible effort to bite something back – a witticism, no doubt, at my expense.

'Good heavens,' he said as we went into the drawing room. 'Are you wearing side-whiskers? Or are you going to a costume ball as Billy the Kid?'

'All the fellows on the Côte d'Azur had them this spring,' I said. 'I'll wager you'll be wearing a pair yourself by August.'

'Not unless I want to look like Soapy Sid and lose my entire practice at the Bar. What does Jeeves think of them?'

'His view is of no consequence to me,' I said airily. 'I have not sought it.'

After a bit more of this banter, Woody got down to business. 'The thing is, Bertie, the reason I needed to consult you, or rather your excellent manservant is ... Well, it's a bit sensitive.'

I glanced up at Jeeves, who had slipped back into the room after the old pals' catching-up was done and now stood like an attentive gun dog awaiting the command to fetch.

'Woody,' I said. 'Remember who you're confiding in. Graves are garrulous, tombs talkative when compared to me. Is that not so, Jeeves?'

'Your discretion has frequently been remarked upon, sir.'

Woody heaved a big one. 'It involves a woman.'

'My lips are sealed.'

'Three women in fact.'

'Even more sealed.'

'Her name ... Oh, dash it, I may as well make a clean breast of it ... is Amelia Hackwood.'

'Woody, old chap, this is hardly news. Your engagement was in the paper.'

'Well, it isn't any more. I mean, Amelia's broken it off.'

'I'm sorry to hear that, Woody.'

'I knew you would be, Bertie. The trouble is ...'

'Get it off your chest, old man.'

'Amelia is the sweetest girl who ever drew breath. I worship the grass beneath her plimsolls, the dance floor beneath her evening slippers, the—'

'We catch your drift,' I said.

'You should see her play tennis,' said Woody. 'The way she swoops across the court, the tanned limbs – good heavens, she even has a backhand.'

I tried not to catch Jeeves's eye while Woody filled us in on Amelia's other qualities. These, to keep it brief, included an outstanding knowledge of lepidoptery (or butterfly collecting, as I was able to establish later); a dexterity on the violin that reminded him of Paganini; and – weighing heavily with her swain – an ardent devotion to Beeching, W.

Into the rich unguent, alas, there had entered a substantial fly: this Amelia, it appeared, was one of those girls who, while themselves most liberally endowed with what it takes, are uneasy if the loved one is in the company of another female. At a weekend party in Dorsetshire, at Melbury Hall, the Hackwood family seat in Kingston St Giles, Woody had made insufficient efforts to discourage attention from a couple of local maidens.

'There was absolutely nothing to it, Bertie. A pair of rosy-cheeked village girls were among those invited to tea. I made myself pleasant, but no more. I thought Amelia would like it if the occasion went off with a bang. The next thing you know, I'm being read the Riot Act. Amelia tells me she can't bear the thought of fifty years of me flirting with anything in a dress and that the whole thing's off.'

'That's a bit rough,' I said. 'But surely she'll come round.'

'You don't know Amelia.'

'No, I haven't had the——'

'She used some pretty ripe language, you know. She accused me of "drooling" over one of them.'

'I say, that's a bit——'

'One of them ran her hand up and down my sleeve a couple of times. What was I meant to do? Biff her one?'

'Perhaps get up and hand round the sandwiches?'

'But they were nothing. Nice enough girls, of course, but compared to Amelia, they were ... they were ...'

For once the Chancery advocate seemed at a loss for words, though I had a sense that Jeeves could provide. I looked in his direction.

'Less than the dust beneath her chariot wheel, sir?'

'Exactly.'

I lit a meditative cigarette and sat back in the old armchair. Although I knew that Woody was as honest as the day is long, I wondered if he was giving us quite the whole picture. As well as making F. E. Smith look tongue-tied, Woody, I should have mentioned, is one of those chaps who seems able to turn his hand to anything. He was in the Oxford cricket eleven two years running, played golf off a handicap of two and, as if that were not enough, in his final year picked up a half-blue at boxing.

His features might best be described as craggy, with the old beak pretty prominent, the eyes on the hooded side and the hair generally in need of ten minutes in the barber's chair, but the opposite sex were drawn to his scruffy figure as moths to the last candle before wax rationing. And being an obliging sort of fellow, Woody enjoyed a bit of repartee with the fairer sex; he didn't like to see a girl's face without a smile or a glass without a drink in it. It took a man who had known him since boyhood to see how little all this meant, because the better part of Woody's mind was always turning over some finer point of jurisprudence or wondering how he could slope off to the Oval to catch Jack Hobbs in full flow. The gist of what I'm saying, I suppose, is that while never doubting the old bosom friend, I was also wondering whether Amelia might not have a point.

While the Wooster intellectual juices had been so distilling the data, as it were, Woody was coming to the end of his tale.

'So I'm to go down to Kingston St Giles at the weekend again, but only because Sir Henry insists I play for his confounded cricket team. Amelia said she won't be seen in the same room as me, but Sir Henry's dead set on winning this match against the Dorset Gentlemen.'

There was an imperceptible rustle, neither cough nor sneeze, but an indication that Jeeves was on the verge of utterance, if invited. I invited away.

'Might I inquire, sir, as to Sir Henry's attitude in general to the engagement of yourself to his daughter?'

'Grudging,' said Woody. 'And hedged about with caveats and provisos.'

'Indeed, sir?'

I think I may have missed the odd detail of Woody's story, but not the choice morsel with which he now concluded.

'Yes. Sir Henry needs a very large sum of money to save Melbury Hall, where his family have lived for nine generations. Otherwise it will be sold to a private school. Either his daughter or his ward must provide the where-withal through marriage.'

'And if I might be so delicate as to inquire, sir, whether—'

'I know what you're trying to ask, Jeeves. The Beeching fortune was lost some time ago. An unwise speculation on the Canadian Pacific Railroad by my grandfather. I've no more than what I earn. Sir Henry told me he can't bless my union with Amelia unless his ward brings home the bacon.'

I don't know if you'd spotted anything in the set-up Woody was describing, but if I say a faint tinkling had started in the Wooster brain a minute or so back, I now felt like Quasimodo on New Year's Day as sounded by a bell-ringer with plenty to prove.

'And is she?' I inquired.

'Is who what?' said Woody, rather testily, I thought, as though the two great brains had forgotten I was in the room.

'Is the ward bringing home the bacon?' I glossed.

'Up to a point,' said Woody. 'She's engaged to a chap who has the stuff in sackfuls, but her heart's not in it. She's a dutiful girl, but she's a romantic deep down, like all girls. I'm not convinced she'll get to the church door, let alone the altar.'

'A most parlous state of affairs, sir,' said Jeeves.

His eye met mine and his right hand rose a fraction of an inch – a gesture that in Jeeves's world was tantamount to jumping up and down with a fistful of red flags. I took the hint and kept the lips sealed.

'So what do you suggest I do, Jeeves?' said Woody.

'I regret to say that I have no advice to offer, sir. The situation is most delicate.'

'Is that it? Have you lost your touch, Jeeves?'

'I feel sure, sir, that the problem will be susceptible of a solution in due course. Meanwhile, I would strongly advise a return to Kingston St Giles as soon as may be convenient. An outstanding performance on the cricket field could well go some way towards mollifying Miss Hackwood. As a keen sportswoman herself, she would be sure to appreciate a display of skill from her fiancé.'

'Ex-fiancé,' said Woody gloomily.

'And lay off the girls, Woody. Talk only to other chaps.'

'Thank you, Bertie. I don't know how you come up with these things. I would never have thought of that by myself.'

This having pretty much concluded the business part of the interview, I suggested that Woody might like to join me in a stroll before looking into the Drones for a bite of lunch. Mondays generally saw a rather toothsome buffet, with cold fowl and lamb cutlets *en gelée* to the fore.

'A zonker beforehand, do you think?' said Woody. 'Just to whet the appetite?'

This 'zonker' was a drink whose secrets Woody had been taught by the barman at his Oxford college and had in turn shared with old Upstairs Albert at the Drones. It involved gin, bitters, a slice of orange, some sweetish vermouth, a secret ingredient and then a fair bit more gin, with ice. It tasted of little more than sarsaparilla, but invariably made the world seem a happier place.

'Perhaps just one,' I said.

'No more,' concurred Woody. 'Then I'm going off to do a stint on the Piccadilly Line.'

'You're doing what?'

'Surely even you, Bertie, are aware that there's been a General Strike?'

'I thought that had all been sorted out and that the lads had gone back to work with a song on their lips.'

'It's officially over but there are one or two lines still not back to normal. Some other chaps at the Bar have roped me in. My shift starts at four. You should think about doing it yourself. You might not get another chance to drive a train.'

'I rule nothing out, Woody,' I said. 'So long as I don't get set on by the frenzied mob.'

What with one thing and another it was almost five by the time I got home. After Woody had left for his public transport duties, I picked up a game of snooker pool with Oofy Prosser and Catsmeat Potter-Pirbright, who was resting between dramatic roles, and this, as chance would have it, went to a profitable third frame.

As I latchkeyed myself back into Wooster GHQ, I was aware of the smell of fresh Darjeeling and, unless I was mistaken, a spot of toast. Jeeves has an instinct for the hour of my return and for the sort of fillip that's needed.

I was scanning the evening paper when he duly shimmied in with the needful. Alongside the buttered t. was an unopened telegram, and I didn't like the look of it.

'Who the devil's this from, Jeeves?'

'I should not care to hazard a guess, sir.'

I uttered a small cry as I saw the name of the sender. It took a certain mental steel to read the contents in full.

They were as follows: 'WOULD BE GRATEFUL USE OF YOUR SPARE ROOM WEDNESDAY FOR FIVE DAYS STOP BUILDING WORK MAKES HOUSE UNINHABITABLE STOP URGENT ERRANDS LONDON STOP WILL HAVE THOMAS SUNDAY STOP HALF-TERM. STOP. AGATHA WORPLESDON'.

CHAPTER
=TWO=

I handed the beastly thing to Jeeves without a word. If there is one thing to strike fear into the belly more than the prospect of a visit from Aunt Agatha, it is the prospect of a visit from Aunt Agatha with young Thos in tow.

'Ye gods, Jeeves,' I said. 'It's like piling whatsit on whatsit.'

'Pelion upon Ossa, sir.'

New readers, as they say, start here; the old lags familiar with the Wooster family set-up might like to practise a scale or two on the piano while I bring the tyros up to the mark on the important distinction to be made between my Aunt Dahlia who, though loud of voice and firm of view, is on the side of the Seraphim, Dominions and Powers, and this Aunt Agatha, who is so deeply imbued with shades of darkness that in the aftermath of bloodletting even Vlad the Impaler might have yielded her first dibs with stake and mallet. And that, by way of background, is all I have time for at the moment.

'What on earth am I to do, Jeeves?'

'Might I suggest you offer her ladyship the run of the apartment, sir?'

'Have you gone off your trolley, Jeeves?'

'I trust not, sir. My thinking was that—'

'I know what your thinking was,' I said, as inspiration came to me – suddenly, as it does. 'Your thinking was something to do with my side-whiskers, wasn't it? Rather like your inability to offer any help to young Woody this morning. Tell me, Jeeves, man to man. Is this a General Strike?'

'Not at all, sir. I have no opinion as to your facial hair. It is not my place. Mr Beeching's predicament is one I would wish to consider more deeply before offering counsel. As for Lady Worplesdon, sir, I thought you might wish to make such accommodation available to her on the grounds that you yourself would be absent from the premises.'

I mulled this over for a moment. 'Absent, did you say?'

'Yes, sir. I thought a number of birds might be dispatched with a single stone, as it were.'

'You speak in riddles, Jeeves.'

'The matter is a delicate one, sir.'

'You are among friends.'

'Thank you, sir. Mr Beeching's future happiness seems to depend on the successful outcome of another tryst, or engagement. The lady in question, Miss—'

I held up a policeman's hand. 'One does not bandy, Jeeves.'

'Indeed not, sir. Might I refer to recent events on the Côte d'Azur and to what one might call the Female Lead or Principal in the drama?'

'You might, Jeeves.'

'Thank you, sir. It will not have escaped your attention that this Female Lead—'

'Or Principal.'

'Indeed, or Principal, has a crucial part to play in Mr Beeching's future.'

'The hypothetical bacon bringer-home and the Côte d'Azur Female Lead being one and the same girl, you mean.'

'Almost certainly, sir. It occurred to me that if you were to take up residence at Kingston St Giles for a short time, you might be able to assist Mr Beeching——'

'Or at any rate you could, Jeeves.'

'I should give it my best endeavours, sir. It would further enable you to renew acquaintance with certain persons, should you so desire it, and...'

'I desire it like billy-ho, Jeeves. Though at a distance. And with conditions. She is engaged to another fellow.'

'... And furthermore to relieve yourself of any irksome aspects of the proposed familial visit.'

He had a point, I thought. But there was also a sizeable snag. 'I can't just telephone this Hackwood fellow and invite myself to stay. It's not as though I'm a Ranjitsinhji either. I shouldn't be bringing much to the cricketing party, if invited.'

'I would think it most unwise to alert Sir Henry to your presence, sir. I feel sure that by now he will have been informed of certain events upon the Côte d'Azur and would not wish to issue any such invitation.'

'You mean the Wooster name is already mud as far as he's concerned.'

'I have formed the impression that he is a gentleman of a determined character, sir, and has concluded that the advantageous alliance of his ward is his only hope of financial salvation. One would not wish to be the impediment in his path.'

'And this ward ... You think she will have spilled the beans to him about those innocent evenings on the Croisette?'

'Perhaps not directly to Sir Henry, sir, but almost certainly to her coeval, Miss Hackwood. And once such intelligence has entered the distaff side, it is generally only a matter of time before—'

'Lady H gets to hear the hot gossip and fills in the old boy.'

'I fear it is inevitable, sir.'

I drew in a pensive one and let it out again slowly between the front teeth. 'What do you suggest?'

'It has been our wont on previous occasions, sir, to avail ourselves of a small cottage, there to observe and await developments.'

'Like Wee Nooke, you mean.'

'Yes, sir.'

I shuddered. 'Though less likely to go up in flames, I hope.'

'A lack of such combustibility would be a decided advantage, sir. I took the liberty while you were at luncheon of making some inquiries by telephone. A local agent has offered use of a three-bedroom dwelling by the name of Seaview Cottage. It is within walking distance of Melbury Hall and enjoys fine views to the south.'

I drained the last of the reviving cup and put it firmly back in the saucer. I had made up my mind. 'Jeeves,' I said. 'All roads lead west. Please compose a gracious telegram to Aunt Agatha, giving her the run of the whole bally place. And apologising for my absence on urgent business. Key to be left with Mrs Tinkler-Moulke.'

'As you wish, sir.'

A thought struck me. 'I say, Jeeves, won't you mind missing Ascot?'

'I feel my duty lies elsewhere, sir.'

'Jolly decent of you. I'm sure we can find a book-maker in Sherborne or somewhere. Pack at least two bags. We could be in for the long haul.'

'I have already done so, sir.'

'Good. We leave at dawn. Or ten-ish, anyway. And, Jeeves?'

'Yes, sir?'

'I suppose you'd better bung in a pair of cricket flannels, if I still have any. Just in case.'

'The item was among the first to go into the suitcase, sir.'

Whether it was the fear that Aunt Agatha might arrive early or for some other reason I couldn't say, but the sole of the right brogue was no more than an inch from the floor of the two-seater when Stonehenge slid past to our right. Jeeves was giving me the lowdown on the novels of Thomas Hardy as we turned off and motored over Cranborne Chase into the depths of Dorsetshire.

'Sounds a pretty gloomy sort of bird,' I said, as he reached the big finale of *Jude the Obscure*.

'His is undoubtedly not the sunniest of dispositions, sir. The poetry to which he has returned in later life has—'

'Shall we leave the poetry for another day, Jeeves?'

'As you wish, sir.'

We broke our journey with a ham sandwich and a glass of ale in the small and silent village of Darston. Although we were his only customers, the innkeeper eyed us with a wariness that verged on the hostile. It can't have been the appearance, since we were both wearing simple clothes to let us pass as holiday-makers at our destination. The beer took an age to trickle from the barrel and the ham seemed to have been cut from a porker ill-fated enough to have featured in the novels of T. Hardy.

We did not linger, and with the help of the Gazeteer and a letter from the house agent, it was not long before Jeeves guided us into the village of Kingston St Giles and thence the gravelled area in front of Seaview Cottage. Here I let the faithful motor take a blow while Jeeves unloaded the bags.

Seaview Cottage had a thatched roof and white-washed walls. The accommodations were on the modest side, though adequate for our purposes. While Jeeves unpacked, I pottered round a pleasant patch of garden with some roses just coming out and a few rows of beans. As for a view of the sea, we appeared to be a good twenty miles inland, though I daresay a hawk with a strong telescope hovering a few feet above the chimney pot might have made out a smudge of distant ocean.

In the village, we had driven past a post office, a grocer and a butcher as well as a brace of inns, and I now dispatched Jeeves to send a telegram to Woody at Melbury Hall, advising of our arrival. As I may have mentioned, Woody, though brainy, is about as highly strung as Suzanne Lenglen's tennis racquet. I didn't want him letting off a startled, 'Blow me down, it's Bertie Wooster!' if he bumped into me in lane or meadow. I also instructed Jeeves to bring in some supplies and see what either of the public houses might provide by way of dinner.

Then I took a deckchair into the garden, removed the tie, rolled up the sleeves and opened *By Pullman to Peking*, by Rupert Venables, which I had had sent round from the bookshop before we left. I had been surprised to find that it was signed by the author on the title page, but Jeeves told me it was common for authors to scribble in as many copies as they could, since this meant the bookshop could not return them unsold to the publisher.

It knocked me back a bit. I suppose I had expected something of a yarn or an adventure, but this Venables recounted his journey from first idea, to booking office, to tram, to terminus, in the same tone. He reminded me of someone – though for a moment I struggled to remember who. It was on page thirty-four, in the boat train from Victoria, in which Venables described each of the passengers in his compartment, that it came to me: it was 'Stodgy' Stoddard, the club bore at the Drones, around whom there was always a blast area where other lunchers had evacuated the vicinity. 'The next person to come into the compartment, was a nondescript middle-aged man of oriental or perhaps Eurasian descent,' wrote Venables; but it wasn't worth finding out about this chap because it turned out that after Boulogne he slung his hook and disappeared.

After an hour or so, I put down the book, not without a certain relief, I admit, though also with a fair degree of puzzlement. How on earth had Georgiana allowed herself to become hitched to such a fellow? The only thing I could think of was that he must be livelier in the flesh; and if not, there must have been a dozen others better suited within the county boundary.

I took a turn about the garden, mulling over this oddity. I had just gone back into the house with a view to starting *The Mystery of the Gabled House*, a copy of which I had seen on the hall bookshelf, when Jeeves let himself in.

'What ho,' I said. 'Telegram dispatched?'

'Indeed, sir, though in the event, it proved unnecessary, since I encountered Mr Beeching in person outside the greengrocer's.'

It is not often that one sees Jeeves rattled, but I had the distinct impression that all was not as it should have been. For a start, I had expected to see his arms full of local produce: eggs from contented hens, a slab of yellow butter, peas fresh from the allotment and so forth. But he was empty-handed.

'Is everything all right, Jeeves?'

He coughed a couple of times. 'As we were conversing, we were joined by Sir Henry Hackwood, who was riding a horse.'

'Golly,' I said.

'Indeed, sir. I am sorry to say that Mr Beeching seemed somewhat nonplussed by events. He appeared to think Sir Henry required an explanation of our acquaintance.'

'Even though you're not dressed as a valet or—'

'Indeed, sir. Mr Beeching introduced Sir Henry to

me, but when it came to supplying my name in return, he grew agitated.'

'He panicked, you mean.'

'Doubtless he is anxious to make a good impression on the man he hopes will be his father-in-law and this may account for—'

'What did the silly ass say?'

'He . . . improvised, sir. He introduced me as a friend of his family, Lord Etringham.'

'He did what?'

'He introduced me to Sir Henry as Lord Etringham, sir.'

'Who on earth is Lord Etringham?'

'I have not yet been able to establish, sir.'

'Dear, oh dear. This is no good at all,' I said.

'I suppose that on the spur of the moment, sir, Mr Beeching thought it best not to mention your own name – as a more accurate introduction would have necessitated.'

'Hackwood having me marked down as public enemy number one, you mean? I suppose I can see his point. Anyway, there's no harm done. You won't bump into him again.'

Jeeves coughed. 'I fear matters may develop further. Sir Henry is a gentleman who appears keenly aware of matters of social standing.'

'A corking snob, you mean. Yes, I'd heard as much at the Drones.'

'On being informed, or rather misinformed, that I was a member of the peerage, Sir Henry reined in his horse. His interest seemed to quicken considerably.'

'How quick did it get?'

'He invited me to dine at Melbury Hall tonight.'

I let out a short, mirthless one. 'What a daft old buffer.'

Jeeves looked down at his shoes for a moment, then cleared his throat. 'I regret, sir, that in the circumstances I deemed it best to accept.'

'What? But Jeeves, you can't——'

'There seemed no other available course of action, sir.'

Well, I saw what he meant, of course. He couldn't really say, No thanks, I'd rather have a pork pie and a pint of shandygaff at the Dog and Whistle. Even so ...

'Golly, Jeeves. This is tricky.'

'In the short walk back from the post office, sir, I examined the matter from a number of angles. I feel that

I may be able to carry off the subterfuge successfully so long as Sir Henry is not able to consult any reference books on the peerage and baronetage.'

'Come again, Jeeves.'

'A glance at Burke or Debrett, sir, might inform Sir Henry that his lordship and I are of different ages, for instance. There would be further detail about the seat and the family, and should Sir Henry raise such matters conversationally—'

'You'd be in the soup. Though you could telephone one of your pals and get him to look up the address of the country digs, number of children and so on.'

'Most probably. It is the age question which I fear may be insuperable, sir.'

'His lordship might be a lean and slipper'd pantaloon, you mean.'

'Indeed, sir. Or a whining schoolboy with his satchel and shining—'

'I catch your drift, Jeeves.'

I replaced *The Mystery of the Gabled House* on the shelf, as I needed a spare hand to rub the old bean.

After a few moments, I said, 'We don't know for sure that he has these books, do we?'

'I fear, sir, that for a gentleman of Sir Henry's interests and disposition they would be a *sine qua non*.'

'A cine-what?'

'They would form the cornerstone of his library, sir.'

'So what do you suggest? Burn down the library? Like the chap at where was it?'

'Alexandria, sir. No, I think such drastic action unnecessary. I judge it would suffice merely to remove the volumes in question.'

'To pinch them, you mean.'

'To rehouse them temporarily elsewhere, sir.'

'Then he could just ring up a pal and ask him to read out the entry on old Etringham. You haven't thought this one through, Jeeves.'

'With respect, sir, I had foreseen the problem you raise. It may be necessary for the telephone line to be temporarily disabled.'

'This is all getting a bit much,' I said. 'Don't you think it would be better to beat a swift retreat?'

'Where to, sir?'

The penny dropped with a nasty clang. I couldn't go back to London, where Aunt Agatha had by now installed herself in my flat and for all I knew was at this moment preparing the first of her human sacrifices.

'Anywhere,' I said. 'Cornwall would do. Or we could catch a Channel ferry from Poole and lie low in Dieppe until the trouble blows over.'

'I had the strong impression, sir, that Mr Beeching is relying on our help. The question of his future happiness is a grave one.'

I said nothing for a longish time while I stared out of the back window over the cottage garden. Woody was my brother in all but fact. His plight looked pretty desperate, seeming to hang on the whim of this sports-mad old snob. And then there was the Georgiana complication .... In that particular foggy business, I couldn't at this moment make out the wood for the trees, but one thing seemed fairly certain: this was no time to leave the forest.

'Jeeves,' I said. 'There is a tide in the whatsit of men ...'

'So I am given to understand, sir.'

'So you'd better get up to the Hall pretty sharpish and do your dirty work before Sir Henry gets back from his ride and curls up with Debrett.'

There was a pause, a longish one.

'I say, Jeeves?'

'Yes, sir?'

'You're not saying anything.'

Jeeves went through a bit more of the old coughing and shoe-staring routine.

'What is it, Jeeves? Out with it.'

'I fear it would be ill-advised for a member of the peerage to be seen in the vicinity of the Hall with wire-cutters, sir, or books that did not belong to him. It would give the wrong impression.'

'But you're not going to be seen, Jeeves. This is a smash-and-grab operation. In, out, and back to Seaview Cottage in fifteen minutes flat, books in hand. We lower a snootful to toast your success, bung you into some evening clothes and shove you back up the drive as Lord E.'

'I fear the danger of discovery is too great, sir. After all, the Hall is home to Lady Hackwood, Miss Hackwood and Miss Meadowes in addition to Sir Henry. I gained the impression that there are further house guests as well as a sizeable domestic staff on the premises.'

'Then if it's too risky, we'd better leave old Woody in the lurch and repack the bags. Unless of course . . .

You're not suggesting ... Jeeves, I absolutely ... Under no circumstances...'

'In the event of your being discovered, sir, you would have the advantage of being unknown to Sir Henry.'

'What if he rings the police? Are you suggesting I give a false name?'

'If you remember, sir, on the occasion of Boat Race night—'

'All right, all right, it wouldn't be the first time. I suppose Eustace H. Plimsoll, of The Laburnums, Alleyn Road, could make a comeback by popular demand. For one night only. At a pinch. But it's not a pinch I intend to feel.'

'Such an expedient might be wise, sir. I feel it would be most unfortunate were Sir Henry to discover that an intruder in his house was the same person as the gentleman whose social activities on the Côte d'Azur had threatened to block his path to financial salvation.'

I put my foot down. 'Damn it, Jeeves, I simply can't go through with this. Woody or no Woody.'

I was still protesting silently when I found myself slinking up the back drive of Melbury Hall some ten minutes later.

I am something of a connoisseur of the country pile and I must say old Sir Henry had done himself remarkably well. At a guess I would say it was from the reign of Queen Anne and had been bunged up by a be-wigged ancestor awash with loot from the War of the Spanish Succession or some such lucrative away fixture. This ancient Hackwood had stinted himself on neither grounds nor messuages. The ensemble reached as far as the eye could see, taking in deer park, cricket pitch, lawns and meadows as well as walled kitchen gardens and a stable block that could have quartered the Household Cavalry. The staff needed for such a place must have drawn on every household in Kingston St Giles and I could see that whoever signed the yearly cheque to the electricity company would need a tumblerful of something strong to nerve him for the task.

I got a good squint at the pile itself, a handsome affair in reddish brick with stone bits here and there and a parapet above the second-floor bedrooms. A wide terrace faced south, and I guessed that if I could get there unobserved I could quickly ascertain which of the ground-floor rooms contained the library. Fortunately, the Hackwoods were fond of trees – cedars in particular – and it was easy enough for a chap who had so often played Red Indian scout to Woody Beeching's Masked Cowboy to approach unobserved.

It would be an exaggeration to say that I was enjoying myself, but the sinews were stiffened up like anything as I ducked down beneath the first windowsill. After a pause to regain the breath, I risked a glance inside. It was a half-acre drawing room, with two wooden columns either side of a broad flight of three wooden steps. It also contained three elderly women, one younger one, possibly Amelia, a spindly fellow of about forty, an old codger in full flow and a butler of solemn aspect handing round the teacups. I ducked down sharpish and stole forwards to the next opening.

Raising the beak cautiously over the sill, I was rewarded by a glimpse of books, and plenty of them. I risked another look and got a full snapshot. There was only one thing I wanted more than a library and that was a library devoid of Hackwoods; it seemed that I had hit the bullseye at the second attempt. Gently, I tested the lower section of window. It rose. I looked down to make sure the footing was adequate to heave myself through the opening. As I did so, I noticed a small box attached to the outer wall at ankle height. The Wooster fortunes seemed to be getting juicier by the moment, for unless I was mistaken this was the telephone connection. I have never been much of a one for the practical aspects of life and I feared that if I used the implement that Jeeves had given me to snip the flex I might go up in smoke. I judged it wiser to give the cable a firm upward yank, and to my delight it yielded at once. I concealed the disconnected wires as best I could behind the box and moved on to part two of the operation.

Effecting an entrance was simple enough; finding the relevant brace of volumes looked an altogether trickier prospect. A complete set of *Wisden Cricketers' Almanack* took up one bookcase. Another comprised stud books devoted to matters of livestock and horse breeding. Military history, with special ref to the Hundred Years War, accounted for a sizeable wall. There was frankly not much in the library of Sir Henry Hackwood to appeal to what one might call the general reader. Where on earth, I wondered, did he keep his detective stories? There was something called *The Eustace Diamonds* that looked promising, but a quick flip through its pages disappointed. No hint of a corpse anywhere.

Recalling the urgency of the mission, I pressed on and looked down to the lower shelves. There were a couple of dictionaries and a telephone directory behind a small table with the now useless instrument on it. This looked more promising. And there, between *Bradshaw's Railway Time Tables* and *An Introduction to Numismatism*, lurked a well-used copy of Debrett and a positively dog-eared Burke. Suppressing a small cry of triumph, I bent down and hoiked up the weighty volumes.

I had got one leg out of the window when I heard a soft contralto behind me say, 'Hello, Bertie, what on earth are you doing here?'

I swivelled round to see who spoke, catching the top of the skull a mighty crack on the raised window as I did so. It was Georgiana Meadowes, wearing a summer dress of printed purple flowers, looking if possible even more like something released that instant from the heavenly drawing board than I had remembered.

'I ... was er, I was just ... Borrowing a book, don't you know.'

There was the sound of the old bubbling brook going

over the well-tuned harp, which would no doubt have delighted in other circumstances.

'I can't explain now,' I went on. 'I'm helping a chum. It's all in a good cause, I promise you.'

'I didn't even know you were in Dorset. You should have telephoned.'

'Pointless in the circs.' Suddenly, I remembered my manners. 'Dash it, Georgiana, it's awfully nice to see you. How are you, old thing?'

With some difficulty, I reinserted the whole of the person into the library, intending to offer a peck on the cheek. Unfortunately, I caught my toe on the edge of the sill as I touched down, and this made me trip and pretty much stumble into the poor girl, with Burke and Debrett heading off their several ways.

We brushed ourselves down a bit and I apologised for having cannoned into her like an open-side rugby forward.

'Don't worry, Bertie. At least you didn't actually floor me this time.'

'Absolutely. Anyway, I'd best be off. Books to read, don't you know.'

Georgiana then did an odd thing. She locked the door

of the library behind her. 'I don't want Sir Henry to burst in,' she said. 'Bertie, I think you're in a bit of a pickle. Do you want to tell me about it?'

'I don't think so, Georgie. I think I'd really best be off pronto.'

She let me have the full thousand watts of those brown eyes and I felt the old knees buckle a fraction. A smile began to play around her lips, then lit up the entire physog, like a sunrise speeded up by trick photography.

'Do you often find yourself surprised in the act of theft from country houses where your presence is unannounced?'

There was a bit of a pause while I mulled this one over. 'Not often,' I said. I toyed with the idea of evasion, but we Woosters are wedded to the truth. 'But it's not the first time. I do have a tendency to get into scrapes.'

'Is that all you're going to tell me?'

'It's all I can for the time being. Though if you should clap eyes on me at any time in the next few days and there's someone else there, best pretend you don't know me.'

'Why?'

'I'll explain one day. I promise you.'

'All right, then. I won't recognise or acknowledge.'

'Under any circs.'

'I've got it. Any circs. Now come on. Let's get you out of here. But you must promise to telephone me.'

'I . . . Er, yes, of course.'

'Then maybe you could come and have dinner.'

'I'm not sure I'm top of the list of Sir Henry's desired dinner companions.'

'Well, write to me anyway. There are three posts a day.'

'Oh, rather. I'll be back,' I said, though the words came out sounding more like a threat than I'd intended.

'Don't forget your library books,' Georgiana said as I was halfway through the window.

She passed out D and B, and I hitched up one under each arm.

'Run along, Bertie. I'll keep watch here.'

I had an overwhelming urge to lean through the window and plant a smacker on that lovely face, but discretion being nine-tenths of something or other, I legged it down the terrace, sprinted into the shadow of the cedars and, when I was well out of sight, changed gear into a steady trot that was enough to get me back at Seaview Cottage in less than ten minutes.

It was a pretty relieved Bertram who, mopping the brow, bunged down the weighty vols on the hall table and resumed his seat in the garden, there to catch his breath and take stock of the situation.

I was aware of a discreet rustling behind my deckchair and a moment later a small table was deposited alongside, bearing a trayful of refreshment.

'I was unsure, sir, whether you would require a cold drink or a cup of tea, so I have brought both.'

'Then I shall drink both, Jeeves. I've had a bit of a triumph, though I say so myself.'

'I observed the volumes on the hall table, sir. A considerable achievement.'

I brought Jeeves up to date with the Melbury Hall Raid. Those who witnessed it might have felt that in the telling I rather stressed the fleetness of foot and swiftness of thought over the bruised skull and near-flattening of the divine presence, but all the essentials were there and I could see that the blighter was impressed.

'Most satisfactory, sir. I have already consulted the books in question and it seems that the present Lord Etringham is seventy-eight years old.'

'Golly, Jeeves. Just as well, what?'

'Indeed, sir. I have further established—'

But at this moment there came the sound of someone hammering at the front door of Seaview Cottage and Jeeves disappeared to investigate. I toyed with the idea of picking up *By Pullman to Peking* again, but decided against.

'Mr Beeching, sir.'

I stood up to see the friend of my infancy coming over the lawn with an anxious look on his face. This in itself didn't concern me; he would wear that air of startled apprehension even when the Rev. Aubrey Upjohn was announcing that yet again the Mrs Montague Prize for Latin Verses had gone to Beeching, P.

'What ho, Woody. All well at the Hall?'

Woody let out an exasperated sigh. 'Yes and no. Or perhaps that should be no and yes. In the sense of the background picture, I suppose one—'

'Do get to the point, old chap.'

'Things are looking bleak for Sir Henry. His

accountant is coming down from London. He's in a filthy temper. Amelia won't speak to me. And Jeeves is coming to dinner.'

'Yes, I heard you got into a stew and made up some silly name. Who is this Etringham fellow?'

'I got his name from a friend of mine in chambers. He's a real person, but he's a recluse. He lives in Westmorland and studies fossils. He hasn't left his house for years. This pal of mine always signs himself into the loucher establishments in the West End under the name of Lord Etringham. He says it's an absolutely bulletproof alias.'

Jeeves shimmered up with a cup of tea for Woody.

'It may be bulletproof to the heavyweight on the door of the Pink Owl in Brewer Street,' I said, 'but not to a raving snob like old Hackwood.'

'That's what I'm worried about,' said Woody. 'He's going to look him up in—'

I held up a hand for silence, then broke the good news.

'I say, that was quick work,' said Woody. 'Both books safely out of sight?'

'Think nothing of it, young Woody. Now you'd better brief his lordship here,' I said, nodding towards Jeeves, 'about the Hackwood ménage – subjects to steer clear of, buttons to push and so forth.'

In short – though it was far from short in the oratory of Gray's Inn – the set-up was as follows: Sir Henry Hackwood was a peppery old cove whose main interests were horseflesh, cricket and hanging on to his house. Lady Hackwood was his glacial consort, someone whose manner apparently made the Arctic Circle look balmy and who was deeply disappointed by the turn of financial events. Amelia and Georgiana completed the home team. The visitors included Georgiana's intended, R. Venables – who must have been the lean party I glimpsed through the drawing-room window – and his parents.

'Sir Henry's keen to get the parents onside for obvious reasons,' said Woody. 'So he's rather pushing the boat out for them. You may remember the father. They call him "Vishnu" Venables because he's always going on about his time in India. He bores for Bengal. He made those two speeches when his daughter married Reggie Wentworth.'

'Golly,' I said, 'was that him? I'd forgotten Reggie's bride was a Venables. I knew the name rang a bell.'

Reggie Wentworth was an Oxford chum whose wedding reception had been at Claridge's a couple of years back. The old family friend who was billed to recall bouncing the bride on his knee as a child had cried off sick, so the father took it on himself. But himself was also what he talked about. There was no mention of Reggie and scant reference to the bride. What there was, on the other hand, was twenty minutes of the achievements of Sidney 'Vishnu' Venables as Collector of Chanamasala and how the Viceroy had told the Governor of Uttar Pradesh that S. Venables was the finest thing to have come out of England since the Thames at Tilbury – and a great deal more in this vein. The audience had given him a warmish, if baffled, hand as he sat down. But blow me down if ten minutes later he didn't spring up on to the stage and call us to order so he could have a second innings, including, if I remembered right, details of his exam results at Oxford.

'And what's Mrs Venables like?' I asked. 'Apart from long-suffering?'

'Almost silent,' said Woody. 'She looks like a large cat. She smiles and purrs, but seldom speaks.'

A thought came to me. 'By the way, Woody, are you

sure you can keep a straight face when Jeeves sits down to dinner with you?'

'Of course I can.'

'Might I suggest, sir,' said Jeeves, 'that since Miss Meadowes is already aware of Mr Wooster's presence in the village it would be a good idea for you to inform Miss Hackwood of the true nature of the situation? One would not wish the young lady to betray surprise at any future turn of events.'

'All right,' said Woody. 'I suppose the whole thing's my fault anyway. I'll tell Amelia that Lord Etringham is an imposter and not to be startled if she bumps into some prize lunatic in the village. She knows Bertie by reputation anyway.'

I allowed this slur to pass, and it was a somewhat reassured Woody who made his way off some minutes later to prepare for the wassail, while Jeeves and I repaired inside to consider the delicate question of what he should be wearing.

He was got up in a pretty convincing combination of his and my evening clothes when I shoved him into the old two-seater at the cocktail hour and waved him off Hallwards.

As the car disappeared from sight, I felt a sharp sensation in the pit of the stomach. For a moment I thought it was an unwelcome revisitation of the ham sandwich from lunchtime, but then I thought it might be something else that was giving me the gripe. Could it conceivably be the idea that it was 'Lord Etringham' and not Wooster, B. who would be dining with, and very possibly sitting next to, Georgiana Meadowes?

Turning on my heel and re-entering Seaview Cottage, I dismissed the thought as unworthy and put my mind to the question of how best to reconcile Amelia Hackwood to the worthy case of P. Beeching, barrister-at-law.

CHAPTER
THREE

Whatever course dinner might be taking at Melbury Hall – and the possibilities made the head spin a bit – I felt it important to keep my own strength up for what lay ahead, so soon after eight I sallied out in search of sustenance. The Red Lion was a four-ale bar with a handful of low-browed sons of toil who looked as though they might be related to one another in ways frowned on by the Old Testament. The Hare and Hounds, a hundred yards further up the road, at least had a saloon where the traveller could feel he wasn't dropping in on some Saxon blood feud. I was soon settled into a window seat with a pint of local ale and plateful of hot steak and kidney p. *The Mystery of the Gabled House* helped beguile the hour, and it was a contented B. Wooster who ambled back to Seaview Cottage inhaling the whiff of hawthorn from the hedgerows.

Night had fallen some time since and I had got as far as the discovery of the second corpse in Chapter Five when I heard the rumble of the two-seater pulling up outside. I was already at the front door by the time Jeeves had extricated himself and turned off the headlights.

'Well, Jeeves? I'm all ears.'

'I trust you passed a satisfactory evening, sir. I'm sorry I was unable to be of—'

'To hell with *my* evening. What happened at the Hall? Were you discovered?'

'No, sir. I am happy to say the impersonation aroused no comment.'

'Jeeves, this is no time for reticence. I want a full report. Omit nothing, however trivial.'

'Very well, sir, I shall endeavour to paint a coherent picture.'

After a cocktail in the drawing room, it seemed, the company had moved into a great barn of a dining room at the front of the house. Jeeves had found himself placed between Georgiana Meadowes and Eileen Venables, mother of the intended Rupert.

'And what about Sir Henry?' I asked.

'He seemed keen to impress his visitors. His hospitality was marked.'

'The wine flowed in torrents? Second helpings of foie gras?'

'One gained the impression that this was perhaps a last throw of the dice, sir.'

'I see. And how did the . . . happy couple appear?'

'It was somewhat difficult to form a judgement, sir. The conversation was dominated to a great extent by Mr Sidney Venables, who told a number of stories of his time as Collector of Chanamasala.'

'You surprise me not at all, Jeeves. All of them perhaps reflecting well on S. Venables?'

'The gentleman appears to have been held in high esteem by all who encountered him.'

'And Georgiana? How was she?'

'A most enchanting young woman, sir. I have seldom encountered anyone with whom I have been able to discuss the work of Schopenhauer in a manner so informed yet so light of touch. Miss Meadowes mixes high seriousness with a most playful outlook. She would also appear to have a rare concern for the welfare of others. I formed a most—'

'All right, all right, Jeeves. Don't forget I do know the girl pretty darned well myself.'

'I beg your pardon, sir. I had not intended to—'

'What about young Venables?'

'Mr Rupert Venables seemed most delighted with his situation in life, sir. I had the impression that he had inherited many of his father's characteristics, though he was happy on this occasion to yield the floor, as it were.'

'And what was his attitude towards Georgiana?'

Jeeves considered. One could almost hear the cog-wheels of that great brain whirring as he selected the *mot juste*. It was a pity that, when it came, it was one with which I was unfamiliar.

'I should say his attitude was complaisant, sir.'

'Complacent, do you mean?'

'I fancy either adjective might apply, sir.'

'Hmm.' While unsure of the difference, I was fairly certain neither was quite up to snuff.

'Tell me, Jeeves,' I said. 'One thing I don't understand is how this writer chap is going to rescue Melbury Hall. Do his books sell in such great quantities?'

'I doubt it, sir. The literary life is famously ill-rewarded.'

'So it's the father's loot, is it?'

'No, sir. The Colonial Service pension, even for such a celebrated civil servant, would be a modest one. The family's fortune derives from the mother's side. Mrs Venables is a Spanier.'

'A Spaniard?'

'A Spanier, sir. Of Spanier's Sausage Casings. They are a large Wiltshire company of considerable repute. They hold a royal warrant granted by the late queen. They were recently bought by an American processed-food concern. Mrs Venables was the majority shareholder following the death of her parents. She is now a non-executive director of Hickory Hog Holdings in Cincinnati.'

I let out a whistle. 'That should cover it.'

'The company also owns a proprietary relish, or catsup, that you may have encountered in New York, sir.'

'By golly, Jeeves, not "Hickory Hot Boy"——'

'The very——'

'"It's Smokin' Good!"'

'So I am assured, sir, though I have not had occasion to sample the condiment myself.'

'And you gleaned this from the horse's mouth as it were?'

'Mrs Venables was generous with the details, sir. While less garrulous than her husband, she appears similarly contented with the hand that life has dealt her.'

'I'm not surprised. Which brings us to the case of poor old Woody. Any rays of light there?'

'I fear not, sir. Sir Henry was somewhat offhand in his manner towards Mr Beeching. And Miss Hackwood refused to pass him the salt, repeatedly affecting not to hear his request.'

'I see. The doghouse. Poor Woody. And Venables? Did he throw him a bone?'

'Mr Venables's attitude could I think best be described as patronising, sir. Miss Meadowes was the only person who attempted to include Mr Beeching in the conversation.'

'What about Lady H?' I said. 'Surely the hostess was at least polite?'

'Lady Hackwood's manner was on the chilly side.'

'Arctic?'

'A degree or two above, sir. Enough to attain a modicum of civility, but little more. One had the impression that were it not for the cricket match on Saturday Mr Beeching's presence would not be tolerated.'

I was turning this information over in the mind and I didn't much like what I saw.

'I trust the Côte d'Azur was not mentioned?'

'It was briefly alluded to by Mr Rupert Venables, sir.'

'Really? You surprise me greatly.'

'He appeared to be chaffing or teasing his fiancée, sir.'

'Golly. That's a bit rich. And how did she take it?'

'She was able to make light of it, sir, though I saw her cast a warning glance towards Sir Henry, at which point the young gentleman desisted. Sir Henry's expression was not encouraging.'

'I should think not.'

'Will there be anything else this evening, sir?'

'Hang on, Jeeves. Were there any sticky moments when you thought you might be rumbled? Did Sir Henry mention Burke or Debrett?'

'Neither, sir. The subterfuge passed off with an ease I had not foreseen. Having a long acquaintance with country houses, I was familiar with the etiquette. Mr Venables made it unnecessary for the other guests to speak to the floor, as it were, so I ran no risk of exposure there.'

'You could just have a quiet natter either side with Georgie or Mrs V.'

'Exactly, sir.'

'You didn't find yourself under cross-examination?'

'Knowing who I was, Mr Beeching and Miss Hackwood were naturally discreet, and of course Miss Meadowes was also aware of my true identity. Lady Hackwood appeared too out of sorts to take much interest in her guests.'

'But surely a snob like Sir Henry would have wanted the dope on your coat of arms and all that stuff?'

'After the ladies had retired I did find myself the subject of some questions of a genealogical nature from Sir Henry. I thought it best to steer the conversation on to a subject I knew would interest him even more.'

'Which was?'

'The Turf, sir. I shared with him some information I had gathered about the field in the three-thirty at Ascot tomorrow. A friend of mine at the Junior Ganymede has a brother who works at a well-known Lambourn stables.'

'So you gave him a hot tip?'

'I was in a position to make a number of recommendations, sir.'

'And he was grateful?'

'Sir Henry was already well informed, but we seemed to strike up a considerable rapport. He asked Bicknell, the butler, to bring up his last bottle of Warre's 1885 to drink to our success with the bookmaker tomorrow.'

'A decent glassful?'

'I found it a most helpful digestive, sir.'

'Talking of which, Jeeves, I don't suppose you packed any emergency supplies for a nightcap, did you?'

'I shall prepare it at once, sir.'

Ten minutes later, agreeably capped, I went up to the bedroom to find that Jeeves had laid out my heliotrope pyjamas with the old gold stripe. It had been a long day and I felt ready for a full ration of the deep and dreamless.

I don't know how it is with other chaps, but I tend to feel pretty bobbish first thing in the morning. The tea and newspaper bring a smile to the features; between the ablutions and the breakfast table there is generally a show tune or two to receive its premiere from the Wooster lips.

This June morning was no exception. Jeeves had made

up for lost time at the local shops. The eggs had a pleasing orange glow and the bacon came from a beast far removed from the baleful husbandry of any Jude, obscure or otherwise. Yet despite the cloudless blue sky over Kingston St Giles, the day's task was a serious one, and I felt it would tax my resources to the last drop. Little did I know, as I set fire to an after-breakfast gasper in the cottage garden, what the lead-filled sock of fate had in store for me.

It started well enough, as I moved swiftly on to Chapter Seven of *The Mystery of the Gabled House*, in which a third body was found, this one behind the potting shed. I was contemplating a spin down to the seaside to sniff out a bit of fish for luncheon, when Jeeves came out on to the lawn to announce that he had had some news.

'I have received intelligence from the Hall, sir, that a further house guest is expected this afternoon.'

'Right ho. Who is he?'

'She, sir. Dame Judith Puxley.'

Even on such a sunny morning I felt a shudder run through the lower vertebrae. 'What on earth brings that preying cannibal to Dorsetshire?'

'It appears she is an old school friend of Lady Hackwood, sir.'

I found the mind boggling a bit. 'It's hard to imagine that particular schoolroom, isn't it, Jeeves?'

'It does lie, sir, at the extremity of one's power to conjecture.'

'Had old Isaac Newton done his stuff by then do you suppose?'

'One supposes that the physical sciences were in a markedly less advanced state of knowledge, sir.'

I was about to be a little more humorous at Dame Judith's expense when a sobering thought struck me. 'If Dame Judith was at school with Lady Hackwood, then it follows that Lady H must also have been at school with . . .'

'I believe so, sir.'

' . . . Aunt Agatha.'

'The three ladies appear to have been contemporaries at the academy.'

'Which means that Lady H must also be a friend of Aunt Agatha.'

'Inevitably, sir.'

'This ups the stakes a bit, doesn't it?'

'I see no immediate danger, sir, though it would be as well to remain on the *qui vive*.'

Dame Judith Puxley, I should explain, had featured

in a painful episode in my younger life. She was a house guest at a Victorian pile in Shropshire where, following a crossed wire over the bolting of a second-floor hatch, I was discovered on the main roof late one night dressed as Julius Caesar, and had to be brought down by the local fire brigade. Dame Judith was the relict of the late Sir Mortimer Puxley, a big cheese in the world of chemistry, and was herself a leading authority on – I think I've got this right – Sumerian tablets and the cuneiform script.

'One thing bothers me in particular, Jeeves. If something comes can something else be far behind?'

'Perhaps you have in mind the poet Shelley, sir. "If winter comes, can spring be far behind?"'

'That's the boy. I mean, must we expect Aunt Agatha at any moment?'

'I think we may be fairly sure that Lady Worplesdon is detained in London.'

'I bally well hope so, Jeeves. We left plenty of provisions and a spare key for the juvenile delinquent?'

'Her ladyship was well provided for, sir.'

'Jolly good. And in any event I shan't be going within a mile of Melbury Hall. I'm off to Swanage to get some sea air. When I return, I shall have a solution to the Woody and Amelia problem.'

'Indeed, sir? And what about the question of Miss Meadowes, Mr Venables and the future of Melbury Hall?'

'Jeeves,' I said, 'I think my success with Burke and Debrett has nettled you. I detect a hint of green.'

'On the contrary, sir, I wish you every——'

'I see something of the dog and plenty of the manger.'

'As you wish, sir. Will you be back in time for tea?'

It took me rather longer than I had expected to motor down past Wareham and on towards Corfe Castle, though I must say it was an invigorating drive, with the Purbeck Hills rising gently to starboard. The trouble with these picturesque outings is that the chap at the wheel never gets a decent look at the scenery. I kept thinking how much better it would be if I had a co-driver. And before you could say 'Brooklands' this co-driver had, in my mind, taken the shape of a tallish female in a cotton print dress, long of limb and with eyes the colour of melting chocolate.

I had to remind myself pretty firmly that this vision was betrothed to another and that this ruled her strictly *hors de combat*. I rushed neither the crab salad, the half-bot, nor the soothing coffee and cigarette that followed. Instead, I gazed out to sea a fair bit, and I cannot deny that it was a pensive Bertram who climbed aboard and restarted the engine.

By the time I got back to Kingston St Giles, I had put all such thoughts to one side. We Woosters do not stew in our own juice. My mind had become once more a precision instrument tuned to a single end: the reuniting of P. Beeching with his heart's desire.

'Jeeves,' I called out as I crossed the hall, 'I've got a plan and it's an absolute pippin.'

There was a short pause while the faithful manservant could be heard conducting some business with pot and cups. He emerged from the kitchen with a look one could describe as *distrait*.

'Everything all right, Jeeves? I think I'll have the tea indoors today.'

I took a chair by the inglenook. After a bit of straining and pouring, Jeeves drew himself up to his full height.

'Sir?'

'Yes, Jeeves?'

'There's been a development.'

'What?' There was something in his manner that froze the cup halfway to the lip.

'You will recall that I mentioned Sir Henry's interest in horses, sir, and our animated conversation on the matter.'

'Of course. How did your tips do? Any winners?'

'Three of the horses were successful, sir, and the fourth was beaten by a short head.'

'And had Sir Henry piled into them?'

'As much as he was able to in his somewhat illiquid circumstances, I believe.'

'So he must be happy as a sandboy.'

'He called in half an hour ago to bring the news and—'

'Golly. Close escape.'

'His mood was decidedly improved. He was most generous in giving me credit for the reversal in his fortunes.'

'I should jolly well think so. So why the long face, Jeeves?'

'Sir Henry appears convinced that I can be relied on to effect similar results from the rest of the meeting.'

'And can you?'

'I think it highly unlikely, sir.'

'And you told him so?'

'I did, but he was undeterred. He said that even if he lost on every race he would still be "ahead of the game", and what's more he would have had the pleasure of getting to know a fellow aficionado of the sport of kings.'

'He what?'

'Sir Henry has invited me to stay at Melbury Hall, sir.'

I lowered the cup with a clatter. 'You declined, of course.' Even as I uttered the words, I felt they had a familiar ring – as did the reply.

'I regret, sir, that in the circumstances I deemed it best to accept.'

I let off a gasp like a locomotive on a steep incline.

'This requires some careful thought, Jeeves.'

'Indeed, sir.'

I stood up and paced about the room, catching my head a glancing blow on a beam as I did so.

'Couldn't you just have said no?'

'Sir Henry was most persuasive, sir. He described our present accommodation as a "squalid little arrangement" and said he would be delighted for an excuse to move Mr Beeching out of the corner room, which enjoys particularly fine views of—'

'But this leaves me in the soup, doesn't it? How am I supposed to play Cupid when there's no one to press my evening shirt?'

'Talking of shirts, sir, I have spent some time in planning the sort of wardrobe that might be necessary for Lord Etringham until Sunday evening. The appropriate dress would be—'

'Damn it, Jeeves, there are times when the question of the appropriate dress is simply not on the agenda.'

'I have yet to encounter one, sir.'

I sat down again in the armchair and dabbed away a trickle of blood from the temple.

'I'm stumped, Jeeves. I feel I'm losing touch with the field. Any ideas?'

'It did strike me, sir, that were you to divulge to me your plan for the reuniting of Mr Beeching and Miss Hackwood it might be possible to turn my presence at Melbury Hall to our advantage.'

There was something about Jeeves's manner in this exchange that troubled me. I don't know if you've ever bumped into one of those chaps at parties who go round the merry throng doing card tricks. You're not sure if he's a fellow guest or a hired entertainer. You watch his hands like a vulture, ignoring the patter – and then suddenly he opens a girl's evening bag and whips out the ten of diamonds. You feel a mug. And you don't know whether to bung him half a crown or not.

I wouldn't say I thought that Jeeves had a spare pack up his sleeve exactly, but I felt he was a fraction – what's the word I want ... evasive. I put this down to the success of the Melbury Hall Raid. If Jeeves has a fault it is that he can sometimes allow another's triumph to upset him. It rankles.

Making no allusion therefore to my recent run of form, I went on to outline Plan A.

'I've been doing some thinking.'

'Really, sir?'

'Yes. Let us consider the psychology of the individual.'

'Which individual, sir?'

'Miss Hackwood. Amelia. A well brought-up girl, would you say?'

'Undoubtedly so.'

'An only child. Though for the last ten or so years having a near-sister in Georgiana ... Went to a boarding school or convent ... Kings of England, scripture knowledge, spot of algebra, music and movement, that sort of thing.'

'Miss Hackwood is an accomplished violinist.'

'Then on to Switzerland for a bit of finishing. Gets by in French and German. Goes to London, where she is closely chaperoned by—'

'By Dame Judith Puxley, I believe, sir.'

'My point exactly, Jeeves. Then she's probably had half a dozen temporary situations that Sir Henry's fixed her up with.'

'A summer job at the All England Lawn Tennis Club, I understand.'

'Thank you, Jeeves. And what is missing in all this?'

'I should not care to hazard a guess, sir.'

'Men, Jeeves.'

'I beg your pardon, sir?'

'A knowledge of the opposite sex. No brothers, you see. And quite frankly a couple of foxtrots at Queen Charlotte's Ball and a pen pal in Baden-Baden is no preparation for the red meat that is Woody Beeching.'

'I fear, sir, that—'

'I haven't finished, Jeeves. If this Amelia is of the opinion that Woody is too inclined to flirt with other girls, then we must show her that Woody's way of carrying on is perfectly normal.'

'I'm afraid I don't follow you, sir.'

'All chaps flirt a bit. It's natural. Let her understand that and she'll soon come round.'

'I'm not sure what you are suggesting, sir.'

'I'm suggesting that someone might like to sidle up to Amelia and give her a bit of the old oil – not too much, just some compliments on her appearance, a brush of fingers on the arm.'

'The scheme appears fraught with—'

I held up a hand. 'I am not offering this as a blueprint for discussion, Jeeves. It is more by way of a fait accompli.'

'As you wish, sir. And whom do you envisage in the role of the rake or Don Juan?'

I struggled to suppress a smile. 'Someone of unimpeachable reputation, I should say. Someone she would look up to and know was a thorough-going gentleman. That's the nub, you see. She says to herself, "If even this gallant and respectable chap is not above a bit of idle hand-touching, how much the more so should my irresistible Woody be allowed the odd—"'

'The young lady would follow the *a fortiori* argument.'

'As you wish, Jeeves. The important thing is the respectability of the hand-holder and eye-gazer.'

'And who might such a gentleman be?'

I suppressed another one. 'It's obvious. Her father's new best friend. Lord Etringham.'

I've encountered many types of silence in my time. The silence funereal, the silence pregnant, the silence that lets you know you've laid an egg ... The one that enveloped the front room of Seaview Cottage at this moment had elements of all the three above – plus a bit more all its own.

It was Jeeves who finally broke it. 'I fear I must enter the firmest possible *nolle prosequi*, sir. The temporary impersonation of a member of the aristocracy was something in which I felt I had little choice. What you are suggesting, sir, would be a crossing of the Rubicon. It would be highly irregular.'

I felt a little chastened by the fellow's dignity. A few moments ago I had been wondering whether he wasn't pulling a fast one. Now I thought I had perhaps taken his extraordinary loyalty for granted.

'Well, you may be right, Jeeves. I wouldn't want to be the cause of any unpleasantness.'

'There is also a practical aspect to consider, sir. While I may be considerably younger than the real Lord

Etringham, the plan you outline would stand a better chance of success were the protagonist to be closer to Miss Hackwood's own age.'

I thought about this for a moment; it had a familiar whiff to it. 'I can see where this is heading. I wasn't born yesterday, Jeeves.'

'Not yesterday, sir, but at least not so very long before Miss Hackwood. And given your success in extracting the volumes from the library, you may feel yourself to be—'

'On a winning streak, what?'

'Indeed, sir.'

I stood up again and did a bit more pacing – though ducking, this time, at the appropriate moment.

'Of course there is one reason why I can't do it myself,' I said. 'And that is that I am *persona non grata* up at the Hall. If Sir Henry makes the Côte d'Azur connection he'll be down to the stables and back with the horse-whip. There'll be only one winner in the three-thirty at Ascot tomorrow and that's B. Wooster – by a distance.'

There was another pause, but of an utterly different kind – the kind that precedes the shedding of new light from that great brain.

Jeeves cleared his throat. 'I think I may have a solution, sir.'

But what it was, I did not immediately find out – as we were interrupted by the sound of squealing car brakes, the patter of gravel hitting the front windows of Seaview Cottage and the soft but unmistakable thump of car on car.

'I say, Jeeves, better go and see what the devil . . .'

But the fellow had already vaporised. A few moments passed – perhaps in damage assessment – before he reappeared in the doorway. 'Miss Meadowes, sir.'

I sprang from the armchair like a roosting waterfowl at the sound of a shotgun being closed. Georgiana held up a warning hand, and for once the welcome peck was administered without the risk of a broken rib.

'Bertie, I'm so sorry to drop in like this without warning.'

'Not a bit. Absolute pleasure. Do sit down somewhere and Jeeves will bring some tea.'

'Thank you. There are two reasons why I've come. Or perhaps three,' said Georgiana, settling herself on the sofa, arranging a fold of cotton dress over an endless limb or two.

'The floor is yours. Speak on.'

'First of all, I want to assure you there's no damage to your car. There was a coming-together, but no more. The bumpers touched.'

'That's why they're called bumpers. It's what they're for. Don't give it a second thought.'

'You are sweet, Bertie. Next, I was a little worried about you. I know it wasn't the right time to talk yesterday, but I just . . .' She waved an elegant hand.

'Quite the wrong time,' I said. 'I needed to get myself off the premises with all speed.'

'Yes, I know, but . . .' She trailed off again.

'But what, Georgie old thing?'

For the first time since I had, as it were, bumped into her in the south of France, I saw this blue-stockinged editress at a loss.

'I just want you to know that . . . Well, we were pretty good pals in France, weren't we? And if you ever needed a . . . Not exactly a shoulder to cry on, I mean, just a good listener. Someone to chat to, I would . . . I could . . .'

I had the impression that she was trying to get at something, but I hadn't the faintest idea what. She seemed relieved to hear the clink of the approaching tray.

'Oh, good. Here's Jeeves with the tea.'

In his short absence the amazing fellow had also put together a small plate of tomato sandwiches, which Georgiana fell on with an appreciative cry.

'I think you've met Lord Etringham,' I said.

'I have indeed,' she said. 'A man of many parts. Woody put me in the picture. Just as well, because I recognised Jeeves from the Côte d'Azur and I might well have blurted something out. He was absolutely marvellous at dinner.'

'Was he?'

'You should have heard him egging on old Venables. All sorts of questions about the Brahmins and the warrior caste. And as for dealing with Uncle Henry ... I've never seen him so charmed by a guest.'

'You are too kind,' said Jeeves. 'I was grateful for your intervention, Miss, at several potentially embarrassing moments.'

There was a bit more of this mutual admiration to grit one's teeth through before Georgiana downed her cup and said, 'Well I suppose I'd better be going. Slightly awkward my being here at all, I suppose. What with one thing and another.'

'Where is your intended this afternoon?' I said.

'He's gone to Bournemouth. He's taken Amelia and his mother. To look at some trams.'

'Life's just one long whirligig of excitement for some, isn't it?' I said. 'Weren't you included in this jaunt?'

'Me? No, I'm just the Sonya Rostova of Melbury Hall.' The gurgling stream went over the well-tempered strings, though only for a moment.

I could tell from the look of quiet satisfaction on Jeeves's face that some cultural reference had been made.

'Is she a ballerina?' I said.

'No, sir, Miss Meadowes's allusion is to a character in *War and Peace*. She is an orphan cousin whom fate and the author treat unkindly.'

'I see.'

'I must say I always thought Tolstoy was a bit hard on her,' said Georgiana.

'The sobriquet "The Sterile Flower" was undoubtedly a cruel one,' said Jeeves.

'When you two have quite finished,' I said. 'Can we get back to the matter in hand?'

'Which was?' said Georgiana.

'I'll tell you what it was,' I said firmly. 'You said there

were three reasons for this delightful visit. We've only had two so far.'

'Ah yes. Do you want this last tomato sandwich, Bertie? Oh, good show. Thanks. Just the right amount of pepper. I wanted to tell you that things are not so hot with Amelia and Woody. I'm very worried. She does love him deeply, you know. I don't want her to cut off her nose to spite her face. I was wondering if Jeeves had had any bright ideas.'

'Oh, I see, so it was Lord Etringham you wanted to see,' I said, and it came out a little more tartly than I'd intended.

Georgiana flushed. 'No, no, Bertie, not at all. It's just that ... Time's running out. We only have till Sunday night.'

I was a little hot under the collar myself. From our seated positions, the pair of us looked upwards like a couple of messengers sent to consult the oracle at Delphi.

It was a sticky moment or two before the oracle pronounced. 'I was on the point of outlining a plan to Mr Wooster, Miss, when we ... heard you arrive.'

'Jeeves, you're a marvel.' The Tolstoy scholar allowed herself a girlish clap of the hands.

'Thank you, Miss. The scheme is not without its hazards. In the vernacular of the card table, it is a question of raising the stakes or indeed "buying for one".'

'Do get on with it, Jeeves.'

'I beg your pardon, sir. It occurred to me that if you are to proceed with your scheme for the enlightenment of Miss Hackwood you will need to be present, or preferably resident, at Melbury Hall. I further reflected that a gentleman of Lord Etringham's standing would be in need of a gentleman's personal gentleman. If you were willing to accept that role, sir, it would make it easy for you to be in Sir Henry's establishment while to all intents and purposes invisible to your host.'

My chin had fallen so far that I was incapable of speech.

'It would be unnecessary for you to venture beyond the green baize door, sir, except for whatever visits to Lord Etringham might be necessary for the purposes of verisimilitude. Such moments might also be useful for further confabulation.'

Georgiana was on her feet. 'It's a marvellous idea, Jeeves. Isn't it, Bertie?'

Speech returned, albeit reluctantly. 'I wouldn't know where to begin. I can't boil an egg.'

'The cook does that,' said Georgiana. 'Mrs Padgett. Heaven help you if she finds you anywhere near her eggs.'

'But you know what I mean. I couldn't manage all the pressing of clothes, the tea, the drinks, the—'

'Bertie, you can pour a drink. I've seen you do it. Jolly well you did it too.'

'I'm sure I should give myself away. I mean, I don't know how to talk to the bootboy or the scullery maid. They'd sniff me out in no time. I'd sound all wrong. I'm—'

'Look at me, Bertie,' said Georgiana.

And I did, knowing the risks full well.

'You're being absurd and, if you don't mind my saying so, a bit of a snob,' said Georgiana. 'I'm quite sure that you can walk with kings nor lose the common touch. Just be polite. Look at Jeeves. He didn't bat an eyelid at sitting down at table and being waited on. He just ... He was a natural.'

'The dramatic requirement is, *mutatis mutandis*, no greater, sir. In fact, since most of the time your work will be unscrutinised, one might argue that yours is the simpler role.'

'What name will you take, Bertie?'

'I'm not taking any jolly—'

'You know that game where you take your second name and then add the name of your street and it gives you a film star? What would yours be?'

'Wilberforce Berkeley.'

'That's marvellous! He'd be an absolute matinée idol. And Wilberforce is the perfect name for a valet. Don't you think, Jeeves?'

I battled on gamely for another couple of minutes.

'"Please bring me a whisky and soda, Wilberforce. Put it over there, please, Wilberforce",' Georgiana was saying – and plenty more such rot.

'I'd love to help,' I said. 'But it's simply beyond me.'

At this moment, Georgiana took my hands in hers. My heart, already skipping the odd one from the prolonged eye contact, now began to beat the sort of rhythm you hear in the Congo before the missionary gets lobbed into the *bouillon*.

'Just do it to please me, Bertie,' said Georgiana, lowering the voice a half-octave and giving the fingers a final squeeze. 'I'll make sure you're all right. We can meet beside the tennis court in the evening and I'll bring you a nice half-bottle of something from the cellar. Do it for Woody and Amelia. It's only till Sunday evening. Please, Bertie, please.'

The packing of the suitcases involved some redistribution of clothing. Jeevesward went the tennis garb, the linen jacket, a pair of new co-respondent shoes (a painful loss), the stiff-fronted shirts and a half-dozen studs in Drones Club colours (the last received with a faint but perceptible flaring of the nostril); among my new effects were two pairs of spongebag trousers and a navy blue tie of singular drabness.

Jeeves, having pushed out the dent in the rear bumper, took the wheel of the two-seater in a sporting tweed cap, while I donned his bowler. Considering all it had to encompass, it came as no surprise that this hat was several sizes too large. Only some nifty work by Jeeves with tissue paper and cow gum round the inner rim prevented the thing from falling over my eyes.

We said au revoir to Seaview Cottage as the engine coughed twice and fired into life. Jeeves was a more careful driver than Georgiana, and it was not fear for my personal safety that caused an odd feeling in the pit of the stomach as we swung off the main village street and up the lime-tree avenue towards the distant prospect of Melbury Hall.

'Once more unto the breach, sir.'

For once I thought I wouldn't let him have the last word in quotations. '"I see their knavery: this is to make an ass of me,"' I spouted from memory. '"To fright me, if they could."'

'Very apt, sir.'

'I played the part of Bottom in *A Midsummer Night's Dream* at school when I was sixteen. It's funny how the lines you learn at that age stay with you for life. I couldn't learn it if you paid me now.'

'The young mind is undoubtedly more receptive, sir. Was your performance well received?'

'Tolerably so. The *Chronicle*, as I recall, said, "Wooster gave it all he'd got."'

'Most gratifying, sir.'

'Why are we going this way?'

'So that I can drop you off, if I may, sir, at the tradesmen's entrance.'

CHAPTER
═FOUR═

Casting an envious eye over the duck downs and woollen coverings of the four-poster where Jeeves sat propped among the pillows, sipping his morning tea, I found it easy enough to picture how well he had slept.

'How's the tea?' I said.

'Most refreshing, thank you, sir.'

'You'd better thank Mrs Tilman. She made it.'

'Ah, yes. She is said to be a most capable woman.'

'Lucky old Mr Tilman, what?'

'Doubtless he appreciated her talents while alive, sir.'

'Oh dear. She seems young to be a widow.'

'He was taken in the prime of life, I believe. How was your own accommodation, sir?'

'Who are those Indian chaps who sleep on nails?'

'Fakirs, sir.'

'Well, if you bump into one, do recommend the top floor back at Melbury Hall. I think he'd find it right up his street.'

'I shall bear that in mind, sir, though in Melbury-cum-Kingston the contingency is a remote one.'

'Is it always so bally uncomfortable?'

'The accommodation varies considerably in my experience, sir. The opulence of the main house is by no means a reliable guide.'

'Go on.'

'Totleigh Towers, Sir Watkyn Bassett's residence—'

'Or castle, near as dammit.'

'Indeed, sir. While it is a most imposing building, the word among the servants is that their rooms have not been touched since the reign of William IV.'

'Stingy old chap, Bassett.'

'Brinkley Court, on the other hand, Mrs Travers's house, is always a pleasure to visit.'

'Leftovers from Anatole's wizardry?'

'It is not merely the excellent table, sir. My bedroom is most comfortably equipped with a view of the garden, a strong reading light and an adjacent bathroom. There is invariably a vase of fresh flowers on the chest.'

'A bit of favouritism from Aunt Dahlia, I suspect. Anyway, enough of this gossip, Jeeves. Today sees Plan A swing into action.'

'Might I suggest that you first have a word with the butler, sir? Since you are working for Lord Etringham and not for the household, there should be little constraint on your freedom of movement. However, I have always found it good practice to consult the butler at the start of the day. Mr Bicknell is well-regarded below stairs, I understand, but somewhat old-fashioned.'

'Go and pay my respects, you mean. Clock in.'

'Exactly, sir.'

'But I'll have some time off?'

'The mornings and evenings are generally busy, but the afternoon should see few demands on your time.'

'Is that when you do your Spinoza-ing?'

'I have always found that the hours after luncheon are the most propitious for the rational philosophers, sir.'

'Any idea when I might be able to corner Amelia for Plan A?'

'I fear not, sir, though Mrs Tilman, I am told, is the *fons et origo* of all such domestic information.'

'Right ho, Jeeves. Shall I take the tea tray? I suppose you can toddle down to breakfast without my help. I think I can smell the bacon now.'

'I wonder if I might ask for a copy of *The Times* before I go down, sir? It is the normal practice to leave two or three on the hall table. A brief study of the form at Ascot would put me in a strong position to withstand Sir Henry's questions at breakfast.'

There seemed little point in quibbling, so I went off like a retriever puppy to fetch his lordship's paper. I managed to deliver it and remove the tray to the servants' quarters without bumping into anyone, then set about finding the butler.

In my younger days – as an undergraduate, say, on a visit to some chum's twenty-first – I had found the butler an awe-inspiring figure and spent many an anxious hour calculating how much and at what instant to tip him on the day of departure. The years between, though few enough in number, had taken the edge off such callow fears and it was with a measure of insouciance that I knocked at the door indicated by Mrs Tilman.

'Come in,' said a voice that seemed to come from fathoms underground.

I did as I was told and then stopped short. It was the sheer volume of butler that was overwhelming. If one of the heads on Mount Rushmore had taken first a body then a breathing form, it could have picked up a hint or two from this Bicknell. Monumental was the word that came to mind. No one would have wished — or dared — to call him corpulent: there was no suggestion of spare flesh beneath that mighty waistcoat; but it would have been unwise to attempt a circumnavigation without leaving some sort of forwarding address or *poste restante*.

'Can I help?'

'Yes, I'm Ber ... Wilberforce, Mr Wilberforce, I mean. Lord Etringham's man ... valet.'

I was aware of having made the most frightful hash of my opening lines. I coughed and pulled myself together.

'I thought I'd just look in and say what ho, what?'

There was a silence. I heard the clock in the servants' passageway strike the hour and felt the success of the whole adventure rather hang on the moment.

'Good morning,' said Bicknell. 'I hope you passed a pleasant night.'

The manner was grave, but the eye was genial.

'Oh, rather. Very comfortable. Slept like a top, don't you know.'

'I'm pleased to hear it. Some visitors find the bed takes a day or two to get used to.'

'Not me, Bick ... Mr Bicknell. Quite used to roughing it. Officer cadet corps at school and all that. Absolute lap of luxury.'

I sensed that I hadn't quite got the hang of this dialogue and thought it best to say as little as possible for the time being.

'We're at full stretch this weekend,' said Bicknell. 'We lost a footman last week. Liddle.'

'Oh dear. An accident?'

'No. Liddle was what you might call a shirker. Bone idle. I don't like shirkers, Mr Wilberforce.'

'Nor do I. No time for them at all.'

'And then he was caught with a dozen Georgian forks in his coat pocket when he went home on Saturday night. Sir Henry is very particular about his silver.'

'What a scoundrel. Was he hauled up before the bench?'

'Sir Henry is the bench, in a manner of speaking. He didn't want to take it any further.'

'But Liddle was shown the door.'

'Yes. The next morning. We have a new man called Hoad who's come to help out while we're full up.'

'Hoad?'

'Yes, he's from the village. He used to work in the stables.'

'I see. And does that complete the picture?'

'There's also Mrs Tilman — and Mrs Padgett, the cook. And the women who come in to clean.'

'Well, if I can help at all, just let me know. Always happy to oblige, don't you know.'

'That's most thoughtful of you, Mr ... Wilberforce. As a matter of fact there is something you could do. Sir Henry has asked me to have the telephone line mended. I've written to the company but that may take a day or two. If you were in the village you could perhaps go into one of the public houses and make a telephone call to report the fault. I shan't have the time myself. I would recommend the Hare and Hounds over the Red Lion.'

'Consider it done, Mr Bicknell. I shall see you later, no doubt.'

So saying, I left the impressive fellow in his den and headed to the kitchen garden for a well-earned gasper. On my return to the house, I found breakfast under way in the kitchen. This meal consisted of what had been brought back from the dining room with a fresh pot of tea plonked down by the cook. This Mrs Padgett was a red-faced old party whose way of speaking indicated that she came from somewhere in the northern wilds – possibly this side of Hadrian's Wall, but not by much.

'Come and sit yourself down, Mr Wilberforce. Don't be a stranger,' said Mrs Tilman.

I did as I was told, and found myself between some sort of charwoman and a short, stumpy fellow with a face like a church gargoyle whom I took to be Hoad, the emergency footman.

'I wouldn't eat them kidneys if I was you,' he said. 'Filthy stuff that is.'

This view being widely shared, I was the only taker. I have always been partial to the dish, though it's one I only seem to come across when staying with people. Mrs Padgett's had plenty of devil to them.

'What's Lord Etringham's plans today, then?' said Mrs Tilman. 'Keeping you busy, is he?'

'His lordship has told me he will be spending a quiet day reading,' I said. Then, thinking this sounded rather feeble, I added, 'But he may need me to accompany him to the bookmaker this afternoon.'

'You'll be needing to go to Dorchester then. He's quite a one for the gee-gees, isn't he?' said Mrs Tilman.

'Oh, rather, yes. Never happier than when he's standing by the rail with a pair of bins clamped to his face.'

'He'll be putting some money on for Sir Henry, I expect.'

'Yes, I shouldn't wonder. Don't change a winning team, what.'

While the table was being cleared, I saw an opportunity and turned to Mrs Tilman. 'If Lord Etringham wanted a private word with Miss Hackwood at some point today, have you any idea when and where might be suitable?'

Mrs Tilman smiled. 'She's a bundle of energy, Miss Amelia. You never quite know where she's going to be. Except at three o'clock.'

'What happens then?' I said, quick as you like.

'That's when she has her tennis lesson. Gentleman comes over from Blandford Forum. County player he was. Twice a week. Other days she tries to get Miss Georgiana to play. Trouble is, she's too good, Miss Amelia. She always wins. But Miss Georgiana's a good sport about it.'

'She's a jolly good sport about everything,' said Hoad.

'Too much for her own good if you ask me,' Mrs Padgett chipped in.

'That Mr Vegetables is a lucky man,' said Hoad.

'Mr Venables,' corrected Bicknell.

''Im being forty if he's a day and all,' Hoad went on. 'You ever tried reading one of them books of 'is?'

'Yes,' said Mrs Tilman, rather to my surprise. 'I'm halfway through *By Tramcar to Toledo*.'

'By Penny-farthing to Piddletrenthide's where I'd like to see 'im go.'

A shadow fell across the table. Bicknell had risen to his feet. 'That's quite enough, Hoad. We don't gossip about Sir Henry's guests. You've got plenty of work to do. Get started on it, please. We don't want another Liddle in this house.'

'All right, Mr Bicknell. Wait yer hurry. Just finishing me tea.'

Tearing myself away from this badinage, I headed upstairs to my cell, there to tidy things up a bit and nerve myself for the three o'clock showdown with Amelia. I was more than ever convinced that a bit of gossamer-light flirtation would lift the scales from her eyes as far as old Woody was concerned. And if that didn't do the trick, I was prepared, as Jeeves had put it, to buy for one.

What I was not prepared for was the exact nature of the beast — if I may refer to Amelia in that way. While I'd given Jeeves a fair bit of guff about the psychology of the individual, it had not occurred to me that there was one piece of the jigsaw missing — viz., that I had never actually met the individual in question. The female of the species is not only deadlier than the m., it's also a jolly sight rummier. No amount of theory can ever prepare one for the true extent of that rumminess. I remember the talk given to us half-dozen leavers by my house-master at Eton on the evening of our final day at school. The wisdom with which he wished to send us out to face the world could be boiled down to three things, he said. First: Never trust a man who keeps billiard chalk in his waistcoat pocket. Second ... I seem to have forgotten the second. But the third was, Women are queer cattle.

A disrespectful titter had passed among those present, but experience had taught me that the old pedagogue knew whereof he spake.

I had discovered from Jeeves that he would be driving the two-seater to the bookies' at Dorchester with his new best friend Sir Henry Hackwood in the dickey rather than with yesterday's news, yours truly. Hurtful, of course, but it freed me for some preparatory work. After an hour scouting out the territory, I had selected an excellent spot for my chance encounter with Amelia. And it happened – as the chap in the Bible says – on this wise.

From the centre of the terrace there ran a path with crazy paving, going in a southerly direction for a hundred yards between lines of small, clipped yew trees. At its end were two solid gateposts crowned with stone pine-apples. The gates were set into a hedge at right angles to the path, and beyond them, tucked away to the right and thus out of sight of the house, was the lawn-tennis court.

Dressed now in sports coat and flannels, I drew on the old Red Indian tracking skills to make a loop through the convenient cedars and positioned myself on the court-side of the Pineapple Gates at ten to three.

I am no stranger to the butterfly belly. A man who has had to pass himself off as Gussie Fink-Nottle to four aunts in a chilly Hampshire dining room with only orange juice in the carburettor knows the meaning of fear. I remembered, too, as a sixteen-year-old thespian, waiting for Helena to finish her interminable complaint before the lads who played the rude mechanicals could come on stage and liven things up a bit. Bottom's palms were too damp for any useful weaving at that point. This tennis court moment, though, was certainly in the top ten, and quite possibly up there in the unholy trinity.

Through a gap in the yew hedge I saw my prey approaching, bang on the appointed hour. Remember, Wooster, I said to myself, this is all for good old Beeching, P., the friend of your youth. Remember Beeching . . .

Amelia Hackwood was wearing a tennis dress to just above the ankle, and a dashed well-turned a. it was, clad in whiteish hosiery. Her hair was held with a bandana and she swished the wooden racket back and forth with a distracted air. In any household that did not contain G. Meadowes, she would have passed for hot stuff; and even so, I could see how Woody must have fallen like a sack of coals going down a hole in the pavement.

For all the schoolgirl complexion and lissomeness of form, however, there was something missing: a light, a spark. Her face was, as I've heard Jeeves describe it, sicklied o'er with the pale cast of thought.

'What ho!' I said, springing out, as she came through the gates.

She leapt back and pressed a hand to the bosom. 'You gave me a fright.'

'Expecting the professional from Blandford Forum, were you?'

'What? No, I'm—'

'Just out for a quick knock-up, what? Shall I act as ballboy?'

'What are you talking about?'

'Awfully nice dress, you know. Very becoming. Flattering to the old figure and all that.'

'Are you feeling all right?'

'Absolutely topping, thanks. Never felt better. But not half as good as you look. An absolute picture.'

'I really must be—'

With every sally, Amelia took a step further away

from me. I tried to remember exactly what it was that she had complained of with Woody and the village girls. Sleeve-stroking, I seemed to recall.

When matters come to a head, we Woosters act decisively. I took a step closer. I reached out ... I stroked.

'Lovely material, this. Now, can I give you a tip on the forehand I had from an Oxford blue?'

So saying, I moved in behind and laid my hand over hers on the racket handle, swung it back and followed through with plenty of elan. Even Big Bill Tilden might have had to grant that this was one forehand drive that wasn't coming back.

Amelia extracted herself from my embrace, somewhat red in the face. I hoped this was the first sign of the flush of forgiveness she was determined to extend to poor old Woody. I wasn't putting a lot of money on it, though.

Straightening her sleeve, she said, 'Who are you?'

I felt a slackening in the jaw muscles. I hadn't quite prepared for that one, and I wobbled a bit between Wooster and Wilberforce. Unable to plump for one or the other, I decided to take speech out of the equation altogether. I leaned in and kissed her on the cheek. I clung on for a moment, long enough to hear her say, 'Georgiana!'

Releasing my grip like a Boys' Brigade lightweight at the sound of the bell, I sprang back to see the above-named, also kitted out for tennis, standing a few feet away.

It was as though Amelia ceased to exist. The limbs that a moment ago had seemed the acme of elegance now reminded me of a chap Jeeves knows called something like Ozzy Manders, whose vast and trunkless legs of stone stand in the desert. Not that Amelia's were trunkless, obviously, but you get the gist.

As the gaze travelled northwards up Georgiana's outline, it came to rest on the face, which was pale, with the eye clouded. To say she looked disappointed would be undercooking it a bit; she looked like a child on Boxing Day who has just been told that Father Christmas is only Uncle Arthur in a cotton-wool beard.

Then a little colour returned, and her face took on the look it had had when she referred to herself as that character in Tolstoy. Sonya Something. Her jaw set bravely.

'Come on, Ambo,' she said. 'Time for the weekly thrashing. I'll see if I can get at least two games off you today.'

'Hang on, Georgie. Tell me something. Do you know this man? Have you ever met him?'

Georgiana looked me slowly up and down. 'No,' she said. 'I've never seen him before in my life.'

So saying, she turned her back and strode off to the tennis court.

The Bertram who slunk back up the servants' staircase to his quarters, there to bury his head beneath the pillow, was far from the gay boulevardier of song and story. No. This was a diminished, a deflated Wooster, whom his friends would have struggled to recognise. Where, they would have asked, was the thumping heartbeat of the Drones Amateur Dramatic Society? Where the man who, for a trifling bet, would swing himself across the swimming pool, suspended from the wooden rings above, in full evening dress? Where was the pep-filled fear-nothing who laughed at tyrants and cocked a snook at fate?

The odd thing is that I couldn't really have told them. Furthermore, I had no idea why I was heaving up and down like a merchantman that's been holed below the Plimsoll Line. Things could have been an awful lot worse. True, I had failed with Plan A: I had not yet been able to put two sundered hearts back together. But there was plenty in the demeanour of this Amelia to give one hope for Woody; I didn't believe she was moping simply because the tennis pro had failed to show up. No, there was a lovesickness there for sure. True also, Georgiana Meadowes now thought I was a cad for making eyes at some other chap's fiancée. Moreover, I had the strong impression that she enjoyed denying knowledge of me. It was not just that she was sticking to the scheme that we'd agreed on; she spoke with a relish that wasn't in the script. But if she now thought less of me, where was the harm in that? She was another man's intended and her feelings towards B. Wooster – supposing that she even had any – were of no consequence.

I had lost a battle, not a war. So, steady the Buffs, I thought – or may even have said out loud, as I rose from the truckle bed and changed back into clothing more fitted to my menial duties. Yet even as I donned the spongebag trousering, I suddenly remembered an afternoon at private school when I was about eleven and had been laid low by an attack of measles. The other chaps were off in a charabanc to play cricket against a nearby rival with a slap-up tea thrown in, while I was left perspiring beneath the blankets like the greater spotted toad.

At dusk the matron came in with a letter from home. As well as the usual stuff about the asparagus bed, Grandpa's gout and the Glossops' summer ball, it contained the news that Horace, the family hound, had, at the admittedly splendid age of fourteen, handed in his dinner pail and would bark no more in Woosterland. I had confided more in this beast than any living creature thus far in my life, and my trust had been well founded. As Matron closed the sickbay curtain, I wondered whether life could get much gloomier.

Why on earth this childish memory should have chosen that moment to ambush me, I had not the faintest idea. So straightening the dull blue tie, I checked that the hair was in place, the shoes shining and set off to find Lord Etringham.

My first port of call was the housekeeper's sitting room, though for once Mrs Tilman was unable to help. She had not heard whether the sporting duo was back from Dorchester, but perhaps a look in the garages beyond the stable block, this excellent woman pointed out, would establish whether the two-seater was still absent.

The advantage of this plan was that it kept me in a part of the estate where I was unlikely to come across any of the increasingly large number of people I did not wish to clap eyes on me. In addition to Hackwoods, Puxleys, Venableses and other rough customers, this list, to my chagrin, now contained Amelia and Georgiana.

If there was something furtive in my manner as I skirted past the thoroughbreds in their stabling, perhaps it can be forgiven in the circs. The Wooster sports model was neatly parked alongside what I took to be Sir Henry's somewhat battered four-door chariot, so I made another longish loop on my way back to the first-floor corner room.

I had never really considered before how little of a house like Melbury Hall is used by the family and its guests. Less than a third, I would have guessed, as I panted over a cobbled yard, through a battered side door, up a linoleum-covered stair, down a dim corridor, past maids' rooms and half-shut store cupboards from which mysterious mops and brushes poked their heads. I had almost despaired of reaching civilisation, when I spotted a passage that led to a distant baize-upholstered door.

This opening gave on to the main house and the huge

right-angled oak landing that hung above the main hall. I looked from side to side, like a dowager afraid to cross at Piccadilly Circus. I took a chance. I scooted, skidded, halted, knocked.

'Come in,' said a welcome voice.

His lordship was seated in an armchair by the window that overlooked the deer park.

'I didn't know you wore glasses, Jeeves,' I panted.

'Only for reading, sir.'

'Eye strain, is it? Too many of those triple-decker Russian novels? I can't say I'm surprised.'

'It is normal for people in their middle years to require reading spectacles. The condition is known as presbyopia. It derives from the Greek word "presbys" meaning an elder or—'

'Does it, by Jove?'

'A weakening of the ciliary muscles is unable to compensate for a loss of elasticity in the crystalline lens, which—'

'Jeeves?'

'Yes, sir?'

'Enough. I've got some bad news. An absolute wagonload of it.'

Jeeves laid down the hefty book and removed the specs. 'I am sorry to hear that, sir.'

'Plan A laid an egg. And I thought it was going to be the goose that ... But it was a turkey. Do you catch my drift?'

'The poultry metaphors are painting a lively picture, sir. Am I to take it that you were out for a duck?'

'Enough, Jeeves. This is an absolute snookeroo. Amelia was appalled by my behaviour and, what's worse, by some utter fluke Georgiana witnessed the whole thing and now thinks I'm the biggest cad this side of Newton Abbot.'

'Most distressing for you, sir.'

'I mean, dash it, I came down here to try to put Woody back on track with Amelia and now Georgiana thinks I'm trying to steal old Woody's girl. It's a disaster.'

'So it would appear, sir.'

'Jeeves, you're not helping. You don't seem to understand the gravity of the situation.'

'The plan or expedient was one about which, as I recall, I did express grave reservations, sir.'

'If you're trying to say "I told you so", you'd better just come out and say it.'

'On the contrary, sir. It merely occurred to me that Miss Hackwood is too much preoccupied with her feelings for Mr Beeching to be able to extrapolate any general rule about the behaviour of the male sex from a chance encounter with an over-friendly stranger, let alone to apply such an axiom to her particular situation.'

There was a longish silence in Sir Henry Hackwood's favoured guest room as I slowly decoded what Jeeves had said. I got there in the end and I had to admit that the chap had a point. I could see that now.

I slid a cigarette from my case and sucked in a pensive lungful.

'What next, Jeeves?'

'I would suggest doing nothing, sir.'

'Nothing? Have you taken leave of your senses?'

'I trust not, sir. However, my observation of Miss Hackwood leads me to suppose that she is very much struck by the charms of Mr Beeching. I believe her coldness to be temporary. If Mr Beeching can remember to contain his friendly impulse towards any member of the fairer sex to a point of simple civility in future, then I am confident that—'

'But what about Amelia? Do you think Woody can point out to her that he can't spend the rest of his life being dashed chilly to anything in a skirt?'

'Miss Hackwood is young, sir, but she is not unintelligent. And her character is not yet set. I see no reason why each party should not learn from his unfortunate *froideur*.'

'You may be right, Jeeves, but don't forget that whether they get hitched or not still depends on keeping Sir Henry sweet. Which reminds me, how did you get on at the bookies' in Dorchester?'

'It was Gold Cup day at Ascot, sir. I am happy to say that Sir Henry followed my lead and backed Solario.'

'So he's in a pretty good mood?'

'Indeed, sir, though it would be even better had he taken my advice and backed Pons Asinorum for a place.'

'Pond's What?'

'Pons Asinorum, sir. Sir Henry was deterred by the Latin name, which he described as "fancy nonsense".'

'But you weren't put off?'

'Not at all, sir. The phrase was familiar to me from the fifth proposition of Euclid.'

'Eh?'

'I beg your pardon, sir. It means the asses' bridge. It is the beginners' hurdle — or first point of a proof that the novice must somehow get across.'

'And this nag did well?'

'It ran on strongly to finish third, sir.'

'And you trousered a second bagful of silver?'

'A quite satisfactory sum, thank you, sir.'

I bunged the cigarette end into the fireplace. 'I'm very happy for you, Jeeves. But what am I to do about Georgiana? She's going to tell Woody that I've been making up to his fiancée.'

'I somehow doubt it, sir.'

'Why?'

'I can think of two reasons, sir.'

'I'm all ears, Jeeves.'

'Miss Meadowes is a good-hearted young lady, sir. She is disposed to think well of people. She is also quick-witted and may suspect there was an ulterior motive in your behaviour. Furthermore, she is devoted to her cousin, Miss Hackwood. She would do nothing to threaten her happiness.'

'Even though Amelia regularly gives her a pummelling on the tennis court.'

'Indeed, sir. I believe she is most sporting about it.'

'Well, that's one reason. I take it that it *was* just one, wasn't it? Even if it had half a dozen subclauses?'

'Indeed, sir, it was intended as a single entity.'

'Right ho. So what's reason number two? And any chance it might dash the Dorsetshire Bounder of the Year cup from my unwilling grasp?'

Jeeves cleared his throat and looked out of the window as though he had spotted something. I followed his gaze but could see nothing of moment beyond the railing of the park and a few contented deer cropping the verdure.

'The second reason is a delicate one, sir. It raises questions of feelings contingent on your own person.'

'Would it be possible to speak in plain English, Jeeves? I'm in a spot of bother here.'

'I shall endeavour, sir, to . . .' Jeeves coughed.

'Would you like a glass or water?' I asked.

'No, sir, I . . . Forgive me if this appears in some way *ultra vires* but—'

'You're at it again.'

'Very good, sir.' After one final throat clearance and wistful glance towards the grazing herbivores, he finally gave voice. 'Had it occurred to you, sir, that Miss Meadowes may entertain certain feelings for you?'

'Feelings? What sort of . . . Good heavens, Jeeves, you don't mean . . . Surely not . . . Not *that* sort of feeling?'

I sat down heavily on the end of the bed. My emotions at this moment can best be described as confused. There was a bit of exhilaration, a hefty dose of doubt, a worry about Jeeves's mental stability and the usual unease about bandying a woman's name. When the roiling waters of the Wooster mind had calmed a fraction, however, there was only one thing visible: disbelief.

I chose my words with care. 'What on earth makes you think that a woman who edits books and shoots the breeze with you about . . . what was that chap's name . . . Something-hour?'

'Schopenhauer, sir.'

'. . . and furthermore looks like an angel in human form on a quite exceptional day for angels would care for a complete ass like me – an ass, what's more, she's just seen manhandling her cousin?'

Jeeves passed a hand across his mouth. 'Miss Meadowes is undoubtedly a well-educated young woman, sir, but there is nothing of the intellectual snob about her. She told me that her time at Somerville was spent mostly at the Oxford University Dramatic Society. I believe her Rosalind in *As You Like It* was especially admired.'

'She mentioned something about Rosalind one night in France. I thought she was referring to a girl I knew in St Hilda's.'

'When not treading the boards, Miss Meadowes spent a good deal of time organising picnics or entertaining friends to dinner on a flat roof reached by way of the Principal's fire escape.'

'But she got a degree, didn't she?'

'Of the second class, I believe, sir.'

'That's a bit showy, isn't it? Anyway, the point is there's no reason in the world why she should have any of the feelings you're suggesting.'

'You spent a good deal of time together in France, sir.'

'Brother and sister stuff, Jeeves. Catsmeat and Corky dine together at every opportunity. And one doesn't want to put on the bib and tucker alone every night.'

'I believe you hold the young lady in high esteem, sir.'

'I do. The highest possible, in fact. But that's a completely different matter. That doesn't mean that I'm any more than the dust beneath her thingummy.'

'At dinner last night, sir, I observed a look in her eye when Mr Venables brought up the subject of the south of France.'

'A look in her eye! Egad, Jeeves, these are slim pickings.'

'A wistful look, sir. Accompanied by a degree of moisture.'

'Enough of this childish nonsense, Jeeves.'

'As you wish, sir.'

'And in any event, I feel we may well have been bandying, don't you?'

'It was difficult to convey my meaning without identifying the individual, sir. I might, perhaps, have chosen the form of a parable, as did the prophet Nathan when seeking to enlighten King David, but—'

'Yes, I remember. But I suppose you thought if you'd done the parable routine there was the risk that I wouldn't have known what you were on about.'

'The more direct approach seemed on balance—'

'Do you mind if we just stop there, Jeeves?'

The waters had started roiling again and the cardiac muscle was giving the inside shirt-front a bit of a pasting.

'As you wish, sir. Might I just add that it is still

conceivable that Mr Beeching might hear of this afternoon's misunderstanding from a different source.'

'From Amelia, you mean?'

'The young lady is so out of sorts that I feel she cannot be relied on.'

'She's cornered, you mean. Desperate. She might lash out.'

'The situation is fraught, sir. Miss Hackwood may feel she no longer has an interest in preserving the fiction of Lord Etringham and his gentleman's personal gentleman, Mr Wilberforce.'

'That's pretty serious, Jeeves.'

'I fear so, sir. It would mean an early end to our visit.'

'And Lady Hackwood would be straight on the blower to Aunt Agatha.'

'It is as well that the instrument is temporarily disabled, sir.'

'I tell you what else it would mean if Amelia tells Woody.'

I think I may have mentioned that in addition to everything else, Woody secured a half-blue at boxing in his final year at Oxford. Those of us who made the journey down to the Savoy hotel for the match against Cambridge will never forget the one minute and twelve seconds that made up the full extent of the middleweight bout, the amount of claret splashed about the ring nor the look on the face of the opposing undergraduate as he was helped back to his corner before resuming – with all speed, one imagined – his restful studies at Gonville and Caius.

I was not at all keen to find myself in the shoes of that young man, especially since in the intervening years Woody had almost certainly moved up a division.

'Golly, Jeeves. How on earth are we going to keep Amelia sweet until Sunday night?'

'I have been reflecting on the matter, sir and I have—'

But what exactly he had, I did not at once find out, as there was a knock at the door.

'Come in,' we said in unison.

The door opened and the space filled. When I say 'filled', I mean that there was nothing between lintel, jamb and floor that was not solid butler.

'I beg your, pardon, my lord,' said Bicknell. 'I was looking for Mr Wilberforce.'

'You came to the right place, Mr Bicknell,' I said.

'With Lord Etringham's permission, I wondered if I might ask your assistance, Mr Wilberforce.'

'Of course,' said Jeeves.

'Anything you like, Mr Bicknell,' I said. 'As I told you this morning, we Woo ... Wilberforces like to make ourselves useful. No General Striking for us.'

'Hoad, the temporary footman, finds himself indisposed. We sit down ten to dinner this evening and I need you to wait at table.'

'Love to help,' I said, thinking rapidly on my feet, 'but I haven't yet had a chance to get down to the village and make that call about the telephone line, so—'

'There's no hurry for that, Mr Wilberforce. I can go tomorrow.'

'It's just that I can't ...'

I looked across to Jeeves for salvation, but his face was expressionless and his lips remained sealed.

'I am most grateful,' said Bicknell. 'I shall be serving cocktails in the drawing room from seven o'clock and Sir Henry likes to sit down no later than eight. Perhaps you could report to Mrs Padgett at seven-thirty.'

The doorway emptied.

I may have got out a weak 'Right ho', or I may not. It is immaterial.

CHAPTER
═FIVE═

'Jeeves,' I said, when I had finally regained the power of speech. 'This is the bally end.'

'It would appear that confusion now hath made his masterpiece, sir.'

'Well, I jolly well wish his masterpiece didn't involve me in a starring role.'

'It is a most vexed state of affairs, sir, though perhaps not beyond hope.'

Then I noticed that Jeeves had a glint in his eye. There had been times over the last forty-eight hours when I had doubted the fellow. I had thought he was perhaps partaking in the work-shy public mood; I wondered if as well as

Spinoza he had been dipping into a bit of Karl Marx. Not for the first time, I had underestimated him.

'It is a fact of life, sir,' he said, 'that in the course of a large dinner party those at table barely notice those who wait on them.'

'Unless they make an ass of themselves.'

'Indeed, sir. Otherwise, the company tends to take the service for granted and to be absorbed in its own conversation.'

'That sounds a bit ungrateful.'

'It is the way of the world, sir, and not ours to question. Might I for instance ask you who waited on you last time you stayed at Brinkley Court?'

'Seppings?'

'No, sir. Mr Seppings was indisposed. It was Mr Easton, a young man from the village.'

'I didn't notice.'

'Exactly, sir.'

I pondered this for a moment. 'It's still a blood-curdling prospect.'

'I understand your trepidation, sir. Remember, however, that your disguise has been unremarked thus far. Then, to make assurance doubly sure, as it were, it might be advisable to alter your appearance in a small way.'

'A false beard?'

'No, sir. The footman you are replacing—'

'Hoad? The gargoyle?'

'Mr Hoad also has a pair of side-whiskers.'

'Are you saying the whiskers naturally go with the corkscrew and the folded white napkin?'

'They are more frequently worn by the serving classes, sir.'

There are times to take offence, but this was not one of them. I left my high horse unmounted – though tethered pretty close. 'What else?'

'If you were to part your hair centrally, sir ... It is surprising how much difference such a small alteration can make.'

'Anything further? An eyepatch? A kilt and sporran?'

'Nothing so drastic, sir. I think that if you were to wear my reading glasses for the evening the disguise would be complete without being histrionic.'

I went over to the window and did a bit of the fashionable deer-gazing.

The diners, I thought, could be divided into three

camps. There were those who had never clapped eyes on me: three Venableses and a brace of Hackwoods. There were those who were in on the plot and could be relied on: Lord Etringham and Georgiana. Then there was the problematic trio of Woody, Amelia and Dame Judith Puxley.

The episode of J. Caesar and the Shropshire roof had taken place some years earlier, and I was the last person Dame Judith would expect to see shovelling round the *petits pois*. Even if she deigned to look my way, the disguise should suffice. The danger lurked with Woody and Amelia. Woody, for all I knew, was even as we spoke planning to flatten my nose, while Amelia . . . Well, who could say what Amelia planned – or thought, or felt?

I outlined the above to Jeeves, who did not disagree.

'Might I suggest a division of labour, sir? If you take it on yourself to find Mr Beeching, explain your behaviour of this afternoon and beg his indulgence, I shall draw Miss Hackwood aside before dinner and endeavour to explain that her best interests could be served by allowing the subterfuge to continue.'

'But won't the other servants think it odd that I've changed my parting and taken to wearing gig lamps?'

'I doubt it, sir. They hardly know you, and would think it only a mild eccentricity at worst.'

'Right ho, Jeeves. Give me the specs. There's no time to be lost. Where can I find Woody?'

'I suspect he may be in his bedroom, sir. He has not been made to feel welcome downstairs.'

Woody had been moved from the corner room to a modest bolt-hole on the second floor. Following Jeeves's instructions, I made it up there in no time, but there was something a fraction tentative in my knock at the door.

'Come in,' said a voice. And if a voice can be described as listless, this was that v.

Woody was sitting in an armchair with his feet up on the windowsill, looking down the crazy paving towards the yew hedge. He was smoking a cigarette and his eye seemed fixed. It was as though he was trying somehow to see through the hedge to what lay beyond.

'Sit down,' he said, the v. still l.

The only place to sit was the end of the bed and it struck me I was conducting a pretty extensive trial of

Melbury Hall mattresses. This one gave a bit, but nothing like the model in the Etringham corner room.

'I was wondering when you'd pluck up courage,' said Woody, still not looking at me.

'Did Amelia mention that we'd ... Had a slight misunderstanding?'

'No.'

'Oh.'

Woody ground out his cigarette in a not altogether friendly way. 'Amelia,' he said, 'told me she had been set upon by a lunatic who started stroking her arm and then had the impudence to kiss her. I don't think there is any "misunderstanding" there, do you?'

'Well, no ... I mean, yes.'

'You're babbling.'

'Listen, Woody old man, let's not fall out over this. I was making eyes at Amelia in order to help you.'

'To help me? Have you lost your last brain cell? Shall I finally place that telephone call to Colney Hatch?'

I didn't think this sort of language would have gone down well in the Court of Appeal; there was also the matter of the telephone being out of action, but I let that pass.

'Let me explain, Woody. Look at me, please.'

Woody finally unhooked his ankles from the window-sill and swung round to face me. I had half a mind to ask him to turn back again, as the new vista did little for the Wooster morale. The look on his face was one I had not seen since that evening in the Savoy hotel, when, at seven-thirty on the dot, he stepped into the ring.

After a standing count of ten, I launched into an explanation of Plan A. I saw the old pal's features register curiosity, disbelief, anger and then something I couldn't put my finger on.

I finished and waited.

Finally, he spoke. 'I'd like you to understand something, Bertie. Once and for all. Amelia is out of bounds. No touching, pawing, kissing, slobbering or anything else. Do you understand?'

'Couldn't be clearer, Woody, old man. Daylight itself is murky when compared to—'

'I haven't finished. Amelia is a very clever young woman, well educated and—'

'I should say so! Brainy as anything.'

'Will you please put a sock in it, Wooster. I'll tell you when I want to hear from you next.'

Woody was now standing up, a couple of feet away,

and I had that old Gonville and Caius feeling in the knees. 'Right ho, Woody. Speak on.'

'As well as being an exceptionally bright girl and a very beautiful one, she is also an innocent. She's lived a sheltered life. I see in her great qualities which have yet to come to full maturity. They are there to be nurtured carefully over the years. What that girl doesn't know about butterflies is not worth knowing. She has the finest collection in the west of England. Amelia is the girl I am going to marry and I don't want any bunglers getting in the way. I'm going to marry her even if old Hackwood doesn't give his blessing. We'll elope if necessary. For old times' sake I'm prepared to believe your ridiculous story. I wouldn't credit such a hare-brained tale from anyone else. And you can take that whichever way you like. I'm not a jealous type and I don't want to become one. Let's not mention the incident again. But I warn you, Bertie, I shall be watching you. Like a hawk.'

I said nothing, as per instruction.

'Well?'

'Am I allowed to speak now?'

'Yes. Have you the faintest idea what I've been talking about?'

'Yes, I have. You love Amelia and intend to make her Mrs Beeching if it's the last thing you do.'

'Oh, hallelujah! He's got it. Hold tight to that thought, Bertie. Don't get confused or misled by anything else. And don't try to imagine the feelings that lie behind it. You wouldn't understand.'

'You never know, Woody. Perhaps I might.'

There was an awkward one, during which I caught sight of that look again.

'Or possibly not,' I footnoted, as I made my escape.

It being now almost seven o'clock, I went down a floor, through the green baize and up the back stairs to my quarters. I had fulfilled my share of the division of labours between Jeeves and me, and though Woody may have been a little graceless, I felt he had a point. A chap who's completely lost his head over a girl doesn't want some other chap giving her the come-on. It confuses. It enrages. I had no doubt about his passion for this Amelia, mysterious though she remained to me. And I had at least avoided a series of left-right combinations to the person. I could only hope Jeeves had pulled off a result with Amelia.

A bracing encounter with the chill waters of the bathroom was followed by a change of clothing and a re-parting of the hair. When I peered into the glass above the basin, it seemed to me I looked like Dan Leno about to go on stage at the Shoreditch Empire, but I trusted Jeeves's judgement. I took the spectacles he'd lent me and hooked them over the ears, thinking as I did so how much of Plato and the gang had passed through the lenses on the way to that great brain. It was an honour to wear them. Then I went downstairs – rather unsteadily, as the glasses seemed to make the steps rise up to meet me, like the gangway of a Channel steamer.

In the kitchen, Mrs Padgett filled me in on what to expect. The first course was soup, unfortunately. There was to be no less than five minutes but not more than ten between courses. Bicknell was on wine duty, but would help distribute the plates if I was getting behind.

'But 'ark at me going on,' said Mrs P. ''Appen you've done this all an 'undred times before.'

'Not really.'

I shall never, if I live to be as old as Methuselah, forget my first sight of the dining room at Melbury Hall. As I think I've mentioned, the Hackwoods used only a few rooms for themselves: drawing room, library, long room with billiard table and this dining room, with conservatory off. But what rooms they were.

The dining table could have seated thirty; and if you'd shoved it to one side of the room, you could have got another thirty down a second table alongside. No wonder a private school was baying at the gates.

I entered through a swing door in the corner, bearing a tray with several bowls of cold cucumber soup. I put it on the sideboard, as instructed, turned, and let my eyes take in the awful scene.

The company was in the process of sitting down. At the head of the table was Sir Henry Hackwood, a rubicund old villain with a face like a fox and a glittering eye. Desperation and bad temper had coloured his features, though Scotch whisky may have lent a hand. On his right was what looked like a Persian cat in human form, which, I took it from Woody's description, was Mrs Venables.

Georgiana wore a plain satin dress and a distant look. Amelia was in blue, though the rims of her eyes were red. Lord Etringham in his Drones club shirt-studs and exact bow tie was placed between them, exuding poise.

Woody was below the salt, brooding. The Venables father and son filled in the gaps, the latter without drawing breath as he told a story about a visit to the Maharajah of Jodhpur.

The real horror lay in mid-table where, opposite one another, sat Lady Hackwood and her old school friend Dame Judith Puxley. Dame Judith had rows of black beads over her evening dress and an unblinking gaze, like a rattlesnake that's just spotted its lunch. In appearance, her old classmate, Lady H, ran more to the blowsy end of things, but her voice was a pure icicle of disappointment. Between them they were about as welcoming as Goneril and Regan on being told that old Pop Lear had just booked in for a month with full retinue.

It was with a palsied hand that I began the soup service.

'Damned annoying thing just happened,' Sir Henry announced to the table. 'Shields and Caldecott, couple of my best players for Saturday, have pulled out. Motoring off to Kent to play for some wandering outfit. It's very short notice to replace batsmen of that quality.'

'Really, Henry, it's just a game,' said Lady H. 'What does it matter who plays for you?'

'Because, my dear, the rest of the team are fellows

from the house – guests and staff. We need a couple of strong players. Beeching?'

Woody looked up from his soup. 'I'll see if I can think of someone, Sir Henry. It's Thursday, so—'

'I know what day of the week it is, man. I thought you were supposed to be a sportsman.'

'My work at the Bar has meant that I haven't had much time recently, but I could try a few old friends from the Oxford eleven.'

'We don't want swots, you fool, we want batsmen.'

'We did beat Surrey that year, and drew with York-shire, so ...'

It was a couple of furlongs from Sir Henry's seat to the Coventry occupied by Woody, but a glare made itself felt across the gulf and silenced the playmate of my youth.

'Might I make a suggestion, Sir Henry?' said Jeeves.

'Ah, Etringham. I knew I could rely on you.'

'My man Wilberforce is a keen cricketer. He has fre-quently boasted to me of his triumphs with leather and willow. I believe that when younger he had a trial for the county.'

I had got four soup bowls almost back to safety, but at this moment they broke into a spontaneous dance, the spoons going like castanets as I plonked the whole lot on to the sideboard.

I was about to protest, when I heard Jeeves continuing, 'I feel sure that he would be able to find another player or two at short notice. His acquaintance is formed in large part from the sporting underworld.'

'Sounds like an excellent chap,' said Sir Henry. 'Tell him to see what he can do. He's got carte blanche.'

I don't know if anything about this exchange has struck you as odd. No? Well, the thing that seemed peculiar to me was that no one consulted the fellow Wilberforce himself. It was as though I wasn't there.

I heard the high horse neigh impatiently, and I cast a wistful glance in the direction of the saddle. Then I remembered what Jeeves had told me about Easton, the stand-in butler at Aunt Dahlia's; I bit the lip and took the tray back to the kitchen.

By the time I came back with some sole fillets, Sidney Venables was addressing Lady Hackwood at the top of his voice.

'The Pathan,' he bellowed, 'is a splendid chap and we always got on well with them, didn't we, my dear? The Bengali, on the other hand, is a slippery customer.'

'And did you spend much time in Calcutta?' asked Dame Judith Puxley. 'My late husband once lectured there.'

'Heavens, no, frightful place. All plagues and bad drains. Appalling climate.'

'Did you in fact ever visit?' Dame Judith persisted.

'I was due to go once, but there was a deal of trouble with the Sepoys in the local cantonment. The CO was out of his depth so guess who had to step in and sort it out! "Send for Venables!" That was always the cry if there was dirty work afoot, wasn't it, my dear?'

'Sidney was ever so busy,' said the Persian cat.

Dame Judith was not deterred. 'I was simply trying to establish, Mr Venables,' she went on, 'how you came to have such a view about Bengalis without having actually visited Bengal.'

If you were a Sumerian tablet beneath Dame Judith's scrutiny, one imagined, you would give up your secrets pretty quick, cuneiform or not.

Old Venables, however, seemed oblivious. 'Oh, it's well known,' he said. 'Kipling couldn't stand the blighters either. Now the Punjab is a different matter.'

'We liked the Punjabis,' said Mrs Venables to Sir Henry Hackwood.

'What?'

Sir Henry had been staring out of the window while the Indian chatter went on, doubtless wondering whether it was too late to send a car to London for Patsy Hendren to open the batting on Saturday.

'I said, we liked the Punjabis, Sidney and me.'

'Did you by Jove!' Sir Henry gave her a quick once-over, as though trying to remember who she was. 'Well, jolly good for you.'

'And then of course,' old Venables boomed on, 'some fool in Delhi raised the question of independence.'

'And what did you think of that?' said Lady H wearily.

'Well,' said Venables, wiping his lips on his napkin, 'I was very interested by my own response.'

On my next return to the kitchen, I found Mrs Padgett dishing up the meat course, with the help of a stout female from the village. This was Mrs P's big moment, and it was all hands to the pump. The noisettes of veal didn't look a patch on those that Anatole's legerdemain conjured up in Aunt Dahlia's kitchen, but in any normal light appeared toothsome enough. While all was being transferred from cooking vessel to china, I slipped back into the dining room to make myself useful.

As I was pouring a glass of water for Rupert Venables, I caught Georgiana's eye across the table. It held an expression I had never seen in all those evenings in France, or in our brief encounters since. Reproach was the first thing I spotted; though there was a lingering friendliness, too. What was new in those deep brown pools was ... I'm not sure what the word is. Melancholy? I can't put my finger on it. But the light that had sparkled when she used to say, 'Come on, Bertie, couldn't we just *share* a few langoustines' had been extinguished.

It hit me hard. Pausing only to mop up the worst of the overspill from young Venables's tumbler, I moved hastily down the row of chairs.

Dame Judith had by now wrenched the conversation from the subcontinent to the question of the female vote, where she seemed to sense blood.

'My dear Henry,' she was saying, 'surely you can't imagine that women will give up the battle until they have the same rights as men.'

'Henry can imagine anything if he tries hard enough,' said his wife. 'He can picture a pot of gold under the mulberry tree in Snooks Farm Lane when he's in the mood. Ask him to imagine selling a couple of racehorses, though, and his mind goes completely blank.'

'A great mistake giving women the vote at all,' said Sir Henry. 'Whatever next? They'll try and form an all-women government.'

'That would be a splendid idea,' said Dame Judith. 'They would make a better job of it than the dunderheads we usually have in office.'

'Absolute stuff and nonsense,' said Sir Henry, blind to Lady H's warning look. 'Anyway, the wretched suffragettes have got their way.'

'Only for women over thirty,' said Dame Judith.

'Quite right,' chipped in Amelia. 'Cousin Toby can vote, and he's younger than I am. He's only twenty-two. It's ridiculous.'

'If you think a couple of young girls like you and Georgiana would know how to cast a vote sensibly then I...' Sir Henry seemed finally to catch his wife's eye. 'I'll eat my head,' he trailed off.

I was manoeuvring the dish of what I took to be *pommes dauphinoises* between Sidney Venables and Georgiana Meadowes when I heard a familiar soft cough –

probably not audible to the untrained ear. I looked up to see Jeeves's eye flicker meaningfully from right to left, telling me that I was on the wrong side.

I had wondered why old Sidney, who looked every inch a potato wallah, was giving me the cold shoulder. I had come in hard to starboard and he was braced for a portside docking. I began to withdraw the heavy dish for a fresh approach, without thinking that what was right to Venables was left to Georgiana, who at that moment reached for the spoon and fork. The combination of her digging and my pulling back caused a sort of leverage to take place. Three slices of King Edward's with accompanying sauce flipped on to the table.

'Sorry, Bertie,' said Georgiana. 'My fault. No harm done.'

She quickly scooped up the stray bits and put them on her side plate.

I was too busy with my 'Sorry, Miss'-ing to be absolutely certain that I'd heard correctly. I docked successfully at the second attempt with Venables senior, who helped himself with a will.

Keeping my head down, I moved on to Amelia and in my mind went back over the last thirty seconds or so. There was no doubt that Georgiana had said, 'Sorry, Bertie.'

As I finished dauphinoise duty and returned to my sentry-go position by the sideboard, I felt four eyes boring into me. Reading from left to right, those eyes belonged to Lady Hackwood and Dame Judith Puxley, and what fell within their field of vision signally failed to please.

'Georgiana,' said Lady Hackwood, 'did I hear you—'

But Georgiana was up and running. 'Dame Judith, what perhaps you need to understand about dear Uncle Henry's attitude to women's suffrage is that it was formed by the outcome of the Derby in 1913.'

It seemed to do the trick. There was a pause.

'I beg your pardon?' said Dame Judith, as though she had stepped in something. 'A horse race?'

'Yes! You remember,' Georgiana went on briskly, 'when that suffragette threw herself beneath the hooves of the king's horse—'

'Anmer,' barked Sir Henry. 'Thoroughly second-rate colt. Disgrace to the king's colours.'

'. . . And caused a commotion,' said Georgiana, forging on. 'Well, what some people seem to have forgotten about the race is that it ended in a stewards' inquiry. The winner when they crossed the line was the favourite, Craganour. He had just overtaken a horse called Aboyeur, a hundred-to-one outsider.'

I remembered Georgiana telling me she had spent most of her childhood in the saddle, but I'd no idea she was quite such an historian of the Turf.

'It was a disaster,' said Sir Henry.

'Like most people,' said Georgiana, 'Uncle Henry had put all his money on the favourite. But the stewards disqualified him and gave the race to Aboyeur.'

'Absolute scandal,' said Sir Henry.

'Uncle Henry maintained that Craganour had had to change course after the suffragette incident, whereas Aboyeur was unaffected.'

'Without that wretched woman,' said Sir Henry, 'Craganour would have won by a good two lengths.'

'And that, Dame Judith,' Georgiana concluded, 'is why Uncle Henry is against all forms of female emancipation.'

'I was set to win thirty-five guineas,' said Sir Henry sadly.

Woody was trying not to laugh, while Rupert Venables

let out a shrill one. Goneril and Regan seemed to have been distracted, though I was not convinced the danger had fully passed.

Jeeves may well have felt something similar. As Georgiana fell back, flushed with her effort, he stepped up smoothly.

'A most distressing day,' he said. 'I remember it well.'

'I suppose you were on the favourite, too, Etringham,' said Sir Henry, sympathetically. 'We all were.'

'Indeed,' said Jeeves. 'Though I was placing my bet with Honest Sid Levy, I could not help noticing the extremely generous odds on Aboyeur. It seemed to me that a small saving wager at such a price was well worth the gamble.'

'You really are quite a fellow, aren't you, Etringham? When the ladies leave us, you'd better talk me through the card tomorrow.'

'It would be a pleasure. Though no one of course can guarantee—'

'Don't be so dashed modest! Never known a tipster like it.'

I left them to their mutual admiration, but I have to say it was a pretty shaken Bertram who rejoined the galley slaves.

'By 'eck, you look all in, Mr Wilberforce,' said Mrs Padgett. 'Them folk giving you the runaround are they?'

'Not at all. I'm in prime early-season form, thank you, Mrs P.' This equine chat was catching.

'Well, there's a nice bit of veal left if you fancy it later, love.'

We sons of toil had taken our dinner early – some sort of cheese pie at about six-thirty – and it was still exacting a pretty heavy toll on the Wooster digestive system. The only thing I could, with any pleasure, envisage joining it was a glass or two of the distinguished red I'd seen Bicknell hauling out of the cellars that morning.

'And how did that all go down, then?' asked the proud cook. 'Any nice comments?'

'No one said anything,' I replied truthfully, but then thought better of it. 'Mr Venables senior enjoyed himself. He came back for more.'

'And Miss Georgiana?'

'She didn't seem to have much appetite.'

'Oh dear. That's not like her!'

'I know.'

Mrs Padgett gave me an odd look, like a miner's wife who'd found a ferret in the coal – or whatever passed for odd in her native parts.

'I mean, she looks like a healthy girl who'd enjoy one of your excellent dinners, Mrs P,' I embroidered.

'Any road,' the stout woman sighed, 'we're almost done now. Just the gooseberry fool to go, and then we can all put our feet up. I'll make you a nice cup of tea then.'

So saying, she pointed me towards a tray of glassware and I elbowed my way back through the swing door into the lions' den – a Daniel, if ever there was one, come to judgement.

Bicknell helped distribute the cut-glass receptacles, leaving me to lug round the heavy crystal bowl with Mrs P's finest fool on board.

Say what you like about Sir Henry Hackwood's guests, they didn't let themselves get stuck for long on one topic. As I held the bowl out to Lady H, Rupert Venables made a polite inquiry about whether his future aunt-in-law, if that's the term, had any travel plans for later in the summer.

The reply was brief and discouraging. 'Our current situation will not permit us to travel beyond Wareham.'

'Such a shame,' said young Venables, warming to his moment in the spotlight. 'The Mediterranean in late September is at its most charming. That's the time of year I famously travelled by schooner to Sardinia.'

'That's my favourite of Roo's books,' purred Mrs Venables to her neighbours.

I thought I heard a sound of teeth grinding, but I supposed it was only Sir Henry pushing back his chair.

'Yes, I like that one very much, too,' said Georgiana.

'Do you, my dear?' said Rupert.

'Yes, I do. Why?'

'I thought you rather preferred the month of May for your travels in the Mediterranean.'

Young Venables smiled at the company, like an old vaudevillian who has just produced his catchphrase. The response was coolish.

'The promenade at Nice,' he went on regardless, 'the seafront at Cannes ... I thought you found them especially seductive in the spring.'

Well, I could have told him the old one about what to do when in a hole. As to what to do when in said orifice while being scrutinised by Dame Judith Puxley through her lorgnette ... The maxim has yet to be coined, but in addition to a halt to all excavation, it would almost certainly recommend a change of subject.

Like his father, however, Venables the younger seemed a stranger to embarrassment. 'You didn't tell us, my dear,' he went on languidly, if that's the word I want, 'the full story of your springtime adventure.'

Georgiana flushed an angry red, but said nothing.

'Guinevere!' called out Dame Judith, and I looked towards the door, wondering if we'd be joined by some new harridan, bringing the number of Weird Sisters to the optimum three. 'What on earth is the young man talking about?'

'He's talking about a week Georgiana spent in France,' said Lady Hackwood, answering to her Christian name, as I now gathered. 'She was apparently pursued by some lunatic called Gloucester or Worcester.'

'Good heavens,' said Dame Judith. 'Not Bertie Wooster, Agatha Worplesdon's nephew? I thought Agatha had had him put away.'

Quite a number of things happened at that moment, and I suppose the exact order of them is unimportant, but I like to keep the record straight. A small matter you may say, but we authors have our pride.

The crystal bowl of gooseberry fool, into which Dame Judith was dipping for a second time, jerked violently forwards, as though it had taken on an independent life.

Georgiana Meadowes flung down her napkin, pushed back her chair and stormed out of the dining room.

Rupert Venables followed her with his eyes, simpered and looked about the company.

For the umpteenth time, Bicknell refilled his master's glass.

Back at Puxley Central, a desperate attempt was made to retrieve the situation. However, continued dippings into the fool had rendered the surface of the bowl slippery, while Jeeves's reading glasses blurred my focus. It was perhaps a mistake to remove one hand and try to steady the bowl from beneath, as it may have been this manoeuvre that caused the wretched thing to flip over. It was certainly, on reflection, an error of judgement to attempt to remove approximately five helpings of gooseberry fool from Dame Judith Puxley's lap with a Georgian tablespoon.

CHAPTER
SIX

By the time the commotion had finally died down, the dining room at Melbury Hall contained men only; and I hope it's not ungallant to say that it seemed a better place for it.

Lady Hackwood had dispatched Amelia to inquire after Georgiana and had then taken Mrs Venables and Dame Judith up to her boudoir – there, one assumed, to coo over children's photographs, swap horror stories about their husbands and, in Dame Judith's case, to purge the outer garments of gooseberry.

In the dining room, Bicknell placed the port on the table and retired to his position in front of the double doors. I was told to clear the remains of the table while the men pushed up their chairs towards the host.

'I think we're all right for bowling,' said Sir Henry, as though the events of dinner had been no more than a brief interruption. 'I've got a local farmer called Harold Niblett. Runs like a Jehu, bowls like the wind. Useful bat as well. Beeching can open from the other end.'

'Thank you, Sir Henry, but to be honest, I was only ever a net bowler,' said Woody.

'Good enough in this company,' said Sir Henry. 'And that footman Liddle, the one I sacked last week. He can show us his wobblers.'

'Are you happy to have him back so soon?' said Jeeves.

'Not happy, Etringham, no. But needs must. I've paid him a guinea to bowl eight overs and keep his hands off the silver. You can turn your arm over, too, I expect.'

'It has been many a year since I had the opportunity,' said Jeeves. 'I fear time's wingèd chariot may have—'

'Well, go up and have a net tomorrow. Get some practice. What about you, Venables? Do you bowl?'

'No, I'm an opening batsman. The Nizam of Hydera-bad was kind enough to say I reminded him of Victor

Trumper. I field at first slip. Hands like flypaper, they tell me.'

'All right.' Sir Henry ran his eye up and down the ex-Collector like a buyer inspecting the goods at an Irish horse fair, but bit his tongue.

'What about you, young Venables? Fancy a few overs?'

'I barely know the rules, I'm afraid,' said Rupert Venables. 'My tastes always ran more to the aesthetic. At school I was allowed to miss games because I was needed in the art room, and then of course there was Cambridge.'

'What happened there?' said Woody.

'A little punting,' said Rupert. 'And study, of course. As an undergraduate I was already developing my passion for travel.'

Sir Henry let out a noise like a mastiff sneezing and made a long arm for the port decanter. 'Well, you can go in number eleven, then. Anyway, Etringham, we're all right for bowling. What your man has to do is find me a pair of top-order batsmen.'

'I feel confident that he will be able to do so by tomorrow evening. Might I venture to suggest a wager on the outcome of the match?'

Sir Henry's face assumed a look of foxy interest. 'What? A straight bet with their captain?'

'I wonder if there could be a way of interesting the bookmaker in Dorchester,' said Jeeves. 'It is my experience of turf accountants that if they see a likely profit in it for themselves they are prepared to make a book on any event, however parochial. I might be able to link it to events at Ascot.'

'Shall I leave that in your capable hands, Etringham?'

'I should be happy to oblige. I assume that the abilities of the Dorset Gentlemen are well known in the district?'

'They've been around for donkey's years. The bookies should know their form all right.'

'I remember,' 'Vishnu' Venables began, 'the final of the Uttar Pradesh Divisional Cup. One year it was held in Chanamasala, and as luck would have it I received a call from the Deputy High Commissioner saying, "Sidney, you're the only man we can rely on . . ."'

I can't say for what Venables was being relied on, however, as by this time I had finished my clearing and was dismissed by a nod from Bicknell, who was still on duty by the doors to the hall.

It was with considerable relief that I sat down at the kitchen table and passed a hand across the brow. My schoolboy role as Bottom in *A Midsummer Night's Dream* had involved me in memorising and speaking many more lines than had been required of me in the part of Wilberforce, stand-in footman; but the stakes had not been as high. A momentary lapse or fluff from me, and Boggis-Rolfe minor sat ready, text in hand, to provide the missing line. A slip-up from Wilberforce, on the other hand ... I had no doubt that the mayhem that had been narrowly avoided would have made the Four Horsemen of the Apocalypse look like the warm-up act at the Melbury Tetchett Gymkhana.

'Cup of tea, Mr Wilberforce?'

'Thank you, Mrs P. I don't suppose you could lay your hands on something a little stronger, could you? Did I see some of that claret making its way back?'

'I don't know as I should by rights. It's Mr Bicknell's little perk. But seeing as how there's quite a bit ... You wait there.'

A moment or so later, I was clutching a goblet of the blushful hippocrene, which I proceeded to lower with all speed lest Bicknell should come in and dash it from my lips. It seemed a pity to rush it, but it bucked me up no end.

Back in my billet, I stretched out the aching limbs and picked up *The Mystery of the Gabled House*. For once, however, it failed to divert. I was not sure if this was a new corpse in the conservatory or one I had already known about. Oddly, it seemed not to matter.

I was distracted by a certain ferment inside the old bean. Georgiana had almost dropped me in the soup by using my real name – an odd lapse, I thought, for such a clever girl. Then I had blundered by letting Mrs Padgett see I knew that Georgiana's normal appetite tended to the hearty. I thought I could survive a quizzical eyebrow from the cook, but the suspicious glare of Lady Hackwood and Dame Judith Puxley was altogether more ominous.

I consulted the alarm clock with its hideous twin bells. It was almost eleven, and I wondered if Lord Etringham might be needing anything before he turned in. By corridor, stair and landing, under the eyes of nine generations of painted Hackwood forebears, I found my way to his vast accommodation and knocked on the door. It was a relief to hear that familiar voice.

Jeeves was wearing my burgundy dressing gown

over the remains of his evening dress, looking like the wronged husband in a West End comedy. He was seated in the armchair, holding a book at arm's length, minus his reading glasses.

I shut the door behind me. 'Jeeves,' I said, 'what's all this about me being a county cricketer? You know perfectly well I've barely played since private school.'

'Forgive me, sir. It was an impulse I was unable to resist. I felt certain that you would number some able players among your acquaintance and that it would be well for Sir Henry to feel that our continued presence at Melbury Hall was essential.'

'I suppose there's something in that. I could send a telegram to old "Stinker" Pinker. More of a rugby football man, but he'd probably give it a good thump.'

'Undoubtedly, sir. A proficiency of hand-to-eye co-ordination is generally transferable from one sport to another.'

'He'd also welcome a break from ministering to the poor and needy. And he could bring Stiffy. I haven't seen her for ages.'

I ran over some more chums in my mind. Many were hot stuff at darts, snooker pool and other indoor pursuits, especially those that tended to involve the wagering of money; cricket, however, didn't loom large among their pastimes.

Then I had a flash of inspiration. 'What about Esmond Haddock? There's a sporting fellow if ever I saw one.'

'As I recall, his interests run more to the equestrian, sir.'

'Absolutely. He's the John Peel of the South Downs. But I bet he'd enjoy a game of cricket too. And he might bring Corky. I'll go to the post office first thing in the morning and get cabling. By the way, how did you square it with Amelia not to mention that I was the fool who made a lunge at her by the tennis court?'

'I brought her into my confidence in the drawing room before dinner. It was necessary for me to impress on her the possibility that her father could shortly be in a position to make such a considerable sum that he would be happy to bless her union with Mr Beeching, regardless of other considerations.'

'How?'

'I deemed it best not to go into detail with the young lady, sir. But I emphasised that my continuing presence at her father's side was essential.'

'And she bought that?'

'For the time being, sir.'

There was a pause while I steeled myself to broach a rather sticky topic – and I was not thinking of Dame Judith Puxley's evening wear.

'Jeeves?'

'Yes, sir.'

'You know Miss Meadowes?'

'I have that pleasure, sir.'

'Do you think ... I wonder ... You know what you said earlier? About these feelings of hers?'

'Yes, sir.'

'I've decided to pretend I never heard you. I don't like what it does to the pit of my stomach. It's as though I'd swallowed a whole jar of cocktail olives from the bar at the Drones.'

'A most disagreeable sensation, one would be disposed to imagine, sir.'

'Well, "one" would be absolutely spot on. So let's hear no more about it. And if in some ludicrous fairy story these "feelings" you talk of became a reality and some sort of match took place ... Well, I mean ... imagine!'

'Imagine what, sir?'

'The offspring. Suppose they had my brain and not hers!'

'It may not be a matter of inheriting the qualities of one parent or the other, sir.'

'What? Are you saying it's a sort of cocktail?'

'A Moravian monk by the name of Mendel produced some remarkable results using peas or beans in his monastery garden. In the question of the colour and shape of the pod, he deduced that—'

'Jeeves, are you comparing the Wooster offspring to a broad bean?'

'Not as such, sir – though a comparable mechanism is believed to operate throughout the natural world. Certain heritable qualities may predominate – brown eyes over blue, for instance. However, in the event of both parents carrying the potential for blue, then two minuses may make a plus, as it were.'

'Are we still with garden vegetables?'

'No, sir. A close study of fruit flies seemed to contradict the principle, but—'

'One thing we can say for certain, Jeeves, is that Miss Meadowes is unlikely ever to be the mother of a fruit fly.'

'Indeed, sir. The science is as yet in its infancy. For the

time being, the empirical evidence of one's own observation is perhaps as good a guide as anything.'

'Come again?'

'One need only to compare Miss Madeline Bassett or
Miss Pauline Stoker to their respective fathers to see that
many factors were at play.'

'Golly, Jeeves. I see what you mean. Who would have
thought an armour-plated tank like J. Washburn Stoker
could have sired such an absolute popsy?'

Jeeves raised a polite eyebrow, which was as close as
he could come to saying, 'You betcher.'

I stopped my pacing for a moment. 'Let us leave
fantasy behind, Jeeves, and return to the real world.'

'As you wish, sir.'

'It is improper even to speculate on such matters.
By her own choice, Miss Meadowes is engaged to Mr
Venables. All that remains for us is to clear the diary,
press the morning coat and order the silver fish slice.'

'Indubitably, sir. Unless the arrangement were to
be brought to an end by the mutual agreement of both
parties.'

'Yes. Or a flight of Berkshire Whites went oinking
over Melbury Hall.'

'"Dear as remembered kisses after death, sir, And sweet as those by hopeless fancy feign'd On lips that are for others."'

'Is that helpful?'

'It was intended by the poet Tennyson as a consolation, I believe, sir.'

'Well, you tell him from me what to do with his consoling.'

'A certain melancholy doubtless underlies the verse, sir.'

I made for the door. 'Jeeves, would you be so kind as to forget everything I've said since I came into the room.'

'Consider it forgotten, sir.'

'We shall not refer to the lady in question again.'

'As you wish, sir.'

'Just one last thing. I don't suppose you've had a chance to speak to her since the failure of Plan A?'

'No, sir. I feel the explanation of your behaviour towards Miss Hackwood would carry more weight if it came from yourself.'

'I suppose you're right,' I said gloomily. 'What time have you earmarked for tea in the morning?'

'I have arranged with Mrs Tilman that she will bring a

tray, sir. So there is no need to inconvenience yourself if you prefer to rise at a later hour.'

It was another spiffing June day, and for all the lumbago after a second night on the fakir's cot, it was difficult not to feel a certain lightness of spirit as I strode down the back drive of Melbury Hall with a plateful of Mrs Padgett's hot scrambled eggs and bacon inside me.

The post office in Kingston St Giles was in the main street, between the butcher and the Red Lion. It was a musty sort of place that also served as a sweet shop for the local youth. Resting the telegram form between a jar of bullseyes and a box of sherbet dips, I set about composing.

'STINKER URGENT YOU COME MELBURY HALL KINGSTON ST GILES TOMORROW BY NOON STOP KEY CRICKET MATCH STOP YOUR BATTING CRUCIAL STOP MARITAL BLISS DEPENDS STOP DO BRING STIFFY STOP AT ALL COSTS DO NOT LET ON YOU KNOW ME STOP REGARDS BERTIE'.

I passed the form back to the elderly female behind her wire protection. 'Thank you,' I said. 'And please send another exactly the same to the Hall, Kings Deverill.'

The old dear read the message and began to shake her head. Then she peered at me in a way I have grown used to over the years: as though I had been licensed for day release from some corrective institution, but only by a majority vote.

'Oh, and in the second one, though, change "Stiffy" to "Corky". Otherwise Esmond'll think I'm off my chump.'

'Then I'll send them off, shall I? As they are?'

'Yes, though maybe in the first one also say, "No Bartholomew, thanks". Stiffy's Aberdeen terrier, you see. He bites first, asks questions later. Be an absolute menace on the pitch.'

'And that one's for the Rectory, Totleigh-in-the-Wold?'

'Spot on. For the return, put Etringham, Melbury Hall.'

Leaving the good woman to her telegraphing, I strode out in the sunshine; and there being little to detain me in the village, I made my way back to the Hall, found Jeeves and told him to expect some telegrams.

By noon, the first bicyclist was coming up the drive. Lord Etringham was poised at the receipt of custom, or more accurately in the porch, between a couple of hefty Egyptian urns. 'BERTIE YOU ASS WILL BE THERE STOP

NO STIFFY WITHOUT BARTHOLOMEW STOP YEARS SINCE BATTED REGARDS HP'.

An hour later came tidings from Deverill Hall. Esmond Haddock sounded delighted, as I had foreseen, to be spared the company of his aunts for a day or so. 'RUSTY BUT WILLING STOP REGRET CORKY IN HOLLYWOOD STOP TALLY-HO! WHY MUST I NOT KNOW YOU? REGARDS ESMOND'.

I gave the post office till half-past two to reopen after lunch, then sent the following to Harold 'Stinker' Pinker. 'MUCH REGRET MUST BE INFLEXIBLE ON DOG EVEN IF NO STIFFY AS RESULT STOP LUNCHEON AT TWELVE FORTY-FIVE STOP YOU OPENING BATTING WITH VISHNU VENABLES EX COLLECTOR CHANAMASALA STOP REGARDS WOOSTER'.

To Esmond, I cabled: 'WOULD TAKE TOO LONG TO EXPLAIN WHY NOT KNOW ME STOP BETRAY NO SURPRISE IF YOU FIND ME IN UNLIKELY ROLE STOP WOOSTER'.

The elderly female did a bit more head-shaking as she bent to her task.

Since Jeeves had gone off in the two-seater to construct his wager of many parts with Dorchester's answer to Honest Sid Levy, I thought I might try and catch a moment or two of shut-eye in the third floor back. It was with some surprise that I discovered an envelope sticking out from under my door.

'Mr Wilberforce' was written on it in what they call an educated hand – by which I suppose they mean it was clearly not the work of Liddle, Hoad or any rude mechanical. Inside was a folded sheet of Melbury Hall paper on which the same elegant hand had written in blue ink: 'Mr W, Knowing how busy you have been – and perhaps unfamiliar with the servants' eating hours – I have left a small picnic lunch, including a half-bottle, on the bench in the sunken garden, far from prying eyes. Do enjoy it if you can find time.' It was signed with an illegible hieroglyph, or cuneiform, perhaps – though I had no intention of consulting on that particular point.

It's true that I had been at the post office when the other servants took an early lunch; true also that Mrs Padgett had dug out a knob of cheddar for the latecomer, but, while moderation is the Wooster watchword where any form of refreshment is concerned, it had been a busy day and I felt I could squeeze in a little more. The advantage of this sunken garden was that it was far from lawn-tennis court, rockery or anywhere else I was likely to encounter enemy shipping.

I approached via the greenhouse, cold frames and asparagus beds, through a rustic gate. On a wrought-iron bench sat a wicker basket with a sprig of wild flowers on top. From this last touch I deduced – being pretty quick at these things – that my benefactor was female. Inside, the half-bot was a loosely recorked red of a most fruity provenance; the solids included a wedge of veal-and-ham pie that could have jammed open the west doors of Salisbury Cathedral.

A satisfactory ten minutes later, I was just lighting a cigarette when I heard a contralto voice with a warmish timbre say, 'Ah, Wilberforce, I thought I might find you here.'

I leapt to my feet and saw Georgiana in a straw hat, carrying a trug and a pair of secateurs.

'Ah! What ho! Doing some pruning, what?'

Not exactly Mark Antony, I admit, nor even Beeching, P., but I hadn't been expecting company.

She looked down at the contents of her hands, as though remembering. 'Yes . . . Ah, yes, absolutely. Pruning. How was the picnic?'

'Top-hole. Very sustaining.'

'Mrs Padgett does make a good pie. You should try her steak and kidney.'

'I intend to. Cigarette?'

'No, thanks.'

'Looking forward to the game tomorrow?'

'Oh, rather. Amelia and I are in charge of tea. I shall be driving it down through the village in Uncle Henry's car.'

'And then in through the gate in the lane?'

'Exactly.'

'These Dorset Gents are probably a hungry lot.'

'Yes, I expect so.' She breathed in deeply. 'Bertie . . .'

'Yes?'

'You know yesterday, when I . . . I bumped into you by the tennis court with Amelia.'

'Yes, I can explain. You must have thought me an awful cad when I'm Woody's best pal, but—'

'It's all right. Woody told me this morning. I under-stand.'

'Thank goodness. I wouldn't want you to think that I was the sort of chap who—'

'Bertie?'

'Yes?'

'Do you remember that week in France?'

'Rather. Absolutely topping. I never had a sister, but I imagine that's the sort of fun we would have had.'

There was a longish pause. I decided to end it.

'I didn't quite finish the pie,' I said. 'I could easily cut you a slice.'

Georgiana sat down on the bench and raised a polite hand. 'I've rather lost my appetite for some reason.'

'I noticed that at dinner last night.'

I perched at the other end of the wrought-iron seat. Georgiana fixed the big brown eyes on me and began to smile.

'Bertie,' she said, 'how much longer are you going to keep up this act?'

'Just until Sunday. Then Jeeves and I are going back to London. By which time I trust that Amelia and Woody will have buried the hatchet and you and Venables will have named the day. Our work here will be done.'

There was another pause.

'I do hope you don't get found out, Bertie. I know you're clever, but it's quite—'

'Clever! No one's ever called me that before. Bottom of the class, dunce's hat, that was me.'

'Well, we're not at school any more. And there are lots of ways of being clever. I remember at Saint-Raphaël you told me you ran the book on the darts competition at your club.'

'The Drones? Yes, I do. Why?'

'Tell me how you do it.'

'Well, first of all you think who's most likely to win and put the runners in order. You put a price on each one. But you leave a margin for the book. So whoever wins, unless it's a short-priced favourite everyone's piled into, the book should always make a profit of about five per cent of the total stakes. Then you buy everyone a drink with it.'

'And what if someone puts a huge bet on?'

'Well, then you lay it off by changing the odds on other runners. So if Boko Fittleworth has a fiver on Bingo Little and I stand to lose fifty, then I'll lengthen the odds on Oofy Prosser and make Bingo odds-on.'

'You've lost me, Bertie. But has it always worked out?'

'So far. Honest Sid Wooster. But I bet you were top of the class in everything, weren't you?'

'Not at all.' She let out a rich, tinkling one. 'The only prize I won was for baking!'

I couldn't think of anything to say and I felt another silence coming down. It was a jolly odd thing with Georgiana: you were either at it hammer and tongs like a Pat and Mike crosstalk act, or you were pushing through a treacly sort of pause, like the ones actors bung into *Hamlet* when they want to give you time to ponder.

'About Woody and Amelia,' I said. 'Do you think it would help if she could see him resisting the advances of some girl? Then she'd know for sure that he doesn't have a roving eye and is entirely devoted to her.'

'I suppose it might. She's a funny girl, Amelia. I love her like a sister, but she's headstrong. And sometimes she's just plain stubborn.'

'But if she could see some gorgeous girl running her hands up and down his sleeve and telling him what a splendid chap he is, and then him giving her the brush-off, then—'

'Are you suggesting we get those two girls from the village back for tea?'

Georgiana did a bit of the arranging-a-fold-of-cotton-dress-over-endless-limb routine that I'd seen before at

Seaview Cottage. Meanwhile I sprang from the bench like the fellow in his bath when inspiration suddenly struck him.

'Bazooka!' I cried.

'What?'

'It's what that Greek chap said when——'

'You mean "Eureka!"'

'Do I? Anyway. I've had a brainwave. You do the canoodling, Georgie. You sidle up to old Woody. Don't do anything too extreme. Just a gentle hand on the sleeve, a few sweet nothings ... And Woody says, "Listen, Georgie, old thing, I'm fond of you, but my heart is taken." At that moment, Amelia comes on to the scene and sees Woody giving you the old elbow and she thinks, "He's not a flirt at all. He's the one for me. If he can resist Georgiana, he can resist anyone." And then the wedding bells are on again and we all live happily ever after.'

'Bertie, if Amelia sees me making up to Woody she'll tear me limb from limb. It won't just be the straight-sets spanking on the tennis court, she'll grind my bones to powder.'

'But you can explain later. Anyway, you're marrying Venables, so that'll put an end to any lingering doubts.'

Georgiana stood up. 'Yes, that'll put an end to all doubts.'

'So will you do it?'

There had been more silences now than at a Trappist convention – if they have such things – so another one at this juncture didn't much surprise me.

'Bertie,' Georgiana said eventually, 'I have to go back to work next week in London. We've been moving offices, which is why I've been able to have a few days down here. I've been working in my room.'

'Have you by Jove? What on? Another potboiler from the intended?'

'No, it's a novel. It's rather good, as a matter of fact. I'll ask them to send you a copy. It's a love story, but written by a man.'

'Golly, that sounds unusual.'

'Very.'

Georgiana was poised to go, with basket and seca-teurs aligned and ready for the off, but for some reason she hesitated.

She looked at me in a puzzled way. 'You're very kind, aren't you?'

'Am I?'

'Yes. All this malarkey just to help an old friend. And I've seen the way you talk to the servants. Mrs Tilman told me they think the world of you. "A proper gentleman is Mr Wilberforce," she said.'

'She seems a thoroughly good egg herself.'

Still she hesitated. The length of limb, the wooden basket over the arm, the melancholy look ... I wondered where the old Georgiana with the sparkle and appetite for crustacea had gone; the Mark Two version had a hint of the Lady of the Shalott, if that's the girl I mean.

Then an odd thing happened. The big eyes filled and, all in a moment, overflowed.

She put a hand to her face and turned quickly, saying, 'I'd better go back to work', then vanished across the lawn.

I stilled an impulse to run after and console. It took some stilling, I admit; the Wooster code does not allow us to see a girl in tears without at least offering a shoulder and a pat on the back.

I hadn't the faintest idea what had caused her to spring a leak, but some instinct told me to mind my own business as, with a plod like that of a ploughman on his homeward way, I took up the picnic basket and headed for the servants' entrance.

My mood improved considerably when an hour or so later I had a cup of tea with Mrs Tilman in the kitchen.

'You're not needed at dinner tonight, Mr Wilberforce. Mr Hoad's recovered from his funny turn.'

'That's exceptionally good news, Mrs T. I don't think I was really cut out for waiting at table. It takes it out of a chap.'

'Mr Bicknell had to drive Dame Judith's dress to the cleaners in Dorchester. Lord Etringham told me he volunteered to pay the bill, seeing as it was his man who—'

'Quite right too.' I made a mental note to reimburse his lordship. 'What's Mrs Padgett cooking tonight?'

'It's a rack of lamb, come up from the butcher's this morning. And then a tart with some strawberries.'

'Sounds safe enough. Not too much fluid.'

'And Lord Etringham says you're to go up with him and Mr Beeching for a cricket practice at six o'clock.'

'Right ho. You seem to bump into Lord Etringham rather a lot in the space of a single day.'

Mrs Tilman flushed a little. 'It's the housekeeper's job to make sure everyone's happy. Another cup, Mr W?'

The cricket pitch at Melbury Hall was a goodish walk from the house, at the far end of the estate. A five-bar gate beyond the boundary gave on to a lane leading down to the village; through this entrance the local yeomen had come and gone on a hundred years of Sundays, to play out their historic rivalries with Melbury Tetchett, Magnum in Parvo, Kingston St Jude and all points west.

It was a balmy evening as I sauntered up with Woody and Jeeves – or Lord Etringham as he remained until we were well down the crazy paving, through the Pineapple Gates and out of earshot of the house. To keep the charade intact, I was carrying Woody's leather cricket bag, while he and Jeeves walked a few paces ahead.

A stout net stood beside the pitch, with three stumps at the batting end and a single one for the bowlers. To say that I was out of practice at our national game would be a ... What's the word? Li-something. Jeeves would know. Undershooting by a fair whack, anyway. I had once opened the bowling at private school when some plague had laid low the brightest and best; at Eton I had been a wet bob, though an ineffectual one, we Woosters tending to the willowy and the prejudice in the boat running to avoirdupois, and plenty of it. All in all, it had been more than a decade since the cream flannel had graced the limbs and it was with no small trepidation that I donned the protective gear beside the net while Jeeves and Woody windmilled their arms in somewhat menacing fashion.

I entered the net, made a mark in front of the stumps and prepared to take my medicine. Woody ambled in like a thoroughbred going up to the start. A second later, a red pill whipped past my groping bat. Jeeves, with his sleeves rolled up, came off a shorter run-up, with the dignified tread one would have expected. The ball, however, as it approached, hissed and buzzed like a hornet whose siesta has been interrupted. I made a stab at where it pitched, but it was no longer there, having made off sideways.

Woody let out a roar of delight. 'I say, well bowled, Jeeves. I might have guessed you'd be a spinner.'

'Thank you, sir. I fear I am a little rusty. It is a long time since I have had the opportunity.'

Cantering in again, Woody let rip another snorter that I failed to see, though I fancy I smelt the leather as it whipped past the proboscis. I wondered if he was getting a bit of Amelia business off his chest. When Jeeves came in for a second go, I cunningly took a swing — not at where the ball bounced but at where it had finished last time; unfortunately this one zipped off the other way.

Hands on knees, Woody continued his heartless cackling. 'I say, have you ever played professionally? Wasn't there a Jeeves who played for Worcestershire?'

'Warwickshire, sir. A distant relation. I believe he took four wickets for the Players against the Gentlemen at Lord's in 1914. Alas, it was to be his swansong.'

'What a shame. Retire, did he?'

'No, sir, he volunteered.'

'I see. And . . . That was it, was it?'

'The Battle of the Somme, sir. He was in C Company of the 15th Royal Warwicks. The assault on High Wood.'

'Bad show,' said Woody.

It was quiet for a moment; you could hear the rooks chattering in the elms and cedars.

'You ready, Bertie?' called out Woody. 'Slower one coming up.'

For the first time, there was a brief meeting of willow and leather, the ball scraping along the side of the netting and back to the feet of the bowler.

'Good shot, sir,' said Jeeves.

'Keep your left elbow up, Bertie,' said Woody. 'Lead with the left. The right hand's just there for a bit of guidance and punch if you need it.'

'Right ho.'

I doubt whether I connected with more than half a dozen of Woody's languid whizzers, though one of them connected most definitely with the Wooster soft tissues, causing some vigorous rubbing of the affected area and a rather insincere apology, I thought, from the bowler.

'Must you chuck it down so bally fast?' I said.

'Part of your preparation for tomorrow, old chap.'

'Who are these Dorset Gentlemen? Old alumni of the local Dotheboys, I suppose. Sherborne, is it?'

'No, no,' said Woody. 'They're a load of the most fearful toughs, Jeeves tells me. The match against Blandford Forum last year had to be abandoned.'

'Can this be true, Jeeves?'

'I have done some research into the players who

comprise the team, sir. It seems that few of them are from Dorset and none of them are gentlemen.'

'So this is how they'll go after you, Bertie,' said Woody, sending down another nasty lifter.

As for Jeeves's bamboozling slower deliveries, they remained untouched by human bat, as it were. When Woody took his turn with pads and willow, even he treated them with respect, getting his nose right over the top and more or less smothering the wretched thing as it spat and fizzled on the turf.

Jeeves assured us that Sir Henry was placing him far enough down the order that he would be unlikely to bat, so when Woody felt he had got the old juices running again, we called it a day and set off across the grounds towards where cooling waters and preprandial drink would be awaiting the privileged pair, while more sweated labour was doubtless planned for Bertram.

CHAPTER
═SEVEN═

The first player arrived soon after the church clock had struck noon. It was Esmond Haddock, and the time that had passed since I last saw him had done nothing to lessen his resemblance to a classical deity whose noble brow ought to be worth twenty runs to us, I reckoned, before he even faced a ball.

Bicknell was stationed in the porch when Esmond's roadster hove alongside. The trusty butler made for the steps, but I beat him to it and managed to alert Esmond to my new status as I opened his car door.

'Ah well, the first time we met, Bertie, you were

pretending to be Gussie Fink-Nottle,' he said. 'So I suppose this is a slight improvement.'

Esmond was escorted by Bicknell into the long room, where he stood before the fireplace in a blazer of startling colours, sipping a gin cup with a fistful of herbiage in it. At ease, with no aunt or dowager in sight, he held forth to Sir Henry and Lord Etringham with tales from the Hampshire hunt. Things could hardly have got off to a juicier start, I felt. Sir Henry's face was all ruddy delight as he eyed up the Apollo of Andover.

Before I could congratulate myself further, I was distracted by what sounded like a pack of foxhounds in the hall.

Was it possible that all this racket could issue from the lungs of a single dog? Yes, it was – if that dog was the terrier Bartholomew. And if so, then Stephanie Pinker, née Byng, could not be far behind. By the time I got into the hall, the creature was halfway up the main staircase with Stiffy about three steps behind and losing ground fast. 'Come here, you naughty boy!' she was shrieking. 'Stinker' Pinker was at the foot of the stairs in clerical garb and linen jacket, gesturing weakly.

'What ho, Stinker,' I said, sotto voce. 'Don't forget

you don't know who I really am. I'm pretending to be Jeeves's valet. And he's Lord Etringham. It's a long story. And I thought I quite clearly said No Dog.'

'Stiffy said she wouldn't miss the cricket for the world. And she said everyone loves Bartholomew. I tried to reason with her, but you know what she's like.'

At this point, Stiffy returned to ground level, with the yapping Bartholomew cradled to her bosom. 'Hello, Bertie,' she said, planting a smacker on my cheek.

'Don't call me that.'

'But I've always called you that. It's your name, you chump.'

'Didn't Stinker tell you?'

'Tell me what?'

I told her.

'What an absolute riot,' said Stiffy. 'Kindly fetch me a drink at once, Wilberforce.'

The Rev. Pinker rolled his eyes and I rolled mine back as I trotted off to oblige. I don't know what Bicknell put in his gin slings, but with the company on its second refill the volume of conversation had gone from *mf* to *f*, as Hymns A and M has it. It was at this moment that Lady Hackwood and Dame Judith Puxley decided to come in from the hall and join the party.

The effect on Esmond was like one of those sudden freezes on a December afternoon in New York, when one minute you're strolling along the sidewalk whistling 'Danny Boy' and the next you feel that if you don't get inside a cab that instant your limbs will start to drop off. A look of horror came over his face – a look that suggested he had motored across half of England to have a day off from this kind of natural hazard.

Conversation remained sticky until the arrival of Georgiana and Amelia. They had sportingly put their troubles behind them and had dug out the freshest and floweriest of summer dresses; they swooshed into the long room, bestowing smiles to left and right. You couldn't help thinking that their finishing schools would have been proud of them.

While the nobs went off to a buffet luncheon in the dining room, I repaired to the kitchen and was happy to see there was still a quadrant of Mrs Padgett's pie, as well as sliced tongue and a bottle of beer.

I wouldn't say the mood was confident as I set off, refreshed, for the cricketing arena; but as the last smudge of cloud shifted to one side, allowing the sun to get at the uplands of Dorset, even T. Hardy would have had to admit that things could have looked a dashed sight worse.

The pavilion had a low picket fence in front and a balcony on the upper floor under a thatched roof. Pinned to the inside door of the home dressing room was a hand-written batting order, which read:

Melbury Hall XI vs Dorset Gentlemen Saturday 19 June
1. Rev. H. Pinker
2. Mr S. Venables
3. Mr E. Haddock
4. Mr P. Beeching
5. Mr H. Niblett
6. Hoad
7. Sir H. Hackwood
8. Wilberforce
9. Liddle
10. Lord Etringham
11. Mr R. Venables
Start: 2.15 Tea: 4.15 Stumps: 6.30

As I may have mentioned, I had never been much of a cricketer, but just seeing the order of battle did somehow stir the old juices; I felt like a retired war horse in the paddock when he hears the distant sound of a bugle.

The home side arrived in dribs and drabs, well enough refreshed, to judge from the repartee. Farmer Niblett turned out to be a fine specimen of West Country manhood, his face, neck and arms tanned to the colour of a ripe cobnut.

Sir Henry put his face round the door of the dressing room. 'All right, men?' he barked. 'I've won the toss and we're batting. Pinker and Venables, get your pads on. I should say we need at least two hundred on this pitch. Two twenty would be better.'

Outside, the Dorset Gents were limbering up – and an unnerving sight it was. A couple of burly fellows were touching their toes and whirling their arms about, while the others flung cricket balls at each other. They all seemed able to pluck the cherry from the air one-handed, however fast it was travelling. Eventually, they wandered off into the middle and took their places with rustic noises and the odd handclap of encouragement.

From among the cars behind the pavilion, the soft

thump of metal on metal, followed by a loud rattle of clashing crockery announced that Georgiana had arrived with the tea things.

Pinker, H. and Venables, S. went out to bat, to the applause of the crowd – which, with the entire household of Melbury Hall, plus supporters of the Gents and sundry sporting folk of Melbury-cum-Kingston, must have numbered almost a hundred.

I found that Jeeves had materialised by my side.

'Did you manage to place your bet?' I said.

'Yes, thank you, sir. The turf accountant was most obliging. I was able to link the outcome of the match to that of the daily double at Ascot this afternoon.'

'And did Hackwood have enough of the stuff to make it a worthwhile wager?'

'Emphatically so, sir. Sir Henry was able to negotiate the loan of a substantial sum from Mr Venables senior.'

'But you told me the Colonial Service pension was paltry.'

'I believe the Collector was obliged to draw on Mrs Venables's means, sir. Yesterday was a day of intense financial activity. In the end, a telegraphic transfer was effected from London.'

'So the moolah's wrapped in Spanier's Sausage Casing?'

'One might so describe it, sir, though in this instance the casing forms the meat of the wager and Sir Henry's contribution merely the outer membrane.'

'How much is the old villain in for?'

'I fear I am not at liberty to disclose, sir, though if the bet were to come good, it would certainly enable Sir Henry to refuse the importuning of the private school for a considerable period.'

'Hickory Hot Boy, Jeeves!' I said.

'A most apt summation of—'

'That's smokin' good.'

'One can but hope so, sir.'

Out in the middle, hostilities had commenced.

'But, Jeeves,' I said, 'suppose the nags don't win. Or we come a cropper here, in the cricket. More than likely, I would have thought. Do you need all three parts to bring home the goods?'

'Indeed, sir. Two winners would not suffice. It is a case of all or nothing.'

'But if we lose, how will Sir Henry pay back old Vishnu?'

'I did put that question to Sir Henry myself, sir, but it was not an eventuality he was willing to contemplate. He has developed an unshakeable faith in my equine selections and is confident of his ability to captain the cricket side to victory.'

I felt a slight queasiness when I finally cast the eyes pitchward to see Sidney Venables crouched, willow in hand, and the Dorset Gents opening bowler thundering in from the village end. I haven't the faintest idea who Victor Trumper was, but unless he wore a striped tie beneath his belly and waved his bat like a dowager attempting to swat a wasp, his resemblance to S. Venables can have been no more than fleeting. The Nizam of Hyderabad, one felt, must have been quite a one for dishing out the old oil.

Things were on a firmer footing, in all senses, at the other end, where Stinker seemed to be taking root. His lower half remained attached to the turf, but he met the ball with a meaningful thump that sent it into the long grass. The Gents bowler stood with his hands on his hips and let him have what appeared to be a rather un-Christian appraisal of his batting style. Stinker simply turned the other cheek and carted the next one into a group of small boys on the opposite side of the ground.

'Good shot, Pinker!' called out Sir Henry.

I settled into a deckchair and picked up my copy of *The Mystery of the Gabled House*. My amateur sleuthing was interrupted by a tremendous commotion from the middle, where Vishnu Venables was being given his marching orders by the umpire – the finger of doom belonging to a tallish cove I recognised as the landlord of the Hare and Hounds.

Esmond Haddock now made his way to the wicket, with a consoling word for the Collector as their paths crossed. If Esmond's pre-lunch blazer had been on the loud side, the cap he had selected from a number in his bag made the many colours of Joseph's coat look as dull as an army blanket. It appeared to be the cause of some ribaldry among the Dorset Gents, and the first ball sent down in Esmond's direction made a good stab at removing it, peak first, from his head.

'Hello, Wilberforce,' said a friendly voice in my ear, and the next thing I knew the adjacent deckchair was full of summer cotton and dark, waving tresses. 'Enjoying the cricket?'

'Rather,' I said. 'Everything all right with the tea things?'

'Yes, thank you,' said Georgiana. 'Why shouldn't it be?'

'It's just that I heard you arrive and . . .'

'Yes. Well, one of these wretched Dorset Gents had parked in the wrong place.'

'So you nudged him out of it.'

'Not deliberately.'

I didn't want one of those *Hamlet* pauses developing, so I ploughed on. 'You seem friskier today.'

'Yes, I am. I don't know what came over me yesterday. I wanted to apologise. I hope I didn't embarrass you. Please forgive me.'

'Think nothing of it. I'm sorry I was no help. I didn't want to get under your feet.'

'Absolutely. Now who's this fellow in the hideous hat?'

'Esmond Haddock,' I replied. 'Huntsman, sonneteer and all-round good egg.'

The next half-hour went by in a sort of dream as we chatted pauselessly to the background noise of Stinker and Esmond bashing the ball about. It wasn't until Woody had his turn that I saw what we'd been missing. The only way I can describe it is to say that it was like hearing a string quartet after an oompah band. Where the other chaps had humped and heaved, Woody eased the little red ball across the grass with a flick or a caress. Once he just seemed to lean over and whisper in its ear, yet when it rattled into the fence in front of the pavilion it snapped one of the pickets.

He was joined by Harold Niblett, who applied the long handle, as I believe the expression is, coming down the prepared surface to dispatch the Gents' slow bowler over the top of a particularly tall cedar tree and into the lane. Great was the excitement among the half-dozen small boys who ran off to find it. While Niblett took the high road, Woody stuck with the low, continuing to bisect the sweating Dorset Gents, wherever their captain placed them; you almost expected to see scorch marks through the green.

'I hope Amelia's enjoying this,' I said.

'I think she is,' said Georgiana. 'Look, she's stopped buttering the bread.'

I thought of pointing out that Amelia's open mouth was a trap for passing insect life, but chivalry prevailed.

'I'd better go and give her a hand and see how the urn's coming on,' said Georgiana.

'Must you go?'

'Yes, I must.'

The fun eventually came to an end when a steepler from Niblett was caught on the boundary and there arose the awful prospect that I might soon have to don the pads and gloves myself. The next man in was Hoad and I was relieved to see that he had based his attitude on that of Stonewall Jackson. It didn't matter what they chucked at him; he met it with the same hunched prod, while the ball dropped on roughly the same spot near his feet.

If Hoad could best be described as inert, Beeching, P. was about as ert as they come, waltzing down the wicket to send the ball humming to all points of the compass. An excited murmur had started among the small boys and had now reached the pavilion – viz., that Woody was nearing his century. The entire ground seemed rapt; even Dame Judith Puxley for a moment set aside her *Letters and Inscriptions of Hammurabi* and raised her lorgnette.

To signify Beeching's score, a boy propped a nine and a five on the grass against the scoreboard, where the total stood at 186. Woody glanced in the direction of the board, stepped down the wicket and, for the first time, lifted the ball from the turf, up into the air, and into the hands of an astonished fielder.

There was disappointed applause as Woody returned to the pavilion – unruffled, it seemed, and undampened by so much as a bead of p. The next man in was Sir Henry Hackwood, who set about the opposition with a relish I wouldn't have thought the old boy to have had in him. He loudly instructed Hoad not to run, as he would be dealing in boundaries only.

Perhaps it was the honour of batting with his employer or perhaps the prospect of finally registering a run after twenty minutes at the crease; in any event, Hoad suddenly hit the ball and bolted like a jackrabbit from his home ground with a screech of 'Come on, Sir Henry!' He arrived at the other end to find the baronet unmoved. The ball made its way back to the wicket-keeper, followed by a few choice comments.

Hoad's return to the hutch meant that there was no longer any means of postponing the entry of Wooster, B. It's a funny thing about cricket, but what from the sidelines looks like a gentle pantomime, white figures flitting to and fro, is quite different when you arrive in the middle. It's hostile. The ground is hard and dusty; it bears

the spike marks of battle. There may be a few 'Good afternoon's, but there are also some less cheery words. As the
bowler starts his run-up, a silence descends on the fielders; the new batsman's mouth is dry and his tongue flicks
out in vain; the silence seems to close about his head. You
see the straining, angry face of the fellow about to bung it
down at you as hard as he can; the instant before the first
glimpse of red is about as lonely as a chap can feel . . .

And then the wretched thing whipped past my
groping bat to a chorus of oohs and aahs and a general
sense that if there was one lucky blighter in England on
this summer's day his name was Bertram Wooster – or in
the circs, I suppose, B. Wilberforce.

'Eye on the ball, man,' Sir Henry advised. 'Keep your
head still.'

As the Dorset Gent went back to the end of his run,
I happened to glance over to the pavilion. Amelia and
Georgiana, their tea preparations presumably complete,
were standing by the picket fence, arms folded, chatting
and watching the action. They were pointing at something that seemed to amuse them. I hoped it wasn't me.

His face contorted with effort, the bowler chucked
another fearsome one my way. I kept the old bean still, as

per instruction, but forgot to do much with the bat. By the time I shoved it forwards, it was too late; there was a sound of splintering timber just behind me and a rather unsporting roar from the wicket-keeper.

I slunk back to the pavilion, trying not to catch anyone's eye before I reached the lonely solace of the dressing room.

Liddle was the next man in and managed to squirt a couple away, while at the other end Sir Henry had a few more heaves. The upshot was that at teatime we had a total of 225 and the captain felt able to declare the innings closed.

The heat of the day was such that tea was taken outdoors. The mighty urn was placed on a trestle amid the plates of sandwiches and several examples of Mrs Padgett's bakery. The home team was still pretty full of lunch, but the Dorset Gents, who had grazed more modestly at the Red Lion, set about clearing the decks. Sir Henry manoeuvred a beer barrel into place and tapped off the first glass for himself, before inviting the others to make free with it.

We were then lined up in teams in front of the pavilion while a Mr Jay, the photographer from the

Melbury-cum-Kingston Courier (incorporating the *Magnum in Parvo Gazette*), took photographs. He spent an age with his head under the black cloth before he was satisfied that we were properly aligned; finally he held up his flash and the ordeal was over.

A reporter in a brown chalk-stripe suit and soft hat went about collecting names and checking them off against the batting order that he seemed to have purloined from the dressing-room door. 'And you're Mr Venables senior? Which one's Lord Etringham? The readers do love an aristocrat. Righty ho. Thank you, gents. And have you any comment on the day, Mr Beeching? Is that "beech" like the tree or "beach" like the sand? That's all tickety-boo. Anything else to say to our readers at all, sir?'

'Oh, do let's get on, shall we?' said Sir Henry. 'We've got a cricket match to finish here, you know.'

A couple of the opposition went off to pad up; the others looked happy to have stopped chasing leather all over the county. They had the satisfied look of labourers at day's end as they settled on the grass with their beer and cigarettes.

The Melbury Hall XI was starting to take the field when I became aware of a discreet coughing in my ear.

'I thought you would like to know, sir, that I sent a small boy to the village during the interval. In return for a sixpence, he placed a telephone call from the post office to the bookmaker in Dorchester.'

'Any luck?'

'Yes, sir. In double measure.'

'I say, well done, Jeeves. So far so good, what?'

'Indeed, sir.'

'Any provision for a draw?'

'Alas not, sir. The win is imperative.'

'Well, I should have thought we've made enough runs.'

'Yes, sir, though securing all ten wickets may prove difficult on such a benign surface.'

'But they won't have a Beeching, will they?'

'They are said to be stronger with bat than ball, sir. Mr Beeching may yet rue giving up his wicket.'

'Are you saying Woody got out on purpose?'

'I believe he may have been embarrassed by the thought of scoring such a large number of runs. A gentle-man should not score more than half his team's total.'

'How do you know that, Jeeves?'

'It is my job to know, sir.'

'You don't just make these rules up?'

'Certainly not, sir. Might I suggest you station yourself on the pavilion side of the field? In the event of a high catch, you will be less likely to be dazzled by the late afternoon sun.'

Sir Henry Hackwood had assumed the wicket-keeping gloves and was now setting his field as the Gents' openers came out.

The umpires were in place and the sun was still high when mine host of the Hare and Hounds called out 'Play!' and Harold Niblett accelerated in from the Hall end of the ground. He leapt up at the crease and propelled the new ball down the track with a manly grunt; it bounced, reared up and touched the outside edge of the opener's bat. It flew straight into the gloves of Sir Henry Hackwood behind the stumps, from where it fell harmlessly to the turf.

'Sorry, bowler,' said Sir Henry.

At the other end, Woody came ambling in with the deceptive canter I'd seen the night before. The Dorset Gent looked surprised when the ball zipped past his defensive poke. He at once called a mid-pitch conference with his fellow Gent, which ended with a good deal of head-shaking and ground-prodding.

Out in the deep, I found my mind wandering a bit. I had no idea why the Dorset Gents, even if they might not have Woody's touch, didn't just give it a wallop like old Stinker.

I was also thinking about Rupert Venables. He was stationed on the other side of the pitch from me, recognisable by his white sunhat. I wondered how much of his time he spent travelling and how much writing, whether he would run out of places and types of transport that began with the same letter, and what the role of the wife of such a fellow might be. I had gone into something of a daydream, and may even have been muttering out loud 'By Tricycle to Torquay' when a cry of 'Wilberforce!' reached my ears and I saw the ball rapidly approaching. I bent to stop it, but as I did so it diverted off some plantain or daisy and carried on its way unmolested to the boundary.

'Get something behind it, man!' the captain called out from behind the timbers.

The afternoon reached a rather sleepy passage, like the slow movement in a bit of music at the Albert Hall when you snatch a bracing forty winks to give yourself strength for the rousing finale and the sharp exit to dinner. The Dorset Gents had reached 85 for the loss of three wickets. A group of small boys were training a magnifying glass on to the back of a wooden bench, with some success. Dame Judith had her nose back in Sumeria, if that's where Hammurabi came from. Amelia had taken up some sewing, and beside her Georgiana was staring silently into the summer air. A few villagers who had a crack at the beer barrel now lay snoozing peacefully with handkerchiefs over their faces.

Liddle came on to bowl what Sir Henry referred to as his 'wobblers' – a curious procedure with a whirling of both arms from which the ball eventually emerged at a friendly pace. It may have swung or wobbled a bit as it went, but from my angle it was hard to see.

'Etringham!' said Sir Henry. 'Do you fancy a couple of overs?'

Jeeves marked out a short run, made some minor adjustments to the field, and came in to bowl. The ball bit into the ground as it landed and turned away from the batsman, who followed it with his bat, edging into the eager gloves of the custodian. A mighty fumble was followed by a curse as the ball trickled down his pad and on to the ground.

'Sorry, bowler,' said Sir Henry, bending down to pick up the ball.

Jeeves had come halfway down the wicket. Sir Henry meant to throw the ball back to him, but managed only to throw it over his head, so the journey was fruitless.

'Sorry, bowler,' said Sir Henry again, a bare couple of seconds separating the two apologies. 'Sorry, bowler.'

Eventually, a catch flew to Woody, who managed to cling on to it.

'Well held, old man,' I said, as he walked past me.

'Thank you. We just have to hope no more chances go to Old Irongloves.'

'A dashed disrespectful way to refer to the future father-in-law, young Beeching.'

The look I received in return could best be described, I think, as stricken. Clearly even 95 of the best had not melted the heart of the young Ice Queen of Kingston St Giles.

The Dorset Gents were making good progress, when Sir Henry threw the ball to Sidney Venables. 'Let's see a few of those in-duckers you were telling me about, Venables.'

Vishnu Venables looked frankly surprised to be called into the attack at this point.

'You remember,' said Sir Henry. 'You told me you took six for thirty-eight against the Bombay Gymkhana.'

I couldn't say what particular delivery Venables senior then proceeded to offer, but it certainly seemed to tickle the fancy of the Dorset Gentlemen, whose total rocketed upwards.

'What sort of bowling is that?' I asked Woody as we crossed again at the end of the over. 'Leg spin or something?'

'It's called cafeteria,' said Woody. 'Help yourself.'

The Gents proceeded to do exactly that, and their total began to approach that of the home side when one of them, a burly youth who seemed to have been at the crease all afternoon, hit one high in the air towards Venables junior.

Readers who have been lulled into a sense of calm by the summer afternoon proceedings may be surprised by what happened next; keener types may have noticed that one character has been notable by his absence – so far.

Opinions later differed as to what it was about Venables junior that got right up the dog Bartholomew's nose. Some blamed the floppy white sunhat; others thought Venables had shown insufficient respect towards the hound before lunch – he being a dog who generally commanded a fair bit of bowing and scraping. Stiffy claimed Bartholomew was 'only trying to help catch the ball, which that useless yard of tap water would never have managed on his own'.

The long and the short of it was that Bartholomew launched himself off his mistress's lap like a terrier who's been told that they were about to close off the last rabbit hole in Dorset. The lung power required to bark and run simultaneously had been developed by years of practice, and he covered the mown grass in a blur. He arrived at his chosen destination a moment before the descending red ball, timed his leap to perfection and, closing his jaws at the *moment critique*, as I believe it's known, landed a juicy one on the Venables rear end.

The fielding side was divided in the aftermath of this event, some inclining to anger at the missed catch and concern for the fielder, others offering ribald suggestions for treatment and who might administer it.

The batsmen were unconcerned, and the game, minus Rupert Venables, left its slow movement behind and came to its noisy climax. The Dorset Gents went past 200 with eight wickets down, and when the ninth man was judged leg before wicket to Jeeves, with the score at 220, Sir Henry called us together.

'There's time for one more over,' he said. 'Beeching, you bowl it. They need six to win, we need one wicket. A draw's no use to me.'

'Surely a draw would be a happy outcome on such a pleasant afternoon,' said Woody.

Sir Henry's face went an odd shade of purple. 'I tell you, young man, a draw is no earthly good. Do you understand? We are going to win this game. We will take that last wicket. No other result will do. Have you thoroughly grasped that now?'

'Yes, Sir Henry.'

'Get back to your places.'

I retreated to my post in front of the pavilion, praying that the wretched thing wouldn't come anywhere near me. Woody went to the end of his run and moved a few fielders this way and that.

The batsman facing him was not the number eleven but the chap who'd been in for hours. Woody seemed to be offering him a single so he could have a go at the tailender, but the Gent was too canny for that. Five balls went by without a run and without a wicket. I was relieved that any chance of my involvement was now almost out of the question. They still needed six to win off the last ball. A draw now looked so certain that even Honest Sid Levy would have closed his book.

In his frustration, Woody banged the final ball of the match hard into the turf, about halfway up the track. Unable to resist, the batsman went back on to his heels and gave it a mighty whack to leg. High in the air it went, hovering up there, like a red bird against the sky. It seemed to have someone's name on it for sure, though it was only as it began its spiralling descent that I understood that name was mine.

I could feel the boundary rope against the heel of my boots. I raised both hands in what may, I suppose, have looked like prayer.

It's a rum thing, but although you could hardly have imagined a closer match, not everyone at the ground was following it with their full attention.

As the ball plummeted towards me, Lady Hackwood said, 'I'm bored, I'm cold and I want a drink.'

In amazed response, there came the sound of a frisky

brook going over the strings of a particularly well-tuned harp.

Sir Henry Hackwood yelled, 'Catch it, you fool!'

A dog unseen began to bark.

I don't know which of these sounds made me jerk my head like a frightened thoroughbred, but my money would be on the harp, since it was Georgiana's face I had in my eyeline as the ball hit my upturned hands. It would have been one thing if I'd simply let it drop, but my sudden movement made me palm the thing upwards, giving it the extra boost it needed to carry over the rope for the winning six.

Dinner at Melbury Hall that night was about as much fun as the burial of Sir John Moore at Corunna, with the role of the corpse — or 'corse', as I seem to remember the poet had it — assigned to B. Wooster.

Hoad had apparently had another 'funny turn' after his impression of a limpet at the crease and the services of Wilberforce, stand-in footman, were once more in demand. It was with a leaden heart that, after an icy visit to the staff ablutions, I exchanged the cream flannel for

the evening wear and went down the lime-wood staircase to old Mrs Padgett's galley.

'By 'eck, Mr Wilberforce, I 'eard all about that cricket
match. Sir 'Enry's been locked in the library since he
come 'ome. Mr Bicknell's run off his feet taking in
whisky and soda. 'E must be on his fifth by now.'

'I envy him, Mrs Padgett. There are times when only
oblivion will do.'

'Ah, don't talk so soft, Mr W. It's only a game.'

'If only, Mrs P. Now, what shall I do?'

'Fetch me over them little pots on the chest there. I've
made soufflés to start. Sir 'Enry's right fond of a cheese
soufflé and I thought as how it might cheer him up.'

'I fear it may take more than a cheese soufflé.'

'Well, at least it's a start.'

And so it was – a start delivered, what's more, without
mishap. The Pinkers had gone home, since Sunday was
Stinker's big day in Totleigh-in-the-Wold and Esmond
Haddock was apparently required on aunt duty back in
Hampshire. This was a shame, as I could have done with
a couple of allies.

Sir Henry sat slumped at the head of the table, head in
hand like one of those grim Dutch self-portraits. Woody

seemed somehow to have got wind of the wager; or if not, there must have been some other reason for the reproachful look in his eye.

'Would you care for some anchovy sauce?' I asked as I leant in with the jug.

'Just a drop, please,' he replied. 'You'd understand about drops, I suppose.'

Venables *père et fils* guffawed in merriment – which was a bit rich, I thought, since they had contributed a total of one run between them and old Vishnu's cafeteria bowling had put the Gents in reach of our total.

'Did you see the dear little Turton girl at the match?' said Woody. 'You never see her without her dolly, do you? Seen a dolly lately, Wilberforce?'

Now old Venables laboured up to the party. 'When I was Collector of Chanamasala,' he began, 'I came up with an excellent scheme for irrigating some of the tea plantations. The trouble is, there turned out to be a catch in it.'

Of this drollery there seemed to be no end, it now apparently being open season on my reputation.

'I was having a splendid game of Snakes and Ladders the other day,' said Amelia. 'I was on the top straight and rolled a four. But what I really needed was a six.'

'Send for Wilberforce!' trilled Rupert Venables. 'He knows how to turn a four into a six.'

I retreated to the kitchen for fear of hearing more. When I returned with the fillet of beef, the conversation, mercifully, seemed to have taken a more serious turn.

Lady Hackwood was explaining her new planting scheme to Dame Judith Puxley and Mrs Venables.

'Of course I don't know whether we shall be in a position to implement it. The future rather hangs in the balance.'

I guessed from the way she looked round about her that she was not privy to the fact that Sir Henry had staked his shirt on the outcome of the afternoon's sport and that the next bit of planting she was likely to oversee would be a handful of geraniums in the window box of a bungalow in Bexhill-on-Sea. I didn't like to think how much frostier she might have been had she known.

I had completed the last of my clearing duties and was on my way back to my room, having paused only for a tumblerful of Bicknell's claret in the kitchen, when I heard a discreet cough. I stopped in my tracks and saw that Lord Etringham was holding open the door into the hall. I cantered up.

'This is a bit of a pickle, Jeeves. An absolute Hickory Hot Boy. And why are they only blaming me? I don't think old Hackwood emerges with much credit, do you? I thought he was supposed to know the game backwards.'

'Indeed, sir. A case of *capax imperii nisi imperasset*, one rather feels.'

'Come again?'

'The historian Tacitus, sir. It was his verdict on the Emperor Galba.'

'What on earth did it mean?'

'It is difficult to translate exactly. I suppose that "A man one would have thought capable of leadership had not his tenure of office proved the contrary" might cover it.'

'Be that as it may, Jeeves. The fact is that if Hackwood hadn't kept old Venables serving up his lobs they wouldn't have got close to our total.'

Further post-mortems, as Tacitus might have called them, were curtailed by the arrival of Bicknell.

'Mr Wilberforce, I am asked by Miss Meadowes if you would kindly present yourself in the library.'

'What? Me? Now?'

'At your earliest convenience.'

'Is Sir Henry . . . Is he?'

'Sir Henry has retired early. He is suffering from neuralgia.'

'I'm not surprised after all that . . . Anyway. Right ho. So she's . . .'

'Miss Meadowes is unaccompanied.'

'Right ho,' I said again. And, knowing not a jot what lay in store, I tootled off across that mighty hall.

CHAPTER EIGHT

'Thank you for coming, Bertie,' said Georgiana. 'I hope it wasn't embarrassing.'

'Don't worry. I'm just the local whipping boy.'

'Would you like some of Uncle Henry's brandy? The top comes off that ottoman and you'll find a decanter and glasses inside.'

While I was fishing around for the needful, I heard Georgiana lock the door.

She was wearing a green number with a floral pattern. She smiled as she sat back in the velvet Knole sofa with a bit of careless limb-crossing. I proffered a snootful, which she accepted with a friendly chink against my own glass as I perched on a chair by the fireplace.

'What are you looking at?'

'To tell the truth, I was looking at your dress.'

'Why?'

'I don't know. It's just that you don't wear the same dresses as most girls.'

The fashion was for a sort of loose sack with no waist, whereas hers looked more like something a flamenco dancer might have worn. I couldn't think of a polite way of putting this. Likewise the hair. Amelia, like most girls of her age, had it cut as though the hairdresser had upended a coal scuttle on the bonce and trimmed round it. Georgiana's was longer and wavier.

'The dropped waist just wouldn't suit me,' she said with a sigh.

'And the haircut they all have?'

'It's called a bob, Bertie. It's fashionable. Ubiquitous, you might say.'

'Might I?'

'Of course you might. I didn't know you were interested in clothes.'

'Oh yes, rather. I once wrote an article for my Aunt

Dahlia's magazine, *Milady's Boudoir*, on "What the Well-Dressed Man is Wearing".'

'And are you going to do the same for the well-dressed woman?'

'I'd need to do a bit more research.'

'Don't start with me, then, start with Ambo. She's much more the thing.'

'Right ho,' I said, feeling I'd pretty much shot my bolt on ladies' fashions. 'How's the editing going?'

'Not bad, thanks. I'll probably finish this manuscript tomorrow. If not, I can do the last bit on the train back to London. We're moving into our new offices on Tuesday.'

I could sense that this conversation might follow the pattern of the one in the sunken garden, with the rat-a-tat-tat alternating with sticky periods. I was about as wrong as you can be, though, because Georgiana came straight to the point.

'Bertie, I wanted to talk to you about your plan for setting up this tableau for Amelia to witness. Woody rejecting the wanton cousin and all that.'

'Yes. Are you on for it?'

'No, I think it's an absurd idea. Amelia just needs

time. She loves Woody, there's no doubt about that. She wants to marry him.'

'But surely a dramatic demonstration of Woody being Sir Galahad and turning away from——'

'I'd get the giggles. And Woody just wouldn't fall for it. He'd smell a rat.'

'Well, perhaps you could talk to Amelia instead. Try and explain that just because her fiancé smiled at a couple of local wenches doesn't mean he can't be trusted.'

Georgiana sighed. 'It's complicated, Bertie. If I don't marry Rupert, then Uncle Henry isn't going to allow Amelia to marry Woody anyway.'

'What do you mean, "if" you don't marry Rupert? You're engaged. I saw it in *The Times*.'

'Yes, I know. But his attitude seems rather odd at the moment. I'm not sure if he's still keen.'

'I noticed. All the south of France stuff.'

'Exactly. I don't know what he's driving at.'

'Look at it from his point of view,' I said. 'He's a splendid chap, no doubt, but he's not ... Well, he's a bit older than you, isn't he? He's no sporting hero like Woody. And he's hardly a Greek god like Esmond, either. I imagine he can't quite believe his luck, to have landed such a ... such a ...'

'Don't be a flatterer, Bertie. Sonya Rostova with no money is not much of a catch ... Oops. Sorry to use that word again. I promise you, it honestly—'

I silenced her with a pitying look.

'I mean it,' I said. 'I don't blame the fellow for acting like an angler who's just netted a five-foot pike. He's giving you a test. To make assurance doubly sure, as Jeeves puts it.'

'I can't quite believe that, Bertie. Though thanks for the giant pike. I'm not sure Rupert really—'

'Have you any idea of the effect you have on people, Georgie? The waiters on the Côte d'Azur ... The poor man on the desk at the hotel ... He didn't know where to look when you—'

'Stop it, stop it, stop it!'

'And on top of that you're so dashed brainy with all your literary stuff and—'

'Rupert's the successful writer. Publishers are just the middlemen.'

'Believe me, I know what he's thinking, because it's just what I thought in France.'

'And what's that?'

'He's thinking, Why am I galloping with this filly in the Grand National when by rights I should be ploughing through the fences at the Easter Monday point-to-point at Kingston Parva?'

Georgiana burst out laughing. 'You really are absurd. Did you know that?'

'Well, if ever I had any doubts on that score, the events of the last couple of days have—'

'No, no, I didn't mean it like that. I meant you really are absurdly funny. And thoughtful.'

'Thoughtful? Try telling my . . .'

'Absurdly so. Yes.'

'. . . Aunt Agatha that.'

'No, thanks.'

'To get back to Rupert,' I said sternly. 'He's a good bet. He's just pinching himself at the moment. To make sure he's not dreaming. And you'll have a splendid time together. Your job, his travels . . . The little Venableses in due course. And Mrs V will be a doting grandmother.'

'Have another brandy.' Georgiana swung off the sofa, dipped into the ottoman and filled both glasses to the brim.

'It's funny your mentioning the Côte d'Azur,' she said, resettling herself. 'I was in a quandary before I went down there. And then I had such a wonderful time. I felt so happy when I got back to London. Everything seemed straightforward. I knew what I had to do. And now . . .'

'Now what?'

Georgiana stared up at the painting over the mantel-piece – an eighteenth-century squire in a three-cornered hat, a moody-looking bird, sitting with his wife beneath a tree.

'Now,' she said, 'I feel I should do what I can to thank my uncle. Although he's a peppery old fellow, I know, they did look after me, you know, he and Aunt Guinevere. I was pretty young when my parents died. It was quite a shock.'

'I can imagine.'

'I know you can. Perhaps that's why we got on so well in France. We'd been through the same thing.'

There wasn't much anyone could say for a moment or two at this point. But it wasn't a sticky silence; it was just one of those things.

'Anyway,' I said, 'Venables knows how lucky he is – and that means he's bound to look after you well. I've noticed the way he sneaks the odd glance at you when he thinks no one's watching. He appreciates you. That's the important thing. And Melbury Hall can be wrapped in cotton wool—'

'Or sausage casings. But before I walk up the aisle with Rupert I need to know that Amelia and Woody are going to do the same. Otherwise the job's only half done.'

'Are you saying that if you weren't certain about Woody and Amelia, you wouldn't marry Rupert?'

'I don't think I can answer that.'

I offered a cigarette.

'No, thanks. By the way, Bertie, there's going to be a big Midsummer Festival in Melbury Tetchett next weekend.'

'Oh, really? What's the theme? Ancient fertility rites? Or just a few charades and a sing-song?'

'I'm not sure. Uncle Henry's dead keen. I think the idea is that it should be a masque based on *A Midsummer Night's Dream*. Some village bod's in charge.'

'A masque?'

'Yes, though I've never quite known what that means.'

'Join the club. I do know the play, though. I was in it once.'

'Were you Oberon?'

'No. I was Bottom. I say, there's no need to laugh quite so hard, Georgiana.'

'I'm sorry, Bertie. It was just the way you said it. It was so forlorn. And Bottom's one of the best parts.'

'I know. We played the rude mechanicals in the voices of some of the best-known beaks. I'm told my voice was a spit for Monty Beresford.'

'Who was Monty Beresford?'

'Lower-fifth classics.'

'Do you still remember the lines?'

'They're engraved on my heart. I couldn't forget them if I tried.'

'I always said you were clever.'

'It's just as well, because I can't remember much else from school.'

'Give me a few lines.'

'Right ho. Another drop?'

'Just a dribble. I had some wine at dinner. But help yourself.'

I did. I saw no reason to mention the hastily dispatched claret — Bicknell's portion, as I thought of it — nor the malty local beer with which I had attempted to drown my sorrows from a jug at the pavilion. The old boy's brandy was a rather mellow one, with plenty of oomph and toffee in the follow-through and it was beginning to blur the memory of the dropped catch.

"'O grim-look'd night!'" I growled. "'O night with hue so black! O night, which ever art when day is not!'"

'Is that Monty Beresford's voice?'

'To a tee.'

'He sounds like Mrs Padgett.'

'You speak true, young Meadowes. He did indeed. "O night! O night! Alack, alack, alack! I fear my Thisby's promise is forgot."'

'Carry on.'

'One of the nobs says something now. It's not my line.'

'Hold on a minute. Uncle Henry must have a Shakespeare somewhere.'

'After the end of the Hundred Years War but before the start of *Wisden*. By the window, therefore, I should say.'

'Have another brandy.'

'Perhaps just a dribble.'

'Here it is. One minute,' said Georgiana, riffling through the pages. 'All right, so Theseus says, "The wall, methinks, being sensible, should curse again." Should I do that with a more aristocratic voice?'

'Not at all. A Midlands garage mechanic is the effect you're after. You're supposed to sound like Bony Fishwick.'

'Who on earth is Bony Fishwick?'

'He was the school chaplain. "We 'ave left oondoon thowse things which we ought to 'ave doon."'

'I'll have another go. More brandy?'

'Just a suggestion.'

What with one thing another, we rather entered into the spirit of it, and Georgiana made a much livelier Thisby than had been on offer from Corbett-Burcher.

'Tell you what,' I said. 'If you stand on the sofa there, I'll stand on the ottoman, and then this standard lamp can represent the Wall.'

'Good idea. By the way, Bertie, I've just had a thought.'

'Doesn't surprise me, old thing. Not one bit. Think on.'

'What I thought was this. You know "The Repudiation of the Scarlet Woman by the Virtuous Lawyer as witnessed by his Innocent Bride"?'

'I thought we'd ditched that.'

'We had. But suppose Woody was in on it. That way

he could keep a straight face when I gave him the come-on. There'd be no misunderstanding afterwards between the two of us. And it would help me in my part, too.'

I swilled the brandy round the glass – in much the same way that I revolved the matter in the cranium. From where I stood, on the ottoman, it all looked rather promising. Foolproof, you might say.

'By Jove,' I said, 'I think you've hit the jackpot.'

'Thank you. Shall I ask Woody, or will you?'

'I think it would come better from you. He hasn't quite forgiven me for making up to Amelia.'

The thought gave me another brief Gonville and Caius wobble, my foothold precarious for a moment on the tapestry-covered lid.

'I shall fix it for five to three on Monday,' said Georgiana. 'It's when the pro from Blandford Forum comes in to give Ambo a tennis lesson.'

'Will Woody still be here?'

'Yes, he's catching the late train for a case on Tuesday.'

'Where were we?'

'"As Shafalus to Procrus, I to you."'

'"O! Kiss me through the hole of this vile wall."'

I leant forward to mime the action, as I had done all

those years ago, when the Wall – some new bug whose name I can't remember now – held up his parted fingers to represent a crack in the masonry.

It's possible that on that occasion I had dined on little more than the house supper and a glass of lemonade; I had certainly not got outside a half-pint of Sir Henry's five-star. Or perhaps the lips I could not reach in Melbury Hall induced a greater sense of urgency.

For some reason, anyway, I lost my footing and pitched forward from the ottoman. An instinct made me grab at the standard lamp as I fell. This deflected me for a moment and may have slightly lessened my impact on Georgiana, who ended up, not for the first time in our short acquaintance, sitting on the floor.

Once the racket had subsided, there was the sound of angry footsteps in the hall.

We looked at each other for a second, then, as one, made for the window. I say 'as one', though of course it took Georgiana a moment to heave herself up from the Aubusson. Meanwhile, ahead at the casement: up went the sash, over went the foreleg, smack went the skull into the woodwork . . . I looked back from the outside world and, as on the previous occasion, felt tempted to bestow a parting peck, when there came a mighty rattling at the locked library door, followed by some hefty thumps on the panelling.

Georgiana called out, 'Stop, thief!'

I did as instructed, stopped and turned, but saw her waving me away even as she cried again, 'Stop, thief!'

Being pretty quick on the uptake, I understood her plan and legged it at top speed.

To steady the nerves and clear the brain, I pulled out the cigarette case and, making sure I was well concealed from the house, set fire to one. I pictured Georgiana explaining to an irate Sir Henry that she had surprised a burglar. She would then be attempting to persuade the old boy that since nothing was missing there was no need to call in the police. It was obviously better if I was not to be seen anywhere in the vicinity until things had calmed down a bit and Sir Henry was re-assured that no light-fingered bibliophile had made off with his *History of the Crusades* in five vols, calf-bound, with slight foxing to the endpapers.

I found myself wandering on a path through some

trees – not really a wood, but what I suppose you'd call a grove. There were cedars, elms and other specimens it was too dark to be sure of: a silver birch or two, perhaps. Spindly chaps, anyway.

In their shade, I paused to take stock. Having missed the servants' high tea, I'd dined later off a slice of unwanted beef fillet with horseradish and a wedge of cheddar; the cognac had settled the whole thing nicely. Up in the branches above me I could hear what I fancied was a nightjar: a churring noise followed by what sounded like someone licking his lips. A garden is a lovesome thing, God wot; and a Dorset grove on a warm midsummer night is about as close to Eden as one can come without going to Mesopotamia, or wherever Dame Judith Puxley insisted the original had been.

I wasn't sure why, in the rather awkward circs, I was having these bosky thoughts. Ask anyone in the Drones and they'll tell you that Wooster, B. is essentially a boule-vardier – a man of pavement, café and theatre. I may be possessed of half a dozen decent tweed suitings, even the odd plus-four and deerstalker, but mine is not – *au fond*, as I believe the French say – a rustic soul.

Yet something had got right in amongst me on this

balmy night, and if I had an inner bumpkin, he was there with straw in his hair, grinning toothlessly and going 'ooh-arrr' along with the best of them. I sat down with my back to a tree trunk. I tried to clear my mind of Hackwoods and Venableses, just to get a good whiff of night air and remember what a deuced lucky fellow I was, dropped catch or no.

Then I felt something with about five hundred feet make a determined effort to get up my trouser leg. That's the trouble with these countryside moments: they don't last. Reality tends to stick an oar in.

A glance at the wrist told me it was some minutes past midnight. I knew that Bicknell went round like a gaoler at eleven-thirty on the dot, securing all entrances. My rude billet, as we know, was on the third floor at the back, with a view – if that's not too big a word – over the yard that led to the stables. The front of Melbury Hall had a fire escape that zigzagged from the third floor to the ground, with a particularly showy landing outside what I took to be Sir Henry and Lady H's bedroom. There was no such provision on the other side of the house, where the servants were presumably expected to knot the sheets or take a flying jump.

Georgiana's calming efforts seemed to have worked. I could see the light in the library go off, followed by one or two on the first floor, including that in the biggest bedroom. There appeared to be no imminent sign of the local constabulary or of the sleeping villagers of Kingston St Giles being roused by their feudal lord to a hue and cry. Then I saw a light on the second floor, in a room that must have overlooked the lawns – a pleasant but modest nook, almost certainly where they would have shoved the junior cousin, the Sonya Whatsit of the estate. I could see that the fire escape extended in a more modest form to this, the south front of the house. I imagined Georgiana doing a final bit of blue-pencil work behind the curtains before snuffing out the candle.

The odds on the ravell'd sleeve of care being knitted up to any appreciable extent as far as I was concerned looked pretty slim. In the sober light of day, it would probably have been clear to anyone in my position that the priority was not to make matters worse. The grounds and messuages of Melbury Hall were sure to contain a hayloft or a stable with some comfortable sacking; it would not have taken much, after all, to try the bones less than the visiting valet's cell.

Unfortunately, the sober light of day was not where I found myself; rather the opposite. It was beginning to turn cold, as English nights do in June, quite suddenly. The thought of bunking down with the horses failed to appeal. It seemed to me, on the other hand, a quite excellent idea to shimmy up the fire escape, go round the south side to Georgiana's light, knock on the window, check that all was well and thence make my way up indoors to my own room. As I cut along back towards the house, I could picture Georgiana's face when she let me in; a hero's welcome and a goodnight peck were mine for the taking.

At private school in Bramley-on-Sea, I used to have a Tuesday rendezvous at midnight on just such a fire escape with a boy in a different dormitory – a freckled lad called Newcome, who later took holy orders. These moonlit shindigs over shared tuck were brought to an abrupt end by the slipper of the Rev. Aubrey Upjohn, but it was with something of this youthful sense of adventure that I mounted the fire escape at Melbury Hall.

It was a solid piece of work, a credit to the ironmonger. It neither squeaked nor wobbled. I averted my eyes from what I took to be the Hackwood boudoir, climbed another floor and turned to survey the scene of which I was monarch. There in the moonlight I could make out the gazebo in the rose garden, and beyond it the rising ground of the deer park. I crept to the corner of the house and along the south front to Georgiana's room, where the light still burned.

Not wishing to startle the dear girl, I knocked softly. I listened hard, but there was no response. I rapped a little louder. Still nothing. I had not thought Georgiana to be so hard of hearing. Then I gave it all I'd got and was rewarded by a muffled shriek, the sound of movement from within, and finally a pulling back of curtains.

I shall never forget the face that met mine through the glass. At first I thought I had seen a ghost, or revenant. The skin was ghastly white; the hairstyle owed plenty to the quills upon a fretful porpentine. The overall expression was that of a Gorgon or Medusa. For what seemed an hour I stood transfixed; but it probably took no more than a second for the Wooster brain, relaxed as it was by the liquid contents of Sir Henry's ottoman, to register that the apparition was Dame Judith Puxley, readied for the night in thick cold cream and curling papers.

Acting of their own accord, the lower limbs whisked me away without demur and up the fire escape. I heard the window being raised but was already one floor higher, beneath the stone parapet – over which I clambered on to a flattish piece of roof.

'Who's there?' the old vixen called.

I feared more activity in the house and determined to press on across the rooftops to the relative safety of the servants' side of things. From this great height I could hear nothing of what commotion might be going on beneath, but I was taking no chances. The roofing arrangement of Melbury Hall was complicated. I knew it had been an especially painful drain on Sir Henry's resources and the roofers had left ample evidence of their visit: pieces of timber, dust sheets and nails – to say nothing of cigarette ends and empty bottles – lay among the broken slates.

As I made my way through the debris, up one pitch and down another into a flat gulley, I had a sudden brainwave. I was still in full evening dress and was therefore unlikely to be taken for a cat burglar: even a distant sighting would confirm an inside job. I therefore grabbed an abandoned dust sheet and wrapped it round the person, tucking it under my collar so no one could make out the dinner jacket.

Just as I thought I was above my own bedroom, a bright light caught me momentarily from below. I ducked down, crawled to the edge and gave it a minute or two. All was quiet. A cast-iron drainpipe seemed to have my name on it. With an agility bred from years of climbing back into my Oxford college, I swung on to it and slid down to where my window, propped open against the sunny day, allowed me a handhold. I clambered aboard, dropped on to the welcome floor and quickly disrobed. With the dust sheet stowed beneath the bed, I was well pyjama-ed by the time footsteps and voices were heard on the back staircase.

It was an indignant visiting valet who appeared a minute later at his door and demanded to know what the infernal noise was about.

Breakfast the following morning was later than usual, but a good deal more animated. I had told Jeeves about the events of the night when I took him up his tea, but I need hardly have bothered since he had already come to the conclusion that there was only one candidate for the role of rooftop intruder wrapped in a builder's dust sheet.

I was not required in the dining room, but Bicknell brought back regular reports to Mrs Padgett, Mrs Tilman and me. It seemed that Georgiana had convinced Sir Henry that she had surprised a burglar in the library when she went in to find a book to take up to bed. To hinder the pursuit, the intruder had locked the door into the hall before making good his escape. All were agreed that it was a relief Georgiana hadn't tried to tackle the fellow, who was described as large and of repellent aspect. There was no question of telephoning the police since the line was still out of action.

'Why did Miss Meadowes want to see you earlier, Mr Wilberforce?' said Bicknell, plonking down an emptied salver.

'She wanted me to ... to ask my advice about something.'

'Really?'

There was something about Bicknell's manner that I didn't much like.

'Yes,' I said. 'About a present for Lord Etringham,' I improvised.

'A present?'

'Yes . . . Yes, I think she wants to give him a present to say thank you for helping Sir Henry with his racing tips.'

'How peculiar,' said Bicknell. 'I would have thought Sir Henry himself would have—'

'Oh, do leave off, Mr Bicknell,' said Mrs Tilman. 'You sound like a police inspector, doesn't he, Mr Wilberforce? Anyway, you were only in there a minute, weren't you, love?'

'Oh, rather,' I said, slightly surprised.

'I seen you going off to bed only a couple of minutes later.'

'Oh, rather,' I said again. Weak, I admit, but I was a bit nonplussed by this unexpected alibi.

'Do they need more bacon, Mr Bicknell?' said Mrs Tilman.

'I'll look after that,' said Mrs Padgett, guarding her stove.

Mrs Tilman poured me a fresh cup of tea and – unless I was mistaken – winked at me. I was still trying to work out what was going on when Bicknell returned in search of more coffee.

'What they're all asking now,' he said, 'is what happened to the man Dame Judith saw outside her window. If he was the burglar, where is he now and how did he escape?'

''Appen as he's the one you saw on the roof, Mr B,' said Mrs Padgett.

'That's as may be,' said Bicknell. 'But I had Hoad guard the fire escape, then go up on the roof first thing and there was nobody there.'

'Sounds like *The Mystery of the Gabled House*,' I said, taking a shot at lightening the tone. 'Not that Melbury Hall has gables, obviously. Jolly good book, though.'

'And who was the murderer?' said Mrs Tilman.

'The butler did it,' I said. 'He always does.'

'Not this butler,' said Bicknell. 'Though I have my suspicions.'

'Well, keep them to yourself,' said Mrs Tilman, using a tone I wouldn't have dared risk. 'Mr Wilberforce, why don't you pop into the dining room and start to clear the sideboard.'

Bicknell gave Mrs Tilman a reproachful look, but said

nothing. I wondered whether she knew things about him, apart from his fondness for the master's claret; perhaps over the years the odd weakness – a pretty housemaid here, a missing silver napkin ring there – had come to her attention and been set aside for a rainy day.

At any rate, I was glad to escape his cross-examination; pottering about in the background of the dining room seemed a safer option.

'But, Dame Judith,' Amelia was saying with some excitement when I went in, 'surely you must have got a good look at the man's face.'

'I've told you, it was dark,' said Dame Judith. 'And I was in a state of shock. So would you have been, young lady.'

'Yes, Ambo,' said Georgiana, 'it's easier for someone outside to see into a lighted room than vice versa.'

'So he must have got a good look at Dame Judith,' said Amelia.

This thought seemed to cause both girls a spasm of silent amusement.

'Were you in your nightclothes, Judith?' asked Lady Hackwood sympathetically.

'Indeed. I had completed my preparations for retiring

and was coming to the end of a most interesting article in the *Journal of Cuneiform Studies.*'

At this point, Amelia had a fit of coughing that necessitated her holding a napkin over her face, while Georgiana leant over and ministered to her, her shoulders also silently shaking.

Sir Henry Hackwood put down his copy of *The Times* and looked down the table.

'Goodwood soon,' he said. 'Any thoughts, Etringham?'

'Not yet, I fear,' said Jeeves. 'But I shall shortly be in touch with a Newmarket friend who may conceivably be in a position to—'

'Splendid. Good man.'

'What I can't understand,' said Lady Hackwood, 'is why, when Bicknell shone a torch up to the roof, the intruder seemed to be swaddled in a bed sheet.'

'A bed sheet?' said Dame Judith.

'Bicknell?' said Sir Henry.

'Yes, Sir Henry,' said Bicknell. 'The party was wearing a long piece of cloth wrapped round him from neck to feet. Like an old statue.'

'Do you mean like a toga?' said Lady Hackwood.

'A toga!' said Dame Judith. 'Good heavens. The last

time a man in a toga was discovered on a roof in the middle of the night, it was poor Agatha Worplesdon's lunatic nephew.'

'Look what you're doing, man!' said Sir Henry, as I bent down to pick up the pieces of a Spode side plate that had slipped from my grasp.

'Yes,' went on Dame Judith. 'It was at a Victorian house near Ludlow.'

'Beautiful county, Shropshire,' I heard Georgiana interject gamely, as I headed out to the kitchen.

The rest of the day passed off without incident, for which relief the entire household, I imagine, gave silent thanks. Lady Hackwood and Mrs Venables went to church; Georgiana played croquet with old Vishnu (the lawn was nowhere near as flat as that of Government House in Simla, it appeared), while Amelia gave Venables junior a straight-sets bashing at tennis. Mrs Padgett had the day off and Mrs Tilman conjured a creditable joint of roast pork for lunch. Woody made himself scarce doing some papers in his room and Sir Henry, I fancy, had another crack at the accounts, hoping that this time they just might come out right. The groans from behind the library door did not fill one with hope. I busied myself disposing of the dust sheet in a bonfire area behind the stables.

Sometimes when you get a breather like that, though, the respite can seem ominous – as though fate is merely taking time off to refill the sock with wet sand. And so it proved; for Monday was the day that mayhem had marked down for her own.

First thing in the morning, I took Lord Etringham his tea.

'Jeeves,' I said, placing the tray beside the bed. 'Plan B swings into action shortly before three pip emma.'

'Indeed, sir? Might I be so bold as to inquire into the nature of the stratagem?'

'Georgiana is to come over all flirtatious with Woody and he's going to give her the bum's rush just as Amelia comes on the scene. She'll see that he's a parfit gentil knight who only has eyes for her.'

Jeeves took a sip of Oolong. 'I am somewhat surprised that Miss Meadowes has consented to such a scheme.'

'She didn't at first. Then she hit on the idea of getting Woody in on the act.'

'A wise precaution, undoubtedly, sir. And Miss

Meadowes is a high-spirited young lady who doubtless enjoys a prank – especially in a good cause.'

'Spot on, Jeeves.'

'And where is the assignation to take place?'

'Next to a rhododendron bush with a bench seat in front of it on the gravel path. Not far from the tennis court. Why do you want to know?'

'I was merely trying to envisage the scene, sir. Assuming all passes off without incident, how will Miss Meadowes subsequently repair her friendship with Miss Hackwood?'

I hadn't really considered this angle. 'I'm sure she'll think of something,' I said.

'One can but hope, sir. They seem the best of friends.'

'I expect when the dust's settled, she'll tell her the truth. Amelia will be so dashed happy she'll forgive and forget. She'll probably thank Georgie as the – who's that chap who brought people together?'

'The willing Pandarus, sir. He was the uncle of Criseyde in the poem by Chaucer, who enabled—'

'That's the chap. Is all quiet on the intruder front?'

'For the time being, sir, though I fear that Dame Judith remains in a state of agitation.'

'And what about me, for heaven's sake? It was one of the most terrifying sights of my life.'

'One can well imagine, sir.'

'So that's it, Jeeves. Back to the old metrop tomorrow and no harm done. Or not too much, anyway.'

Jeeves did a bit of throat-clearing. I knew of old what this meant.

'Something on your mind?' I said.

'Yes, sir. Sir Henry has invited me to return next weekend for the Midsummer Festival at Melbury Tetchett.'

'You declined, I suppose. And don't give me that "in the circumstances I deemed it best to accept" routine.'

'I temporised, sir.'

'You did what?'

'Prevaricated, sir.'

'Come again?'

'I played for time. I told Sir Henry I would endeavour to return, though I warned him that once back in London I should need to confirm that no more pressing matters had arisen.'

'Well, you'd better think of something pretty sharpish, Jeeves. Much as I love Dorset, I can't stand another night on that fakir's couch.'

'I believe it is Sir Henry's intention to reconvene many of this weekend's house party.'

'Why? Has he gone barking mad? Think of the cost, apart from anything else. Say what you like about the old fox, he knows how to push the boat out.'

'The Midsummer Festival is something that the Hackwood family has patronised for many generations. I understand it was Sir Lancelot Hackwood who initiated the celebration in 1705. And I fear that in financial matters Sir Henry has thrown caution to the winds.'

'Might as well be hanged for a sheep as for a lamb, you mean.'

'The gallows image is most vivid, if I may say so, sir.'

'Well, let's jolly well hope something turns up for the old rogue. If Amelia and Woody can bury the hatchet, Georgiana will bring Venables to heel and all will be well. Sausage casings all round. Plan B, you see.'

'Indeed, sir. "All is best, though oft we doubt what th' unsearchable dispose of highest wisdom brings about."'

'I say, that's awfully good, Jeeves.'

'Thank you, sir. It was the poet Milton who so opined in a dramatic work called——'

'As you say, Jeeves. He must be awfully pleased to think that someone's still spouting his stuff.'

So saying, I tooled off to the hall, grabbed a couple of newspapers, delivered them to the corner room and went on my merry way.

The only incident of note in the morning was the arrival of a repair man from the telephone company. Hoad was back in his place to shove round the luncheon plates, leaving me to hobnob with the excellent Mrs Tilman in the kitchen. All seemed to be purring along nicely towards the triumphant enactment of Plan B.

The appointed hour found me secreted in a rhododendron. This tree or shrub makes an admirable hiding place, especially when in full flower, as it was now. You can insert the person without risk of injury and at once become invisible; the genus had given top-notch accommodation to early experiments with tobacco by most of my school friends.

Woody poled up a few minutes early and sat on the bench, leafing through a book someone seemed to have left behind. The path was covered with a fine pea-shingle and gave ample warning of approaching footsteps. I had chosen the spot for this reason, and sure enough a girlish footfall was soon heard, followed by Georgiana's fond hello.

'Shall we have a trial run?' said Woody.

'Right ho. Shall we be sitting or standing?'

'Sitting's better. Then it looks as though as we've been having a serious heart-to-heart.'

'All right,' said Georgiana. 'You sit there, so Ambo gets a good view of you as she comes round the corner. Then I'll stroke your arm like this.'

'You'd better talk a lot of rot at the same time.'

'Right ho. Oh, Woody, I don't know how to tell you this. My heart is yours, you dashing sportsman. I love your broody eyes and your noble nose and your charm and modesty—'

'Steady on, Georgie.'

'Am I overacting? I have a tendency to.'

'Well, I suppose we have to send a clear message.'

'So perhaps I ought to kiss you. I lean in like this and plant a smacker on your lips.'

'Yes, I suppose so. Don't let's spoil the ship for a ha'porth of tar.'

Meanwhile, deep in the concealing rhododendron, the feelings in the Wooster bosom were decidedly mixed. I was aware of a nasty tightening in the pit of the stomach, and it was all I could do not to leap out of the bally bush and tell them to put a sock in it.

'But then I rebuff you sternly,' said Woody. 'I push you away and say, "My heart is only for Amelia. So cut out the funny stuff."'

'Ssh. I can hear her coming.'

Georgiana took closer order on the bench. 'Oh, Woody, you handsome cricketer, you Apollo of the bat and ball, let me wrap you in my arms.'

The footsteps came closer and Georgiana began to lay it on with a trowel.

'Let me stroke your hair, you little spring chicken. I adore you, Woody, you heavenly creature. Let me kiss those gorgeous lips again. Hold me closer, please.'

It was hard to make out through the twigs and branches exactly what had gone wrong, or when. But I can say for certain that it took no more than a second for the lovers to spring apart when they saw that the new arrival was not Amelia but a harassed-looking Rupert Venables.

CHAPTER
≡NINE≡

My services were required neither at dinner nor after it, so I seemed to be in for a solitary evening. By the time the 'quality' put on the nosebag at eight, I could contain my restlessness no longer and set off for the village. I dined once more at the Hare and Hounds, where the landlord's mind was still clearly on the cricket as he shoved a pint of ale across the bar.

'Best use both hands on that. Shall I carry 'im to the table for you?'

Then, when he came over a few minutes later to take my order: 'We got some nice duck pâté. I know you be fond of a duck, young man.'

I was about to remonstrate when I remembered it was mine host's bony finger that had cut down Sidney Venables at the wicket and sent him packing. The fellow couldn't be all bad, I told myself.

A great deal seemed to have happened since my last steak and kidney in the same window seat, and not much of it came under the heading of good news. I had escaped playing host to Aunt Agatha and the blighter Thomas in London, though a part of me – not the largest part, I suppose – felt ashamed of what my late father might have thought of my giving his sister the miss in baulk. The only other item in the credit column was having successfully misled our hosts as to our identity, and my aching back prevented me from taking much pleasure in this minor triumph.

The real business of the trip – the attempt to reunite the sundered hearts of my oldest friend and his beloved – had been an utter washout: a fiasco, a lulu, a damp squib from start to finish. I had tried my best to play Woody out of trouble and give him a decent shot at the green; I had left the poor chap playing five off the tee.

I didn't like to think what the repercussions of the failed Plan B might be. Venables didn't seem by nature a hothead, but no one likes to see his fiancée kissing another bloke. It would take all the oratory of Gray's Inn and the charm of Bedford Square to persuade the tireless traveller that things were not as they appeared.

The time had come to sound the retreat, and it was with considerable relief that I stuffed the spare clothes and washbag into Jeeves's modest holdall the next morning. I said my goodbyes to my fellow scullions, and in the case of Mrs Tilman and Mrs Padgett, they were fond ones.

'I'm sure we'll see you again soon, Mr W,' said Mrs Tilman.

''Appen I'll make another of them pies Miss Georgiana took you,' said Mrs Padgett.

'I hope so. Toodle-pip,' I said – to the obvious amusement of these two good-humoured domestics.

Remembering not to cross Bicknell's mighty palm with silver, I collected Lord Etringham's cases and stowed them in the back of the two-seater.

The dogs barked, but the caravan moved on. Vishnu Venables and his memsahib were collected by a driver in what looked like a hearse; Dame Judith was to take the train after lunch. Jeeves started the engine and we were about to escape when Sir Henry ran alongside and thrust a newspaper through the window.

'By the way, Etringham, I thought you'd like a copy of the *Melbury Courier*. It's just arrived. The report of the game's not up to much, but it's got a splendid picture of the team.'

With a crunch of gravel, we were gone. There was much to say, but I wanted to put a fair bit of distance between ourselves and Melbury Hall. As soon as we agreed the coast was well and truly clear, we swapped hats and places.

'So, Jeeves,' I said, 'what was the aftermath of Plan B like? How did young Venables take it?'

'Mr Venables made an early departure, sir. He left before dinner.'

'He must have driven past me in the Hare and Hounds.'

'Very likely, sir. He is expected back on Saturday for the Midsummer Festival, where he is to read some of his poems.'

'He's a poet, too, is he?'

'Light verse, I gather, sir, of a pastoral nature.'

'I wonder how that'll go down with the lads from the Red Lion.'

'I understand the verses have brevity on their side.'

'Unlike the travelogues.'

'An unkind observation, sir.'

'But not an unfair one, Jeeves. Golly, I felt as though I'd walked to Peking on my own two feet. Perhaps that could be his follow-up. By Shanks's Pony to Shanghai. Anyway, he didn't at once break off the engagement?'

'No, sir. I gather Mr Venables was greatly disturbed by the turn of events, but did not wish to be seen to lose face, as I believe the expression is. I understand he has given Miss Meadowes two days in which to offer an explanation of herself.'

'Stern stuff, eh? And what about Woody?'

'Relations between the two gentlemen were not of the most cordial before the incident. Mr Venables is conscious of a sense of inferiority. He believes Mr Beeching's athletic accomplishments and ease of manner show him in an unfavourable light.'

'That's hardly Woody's fault.'

'Certainly not, sir. But it is conceivable that Mr Venables's natural unease could work to the advantage of all concerned.'

'You mean he'll think twice before making an ass of himself.'

'Exactly, sir. Though if he concludes that he has already been humiliated beyond repair . . .'

'You mean . . .'

'I gathered from Miss Meadowes that his return is far from guaranteed.'

'Then bang goes Hickory Hot Boy, Jeeves. In come the blackboards, the chalk and the cupboardful of canes.'

'So it would appear, sir.'

Back in Berkeley Mansions, I left Jeeves to unpack and make sure that young Thomas had left no bucket of water poised above the bedroom door while I went down to the Drones for a late lunch.

The members would not take kindly to my giving away too much about the premises, but for the sake of a spot of atmosphere I should probably have a go at the broad outline. The place combines the impressive with what you might call the homely. About half Carrara must have gone into making the marble staircase that fills the hall; on a lower floor are courts for squash racquets and a swimming pool. The first-floor bar is where the lads mostly foregather amid oil portraits of former Drones, including a handful of princelings and Cabinet ministers. The main browsing and sluicing is done in the Morning Room, which is a little over twenty-two yards long – a sporting distance at which to try to hit the raised pie on the sideboard with bread rolls bunged from the far end. Then there is the smaller Queen Bee saloon and a card room, where fortunes have been won and lost. Above that are rumoured to be bedrooms for country members.

When I got to the club, the luncheon service was over, but you can always get a plate of kedgeree or a shepherd's pie and a glass of something in the lower bar – a wood-panelled nook that brings to mind the nineteenth hole at a Highland golf course.

This was where I headed on arrival, and was lucky enough to find Boko Fittleworth in conversation with Freddie Oaker. These are two of a handful of Drones professional writers, Boko penning what you'd call wholesome popular fiction – adventures with a bit of uplift for the masses, and Freddie churning out appalling 'true love' mush for the women's weekly magazines under the name of 'Alicia Seymour'. What really binds these men of letters is a shared interest in the folding stuff: who of their acquaintance has sold most copies or which publisher is said to ante up the juiciest sum.

They were finishing a decanter of the club claret, in which they kindly included me, before moving on to coffee and a cigar.

'I've heard good things about Pearson Lane,' said Freddie. 'They bid the most enormous sum for Sir Edward Grey's memoirs.'

'Smith and Durrant still have the deepest pockets,' said Boko. 'And they've got this new girl working there on the fiction side. They say she's got the mind of Jane Austen and the looks of Clara Bow.'

'Are you sure it's that way about?' said Freddie.

'Absolutely. She's a first-class popsy by all accounts, and a good egg with it, but don't get your hopes up, old man. She's marching up the aisle with one of their authors. Chap called Venables.'

'The "By" man?'

'Yes. By Handcart to Hell and so forth.'

'Well, I suppose he's a catch of sorts.'

'How's young Nobby?' I asked Boko, in an effort to ease the conversation on to a less awkward track – Nobby being Zenobia Hopwood, the blue-eyed little half-portion to whom he was engaged to be married. 'Have you named the day yet?'

'Nobby and I are set on a Christmas wedding, but her guardian's trying to put the kibosh on it.'

Nobby's guardian, the old lags will need no reminding but new readers need to be told, is England's premier masochist: he models himself on the Greek fellow who was chained to a rock where a bird of prey dropped in daily to breakfast on his liver – though that might have been light relief compared to hitching yourself to my Aunt Agatha, which was the fate this poor, demented Worplesdon had selected of his own free will.

'The kibosh from the guardian, or the guardian's wife, Boko?' I queried.

'A bit of both, since you ask. I spent the weekend with them at Steeple Bumpleigh. I sometimes have the impression that your aunt doesn't think much of me, Bertie.'

'Did you say you spent the weekend with her?'

'Yes. We had a few practical details to talk over.'

'At Steeple Bumpleigh?'

'Yes.'

'And the Worplesdons were there?'

'I'd hardly go and stay if they weren't.'

'At Bumpleigh Hall?'

'That's where they live, Bertie.'

'And young Thomas?'

'Yes. Why is this so surprising, old man? I know you've never been engaged yourself for more than forty-eight hours, but if you had, you'd know that buttering up the in-laws is part of the process. And believe me the Worplesdons take a fair bit of butter. Think of the United Dairies depot at Melksham.'

'Well,' I said, massaging the lemon a fair bit as I did so, 'it's just that I went off to Dorsetshire so Aunt Agatha could have the run of my digs for a few days over the weekend. Now you say she was in Essex. So—'

'The old girl must have changed her mind,' interrupted Freddie Oaker, who had not been much gripped by the above exchange. 'No great mystery. Anyone fancy a frame of snooker pool?'

It was a pensive Bertram who strolled through Berkeley Square an hour or so later. From the day I had returned from my spring holiday on the Côte d'Azur I'd felt a bit like the sidekick in one of those detective stories – the fellow who's always one step behind the famous sleuth and whose function is to ask questions on behalf of the dimmer class of reader. It was almost as though some master criminal was orchestrating something in which I was a hapless pawn – if a pawn can be orchestrated. But perhaps you see what I'm driving at: a lurking sense that there were Forces at Work of which I Understood Little.

The first thing I wanted to do when back at the flat was to telephone Woody and find out how things stood. I didn't fear the squashed nose or the broken rib so much as I had after Plan A came a cropper because in this second fiasco Georgiana was as much to blame as I was – and so was Woody himself, come to that. Also it was not the Beeching–Hackwood wedding plans that had suffered; it was the Meadowes–Venables team that had been laid a stymie.

After an update on that front, I would come to the Case of the Missing Aunt. I must have been pondering all this pretty deeply when the sound of a motor horn made me leap back on to the pavement from an ill-advised attempt to cross the road. What was nagging at the edge of the Wooster brain was an inkling that all these loose ends could in some odd way be tied together.

'What ho, Jeeves,' I called out on re-entering the domicile. 'Any chance of a cupful of the fragrant Darjeeling?'

'The kettle has just boiled, sir.'

'Dashed odd thing,' I said, as he set the tray down beside me. 'I bumped into Boko Fittleworth at the Drones and he told me he had spent the weekend at Steeple Bumpleigh. With Aunt Agatha.'

'Indeed, sir. It appears that her ladyship was waylaid. I could find no trace of her visit.'

'Or of young Thomas?'

'Still less, sir. One might have expected the young gentleman to have left a calling card, as it were.'

'An apple-pie bed, a broken window or two. A plague of frogs.'

'Indeed, sir.'

'A murrain of cattle.'

'Less likely in the—'

'Stopping only at the slaughter of the firstborn. But why on earth didn't she let me know?'

'I dare say her ladyship telephoned to apprise you

of her change of plan, sir, but if you remember we left London with considerable despatch.'

I did remember. 'Are you suggesting there were panic stations, Jeeves?'

'I recall more of an air of decisiveness on your part, sir: a sense that if it were done then 'twere well it were done quickly. Did Mr Fittleworth mention the building work at Bumpleigh Hall?'

'No. And I forgot to ask. I hope nothing's amiss.'

'Would you like me to establish a connection by telephone so that you can speak to her ladyship yourself, sir?'

I swallowed some hot tea rather faster than I meant. As I sponged down the shirt front with a pocket hand-kerchief, I said: 'I think not, Jeeves. In the circumstances, better just to let sleeping dogs lie, don't you think?'

'As you wish, sir. Will there be anything else?'

The next day, I met Woody for dinner at an oyster bar near Victoria Station, with sawdust on the floorboards – Woody's choice, it being not far from his flat in Elizabeth Street. He had got there before me and instructed the barman in the making of two zonkers that stood ready on the table between us, winking up invitingly.

I had taken along the copy of the *Melbury Courier* to remind him of his triumph at the crease.

'Gosh, what a crew!' he said. 'Who's the shifty-looking one?'

'Liddle,' I said. 'He was out on parole, as it were. Jeeves looks the part, doesn't he?'

'Gifted spinner,' said Woody. 'Bowling must run in the family. It says here Lord Etringham took two wickets, but I'm sure he had three.'

'Sir Henry warned us the report wasn't up to much.'

A waiter came alongside with a variety of shellfish.

'I went to see Rupert Venables at lunchtime,' said Woody.

'That was brave.'

'I thought it was the right thing to do. He took me to his club in Brook Street. He's a rum cove.'

'What did he say about Georgiana? Is he going to hand her the mitten?'

'He was a bit ... elusive. What do you make of Venables, Bertie?'

This was not a subject I was anxious to spend much time on, but I could see I had to have a stab at answering. 'I'm sure he's a solid enough fellow. And they have the old literary world in common.'

'It's funny,' said Woody, digging into the brown shrimps, 'I had the impression that he had ... Well ...'

'Had what, old chap?'

'Well, I could be completely wrong, but I had the impression that he had another iron in the fire.'

'Ouch!' I said. 'Look out, you chump. You just squirted lemon in my eye.'

'Did I? Sorry, old man. I thought you were in pain at the thought of Venables leaving Georgie in the lurch. I can't imagine why, though, since it's quite clear you're potty about the girl yourself.'

'I don't know what you're talking about, Beeching.'

'Oh, stop it, Bertie, for heaven's sake. Your tongue hangs out like Monty Beresford's golden retriever on the Fourth of June.'

'You are referring to another man's fiancée, Woody. That's surely *ultra* something.'

'Do you mean *ultra vires*?'

'I mean it's jolly well not on.'

Woody separated an oyster from its shell and applied the citrus, this time without nearly blinding me. 'Venables talked a lot about his parents,' he said. 'All the years they'd lived abroad and how they wanted a quiet old age in the English countryside. But they don't really know anyone.'

'So the idea is they get their legs under the Hackwood table and Sir Henry introduces them to all the Dorsetshire gentry?'

'Yes. And lucky gentry, you might well say. It was all a bit sad. I think he accepted my explanation of this hare-brained flirting scheme I'd been talked into, but he seemed a bit wistful.'

'Wistful?'

'It was as though he and Georgie were both trying to please the elder generation, whereas Amelia and I are pledged to one another despite anything the old folks can throw at us.'

I speared a moody winkle. 'And what about Amelia? Is she still of the view that you're a modern Bluebeard and that Georgiana's a scarlet woman?'

'I've been asked back this weekend. That must be a good sign. As for Georgiana's behaviour, Amelia accepted her story. She presumed Georgie had been talked into this typically loony scheme by you.'

'Thank you. You've been on the blower, have you?'

'Yes. Now it's been mended, Amelia's been in touch a fair bit. Between you and me, Bertie – but please don't tempt providence by blurting this out – the whole thing's on again.'

'Congratulations, old man. I couldn't be more pleased. She's a splendid girl.'

'She certainly is.'

'I hope one day she'll show me her butterfly collection.'

Woody's eyes narrowed a fraction. 'You keep away.'

I poured a glass of frosty white to toast the news. 'So what's this other iron in the Venables fire?'

'He mentioned no names,' said Woody, 'but he spoke of someone he'd met on his travels. In Constantinople, I think. Her parents have a place in Nottinghamshire.'

'Well, that's far enough away.'

'And it's where the Persian cat comes from originally.'

'So they'd know a few people,' I said.

'Presumably, yes, and I gathered the family had some scratch of their own so they wouldn't need the Spanier riches.'

'Better and better,' I said, replacing the glass on the table. 'Meanwhile, all is for the best though often we doubt what the unsearchable something of whatsit brings to pass.'

'What are you on about, Bertie?'

'The poet Milton, Woody. Jeeves passed the thought my way.'

'It may have lost something en route.'

'Possibly,' I conceded. 'Talking of routes, are you still driving your Underground train?'

'No, sadly that's all gone back to normal. Jolly good fun, the General Strike. It just didn't last nearly long enough.'

'It more or less passed me by,' I admitted.

'You chump, Bertie. Even the girls came up from Kingston St Giles to lend a hand.'

'Really?'

'Yes. Amelia sold tickets and Georgie drove the 27 bus.'

I managed to keep a grip on the slippery glass as I stopped it halfway to the lips.

'Georgiana drove a bus?'

'Yes.'

'With people on it?'

'Yes. The 27. From Hounslow to Muswell Hill.'

'Were there many . . . injured?'

'I gather not, though it was believed that she set an all-comers' record for the time from Twickenham to Kew. An expectant mother went into labour on the upper deck at Richmond. A schoolboy tumbled down the stairs but only grazed his knee.'

'Was that it?'

'Yes. She was replaced at Turnham Green.'

The next morning, when Jeeves shimmied in with the tea tray, there was a letter with a London postmark and the handwriting that had alerted me to the presence of a picnic basket with my name on it in the sunken garden.

'What's it like outside?' I asked.

'The weather continues to be exceptionally clement, sir.'

'Jolly good,' I said, slipping the paperknife through the envelope. 'I'm going to Curzon Street for a trim at the barber's.'

I thought I saw a small lift of Jeeves's eyebrow. I raised

a hand to the side-whiskers. 'Just a trim,' I said. 'Nothing more.'

'Very well, sir. Shall I telephone for an appointment?'

I didn't answer at once, since I was scanning the letter – an elegant scrawl in black ink. 'Dear Bertie,' it said, 'I know Uncle Henry has invited Lord E back this weekend and it would be lovely if you would come too. Your employer will surely need your help! There is also the question of the entertainment at Melbury village hall. Uncle Henry's plan is that it should include the enactment of a scene from *A Midsummer Night's Dream*. We are short of rude mechanicals. Your experience – and expertise – could save the day. It might also be fun. With love from Georgiana.'

'Jeeves,' I said, 'have you had any further thoughts about the weekend?'

'No, sir. I don't feel it is my place to accept or refuse Sir Henry's invitation. I am awaiting your instruction.'

I finished the refreshing cupful. As usual, it seemed to fill me with a sense of pleasant possibilities.

'Telephone the barber, please, and make an appointment for noon. Then send a telegram to old Hackwood. Did he specify a time?'

'No, sir. There is a summer fete in the grounds of the house on Saturday afternoon before the evening festivities at the church hall. I had the impression that as far as Sir Henry was concerned, the revels would begin on Friday evening.'

'Then so be it, Jeeves,' I said. 'On with the motley.'

Thus was the die cast, this exchange taking place, I am pretty certain, on the Thursday morning.

An odd thing I've noticed over the years, chronicling these adventures of mine, is that even in the middle of an absolute corker – the Steeple Bumpleigh Horror, for example – there are days when not much happens. This is ticklish for the author. I dare say that at such a point in one of those novels beloved of Jeeves and Georgiana, old Tolstoy took advantage of a lull in the action to bung in a bit of family history – how the Rostropovs had known the Ilyanovs, for instance, since the first bear was sighted on the Russian Steppe. The author of *The Mystery of the Gabled House*, if in doubt, generally throws in another corpse. Not having any stiffs at my disposal, I can only say that little of note took place in Berkeley Mansions for the next twenty-four hours. Nothing really got going until Friday afternoon, after which things got pretty fruity. End of lull. Now read on.

Though dressed as a valet, I took the wheel of the two-seater as we left the Great Wen once more and headed for the sunlit hills. There is something about this particular road with its signs to Micheldever and Over Wallop that always seems to lift the spirits. The first bright green of May had given way to something lusher, so everything in the countryside looked just the way the Almighty must have roughed it out on his sketchpad; the cow parsley could not have been more rampant, the oaks more oakish or the roadside inns more tempting if they'd tried.

'I say, Jeeves,' I said, waving an arm in the general direction of Stourhead, 'it's odd to think we might have lost all this. During the...' I trailed off, not wanting to put a damper on things.

'The hostilities, do you mean, sir?'

'Yes. Do you think it will all ever just ... disappear?'

'No, sir. A thing of beauty is a joy for ever. Its loveliness increases; it will never pass into nothingness.'

'Hang on, Jeeves. I recognise that.'

'I am pleased to hear it, sir. It was the poet—'

'Don't tell me. It was ... the poet Keats, wasn't it?'

'It was indeed, sir. The lines supply the opening of an early work, "Endymion".'

We drove on in silence for a mile or so. 'I say, Jeeves, do you know, I think that's the first time I've ever recognised one of your quotations.'

'I know, sir. I found it most gratifying.'

'You mean that after all these years something must be rubbing off?'

'I was always given to believe that one's education did not finish with the closing of the school gate, sir.'

'So this moment represents a ... What's that thing on a mountain top where one drop of rain goes to the Pacific and one to the Mediterranean?'

'A watershed, sir.'

'That's the chap. Here's to watersheds, Jeeves. Next left, isn't it?'

Having lunched in London, there was no need to revisit the Death's Head at Darston, though we were making such good time that we did stop at a rather fine converted manor house near Blandford Forum for a cup of tea and an egg-and-cress sandwich.

'I'm rather looking forward to this, Jeeves,' I said. 'I

have a feeling things are all going to work out just fine and dandy.'

'The news about Mr Beeching and Miss Hackwood is certainly encouraging, sir.'

'Yes, and I'm sure Venables will see sense. They'll be very happy together. We'll say no more about that idiotic idea of yours that Georgiana had – what did you call them?'

'Feelings, sir.'

'Yes. Imagine! She would have tried to improve me. It would have been worse than Florence Craye. I'd have been forced to go to concerts by Stravinsky.'

'Not necessarily, sir. When Dame Judith brought up his name once at dinner, Miss Meadowes affected to believe he was a member of the Politburo.'

'Still, better off as we are.'

'As you wish, sir.'

It was shortly after six when the two-seater, with Lord Etringham now at the wheel, turned off the high street of Kingston St Giles and into the lime-tree avenue that led to Melbury Hall. Mrs Tilman was at the tradesmen's entrance, as though she had been listening for the sound of a car; to my embarrassment she welcomed me with a peck on the cheek.

Being back so soon felt pretty odd – like returning unexpectedly to school only five days after you'd signed off for the summer hols. You somehow imagine that such establishments cease to exist when you wave a cheery goodbye in July, rematerialising only in time for the new boys' tea in late September. I went meekly to my quarters, an old lag who knows the ropes, and was surprised to find a small pot of wild flowers on the table. Something about the bed looked different, too. I gave it a tentative prod. All clear. I gingerly lowered the posterior. To my surprise, I was not impaled, but sank an inch – and then some. Whipping back the bedclothes, I saw that someone had laid a sort of over-mattress on top of the old fakir's palliasse.

I was wondering whether I should take the early dinner with my fellow servants or if I could face another solitary evening at the Hare and Hounds when there came a knock at the door. It was Bicknell.

'Mr Wilberforce, I'm afraid I shall have to call on you for an extra pair of hands again.'

'Hoad?'

'I'm afraid so.'

'He's not much use to you, is he?'

'It was a temporary appointment. I don't think it's going to be made permanent. He's not reliable.'

I had a sudden thought. What could make a chap have funny turns, be both sluggish and impetuous, then liverish? I made a gesture with my right hand to suggest the raising of a substantial glass.

Bicknell nodded, gravely. 'He was discovered flat out in the cucumber frames at teatime. Mrs Tilman tried to revive him with a glass of water. She got him on his feet but then he started singing "The Battle Hymn of the Republic".'

'So he's trampled out the vintage where the grapes of wrath are stored,' I said, aiming for the light touch.

It didn't wash. Bicknell's face was impassive. 'He's locked in the stable. He won't be let out till morning.'

'Won't he frighten the horses?'

'He's on his own. He's in Jude the Obscure's box.'

'And where's Jude the Obscure?'

'He's standing at Newton Abbot.'

'Well, jolly good luck to him. And to the mares. I hope they don't have gloomy foals.'

Bicknell turned to leave, then stopped in the doorway.

'Hoad said he found a half-burnt builder's dust sheet near the cold frames.'

'In the bonfire area?' I asked airily. 'I mean, that's where it got burnt, I expect?'

'Yes. Odd, don't you think?'

'Not really. Messy chaps, builders.'

Bicknell gave me a long, hard stare. A lesser man, I dare say, might have flinched or looked away. Not Bertram, though.

Eventually, the mighty butler spoke. 'Seven-thirty in the kitchen would be best.'

'You can rely on me, Mr Bicknell.'

'I thought I could, Mr Wilberforce.'

Those gathered for dinner comprised the entire cast as before, with additions. Of the old-timers, Woody had the hawkish twinkle back in his eye and Amelia looked like the fourth seed at Wimbledon who's just discovered the defending champion's gone lame. 'Perky' would about cover it.

The Venables trio had arrived in the family hearse, while Dame Judith Puxley had once more been lured from the Reading Room at the British Museum, though on what pretext I found it hard to imagine – a village fete and an evening in the church hall hardly adding up to her idea of culture.

The additions were the vicar and his wife and a local worthy called Major Holloway, who had taken it on himself to organise the Saturday evening show. He was accompanied by an apple-cheeked female, presumably his wife.

Sir Henry Hackwood wore a green smoking jacket and an air of desperation. I've seen chaps with the same hunted look during the final hand of cards at two in the morning at the Drones; the three kings are securely in the hole, but they're wondering how to keep the other players interested for a few more minutes.

The last in to the dining room was Georgiana, and her appearance brought me up short. I'd seen those lovely features in countless moods, the 'let's just share a few langoustines' one, the unsuccessfully resisted water-works, the wounded but forgiving, the quizzical 'Do you think that's what Pushkin really meant?' and the smiling 'I'm fine, but you have another glass' variants.

This one, as I've said, was a new one on me. She looked

like a messenger charged with calling on King Harold's bedchamber to tell him that the Normans had splashed ashore in force near a spot called Hastings. Foreboding was writ big in those chocolate-coloured eyes.

Lady Hackwood and the girls, it seemed, had the afternoon fete pretty much under control with the help of the vicar's wife, so Sir Henry took the opportunity to run through the evening programme with Major Holloway.

'Our contribution is a scene from Shakespeare,' said Sir Henry. 'Very apt, I'm told. My niece Georgiana will be rehearsing the players in the morning.'

'I remember mounting a performance of *The Merchant of Venice* in Bangalore,' said Sidney Venables. 'The local paper said my Shylock was the finest since Henry Irving at the Lyceum.'

'Perhaps you can play the duke, then,' said Sir Henry.

'Or maybe you might find room for a crosstalk routine?' said Venables.

'Oh yes,' said Mrs V. 'Sidney was famous in Chanamasala for his crosstalk acts. He'd make up the jokes on the day so they were nice and topical. People did love them.'

'I'd need a straight man or feed,' said Venables.

'It's rather late notice,' said Major Holloway.

'I'm sure we can manage something,' said Sir Henry. 'What about the rest of the programme?'

'We have the Melbury Glee Club,' said Holloway. 'They'll be singing "'Twas a Shepherd and His Lass" and "The Ballad of Cranborne Chase", accompanied by the vicar's wife at the pianoforte. A schoolgirl from Kingston St Jude is doing a dramatic recitation and we've some conjuring tricks from my wife's brother. Next we have a barbershop quartet from Puddletown, then there'll be refreshments. After which the Melbury Tetchett string quartet – with my lady wife playing second fiddle – will give a short recital. Then there'll be a *tableau vivant* from the Ladies' Sewing Circle. And after that we come to the grand finale, which is your ensemble scene from Shakespeare.'

'I thought young Venables was going to be reciting some of his verses,' said Sir Henry.

'I'm afraid I shan't be able to do that,' said Rupert Venables.

'Why on earth not?'

'Because I shan't be here.'

'"Shan't be here"! But you've only just come back!'

'I think in the circumstances it would ill become me to remain at the Hall, Sir Henry.'

'Ill become you! What the devil are you talking about?'

The room was silent as it waited for young Venables to explain. 'I regret to say that I am no longer engaged to be married to your niece, Sir Henry. I returned to Kingston St Giles to terminate the engagement in person.'

'Oh, Roo!' said Mrs Venables. 'Why didn't you tell me?'

'I'm telling you now, Ma,' said Venables.

The silence came down again, a bit thicker this time. I looked at Georgiana, who was staring straight ahead, pale but unspeaking.

'This is a fine pickle,' said Lady Hackwood – an unfortunate choice of word, one couldn't help feeling, since a proprietary pickle or relish was just what seemed to have gone missing.

Amelia began to sob. I shuffled about doing a bit of plate-clearing, hoping that some stage business might ease the tension.

Bicknell responded to his stricken master's gesture and refilled his glass to the brim.

Rupert Venables glanced up and down the table with

a look that you might, had you not known the circumstances, have taken for satisfaction.

'I'm sorry that the news had to emerge in this way, Sir
Henry,' he said. 'I had hoped for a chance to speak to you
alone before dinner.'

'And what about Georgie?' said Amelia.

'I'm all right, Ambo,' said Georgiana in a very small
voice.

At this point I was required on chicken fricassee
duty in the kitchen. After a hectic few minutes to and
fro, I settled into a steadier rhythm of touring with
the broccoli dish — making sure to come in from the
left-hand side. I couldn't help noticing as I did so, the
worrying shade of purple that Sir Henry's face had
taken on.

'I wish you and your family the very best good fortune
in the future,' said Rupert Venables, 'and I trust that in
the circumstances . . .'

He tailed off as a noise like an exploding water main
came from Sir Henry. 'For heaven's sake be quiet, you
ridiculous young popinjay,' said the baronet. 'How dare
you come into my house, sir, make up to my niece then
discard her in this impudent manner?'

Rupert Venables looked round the table for support. He smiled, a touch nervously. 'I think I've explained, Sir Henry. Personal matters which it would be indelicate to reveal have made it impossible for me to—'

'To hell with your personal matters,' said Sir Henry. 'Georgiana's father was my wife's brother. He was as fine a man as ever drew breath, if somewhat overfond of port. I take my responsibility to his daughter very seriously. As for you, young man ... You can pack your bag and leave my house. At once.'

One might at this point have expected either of the senior Venableses to stick in a word for the fruit of their loins or Lady H to offer a calming 'there, there' to her niece. But the next voice to be heard – a warmish baritone – belonged to P. Beeching.

'Sir Henry, might I, with due respect, urge a moment's calm on us all? The happiness of many is at stake. There is another engagement here that is not, if I may say so, *eiusdem generis*. And if—'

'Don't give me that Latin nonsense, Beeching. You're not in the High Court now. And if you still think you're going to marry my daughter, you'd better think again pretty smartly.'

Amelia let out a stricken cry and Georgiana began to sob silently. Lady Hackwood said, 'Really, Henry!'

For all I could tell, Dame Judith Puxley might at this moment have put in her two bob's worth, but all conversation was brought to a sudden end by the sound of the front door bell ringing clangorously in the hall.

With heavy and suspicious tread, Bicknell left the dining room.

A cathedral hush came over the company. I stood like a dummy by the sideboard; I could think of no consolation except to tell myself that things could not possibly get worse.

How wrong I was.

The double door from the hall swung open and filled with butler.

Clearing his throat, Bicknell drew himself up to his fullest height and announced to one and all: 'Lord Etringham.'

CHAPTER
===TEN===

The Woosters are generally acknowledged to be made of stern stuff. We did our bit in the Crusades and, I'm told, were spotted galloping into the French at Agincourt under a steady downpour of arrows. We don't duck a challenge.

When the time comes for a strategic withdrawal, however, we withdraw alongside the best of them. I couldn't see how anything helpful to the happiness of those near or dear to me could emerge in the next few minutes; and just as in the normal day there is a sense of *noblesse oblige*, so in my position of humble footman I could see no way to be of further service. I therefore exercised the historic right of the worker to down tools and call it a day.

I was into the kitchen, through the corridor, up the back stairs and inside my simple quarters – pausing only to gather up an unregarded bottle from the dresser – before you could say Burke and Debrett.

It was a flummoxed, wits-endish Wooster who, an hour later, became conscious of a polite knocking at the door. Wondering only what fresh curses might have been called down on my head, I went to open it.

Outside stood Mrs Tilman. To my surprise, the good woman was neither sobbing nor distraught; in fact she wore a benign, almost cheerful expression.

'Mr Wooster,' she said, 'Sir Henry would like to see you in the library.'

'Mr Woo-Woo-Wooster?'

'You won't remember me, sir. We met some years ago when I was chief housemaid at Sir Henry Dalgleish's house in Berkshire. My name is Amy Charlton. I was married to Mr Tilman soon afterwards. He was Sir Henry's butler.'

'I'd like to say I remember, Mrs Tilman, but the truth is—'

'It doesn't matter, love. Everything's been sorted out downstairs. Sir Henry knows who you are and who Mr Jeeves is.'

'But isn't he furious?'

'Sir Henry is unpredictable, sir. It's his nature. But he's a kindly man underneath. He's become fond of Mr Jeeves. If he takes to someone, he takes to them. His best friend for years was the chauffeur. It broke his heart when he had to let him go.'

'And Lord Etringham? The real one?'

'He's an elderly gentleman, sir. Very mild-mannered. And he's interested in history as well as fossils. He and Sir Henry seem to have taken a shine to each other already.'

This was all rather a turn-up for the book, of course, but I can't pretend there was much of a spring in the step as I crossed the mighty hall, as bidden, and for the first time entered the library under my own name.

Assembled in that bookish room were, reading from left to right: G. Meadowes, looking more spry, less like patience on a monument, as I've heard Jeeves put it, than she had an hour earlier; R. Jeeves, the valet lately known as Lord Etringham, inscrutable, yet visibly at ease; Sir H. Hackwood, foxy, animated; A. Hackwood, flushed and a-tremble; and a white-haired old cove with horn-rimmed glasses, barely five feet tall, with the fussy air of the White Rabbit from *Alice in Wonderland*.

'Ah, Wooster. Glad to meet you properly,' said Sir Henry, extending the hand of friendship from the cuff of his smoking jacket. 'May I now introduce Lord Etringham?'

A second handshake followed. The ensuing explanations rambled over an hour or more, lubricated by the contents of that hospitable ottoman. The salient points, which were few, went as follows.

Lord Etringham (the bona fide one, not Jeeves) had for some time been treated for aggra-something by the well-known loony doctor, Sir Roderick Glossop. Progress was now so marked that he was proposing to join an expedition to Egypt with Howard Carter the following spring. As part of the limbering up, Sir Roderick encouraged his patient to travel in England – beginning with a trip on foot to the village post office and coming to a peak with a steam-train excursion to the Jurassic Coast of Dorset, some few miles from Melbury Hall. Lord E had planned to visit in August, but decided to come at once when an old friend in Sherborne sent him a copy of the *Melbury*

Courier with a photograph of a cricket team under which the caption revealed that his lordship was being impersonated by a stranger.

In the course of the peer's story, Sir Henry established that Lord Etringham had booked into a modest bed and breakfast at Lyme Regis and insisted that he stay on at Melbury Hall, in the corner room that his namesake had previously occupied, using the house as a base for his expeditions. The nervous Lord E was obviously relieved to find himself enveloped in such a welcome rather than take pot luck with a seaside landlady. They had further discovered a shared interest in the Hundred Years War, though Lord Etringham drew the historical line at the Battle of Bosworth – later events, in his view, falling into the 'modern' period.

It was clear to me that not only had Sir Henry turned on the charm he generally kept hidden under a pretty all-obliterating bushel, but that Georgiana had also not been backward in dishing it out. If you had spent the best part of half a century in a draughty Westmorland house with only bits of old rock for company, it must have come as quite something to find yourself caught in the beam of that girl's twin headlights as she discovered a sudden interest in geology. The old boy was clearly wondering whether the Pleistocene era was quite all it was cracked up to be when the modern day seemed to have so much more to offer.

'So, Wooster, Bobby Etringham and I are friends already,' Sir Henry concluded. 'By the way, Bobby, you must feel free to take the car for your fossil-hunting.'

'Most kind of you, Henry, but I have never learned to drive. My condition, you see . . .' The old boy's voice was reedy, and the words hard to distinguish.

'Then Georgiana shall be your chauffeur!'

'With pleasure, Uncle Henry. So long as I'm here.'

Well of course one couldn't help but wonder how much excitement the old nerve-patient could take; but I thought it best not to throw a spanner in the works.

'Sure you won't have a glass of brandy, Bobby?' said Sir Henry.

'No, I really can't. Roddy Glossop is absolutely strict on that point. The powders he has diagnosed must never be mixed with alcohol. He said I should fall asleep almost at once.'

There was the sound of a throat being cleared, and long experience made me glance in Jeeves's direction.

'Might I suggest, Sir Henry, that we leave you and Lord Etringham together? I'm sure that Mrs Tilman will have reorganised the sleeping arrangements by now.'

'Good idea,' said Georgiana. 'Come on, Ambo.'

Sensing that wiser heads than mine were on to something, I shuffled off with the gang and left the peer and baronet alone. Jeeves accompanied me to my new quarters at the end of the corridor on the second floor, a small but charming room with a fine view over the lawns towards the tennis court – in so far as one could see past a giant wellingtonia. Mrs Tilman had done a sterling job in restoring all my clothes to chest and wardrobe.

'Well, Jeeves,' I said. 'Business as usual, what?'

'So it would appear, sir. I confess that I shall be happy to resume my normal duties. I found myself suffering a degree of indigestion after so many of Mrs Padgett's meals.'

'And the bed a fraction soft, was it?'

'I have long favoured a firmer mattress as being beneficial to the posture, sir.'

I glanced round the new arrangements. I felt I should sleep like a lamb.

'Old Etringham's a very forgiving chap, isn't he?' I said.

'A most mild-mannered and agreeable gentleman, sir.'

'A bachelor, is he?'

'Yes, sir. He has no issue.'

'So what happens to the Etringham fortune when he pops off?'

'I did some research at the Junior Ganymede when we were in London and I believe he has favoured a number of educational trusts and charities, sir.'

A thought struck me. 'I say, Jeeves, you don't think Sir Henry has ... that he's planning...'

'I think that *in extremis*, as he now finds himself, Sir Henry would consider all options. It is conceivable that he sees in Lord Etringham a *deus ex machina*.'

'Come again?'

'Perhaps the phrase "a white knight" would be more readily illuminating, sir.'

'It might. But how would it work out?'

'I should not care to hazard a conjecture, sir. However, I felt it imperative that we leave them alone, the better to get to know one another.'

'Well, miracles do happen, don't they, even at the eleventh hour? What I want to know first is how on earth I'm to face Lady H and Dame Judith in the morning.'

'Might I suggest breakfast in bed, sir? After that you will be required for rehearsal in the drawing room, where neither lady will be present.'

'And lunch? Perhaps a sandwich and a half-bottle in the sunken garden?'

'Indeed, sir. Following which the ladies will be occupied by the fete. There will then be only the evening's festivities to negotiate before we can return to London.'

I heaved a deepish one. As I did so, I noticed Jeeves's eye on my burgundy dressing gown with the paisley pattern, which was hanging on the door.

He saw me seeing him, if you catch my drift.

'Go on, Jeeves,' I said. 'Keep the thing. It can be a souvenir of a pretty sticky few days.'

'That is most generous of you, sir. It is a splendid garment.'

The bed turned out to be everything I had foreseen, and the sun was already well up in the heavens when Jeeves came in with the laden breakfast tray. Having missed dinner in all the previous night's excitement, I set to with a will.

'What's the latest from Bedlam?' I said, forking up the last of the kedgeree. 'I hardly dare ask.'

'There has been an alteration to this evening's programme, sir.'

'Oh yes?' I said. And I dare say there was a note of wariness – or even of dread – in my tone.

'Yes, sir. It appears that Sir Henry and Lord Etringham sat up deep into the night. His lordship's agoraphobia—'

'Yes, I meant to ask, what is this aggra-thing?'

'The word derives from the ancient Greek, sir. It means a morbid fear of the marketplace – or by implication of any open space. It is the opposite of claustrophobia, which is—'

'I know, Jeeves. I'm not a complete ass, you know. Carry on.'

'As I was saying, sir, his lordship's agoraphobia has responded well to treatment so far, but Sir Roderick Glossop has advised him that a full return of confidence may come only after he has faced down his worst fear – that of appearing and speaking in public.'

'In the marketplace?'

'Yes, sir. Or in this case the village hall. Sir Henry has offered him the part of Bottom in the scene from *A Midsummer Night's Dream*.'

'But that's my part, Jeeves!'

'I assured Sir Henry that you would not begrudge it to Lord Etringham and that such a gesture on your part would make amends for the small deceit you were compelled to practise on our host.'

I took a thoughtful draught of coffee. 'That's as may be, but you seem to be missing the point, Jeeves. The character of Bottom is a robust one. Old Etringham is about as robust as a feather duster. He wouldn't say boo to a goose even if that goose was served up roast with red cabbage and apple sauce. The standees won't take kindly to a whispering Bottom. Trust me, Jeeves. I have experience of the parish hall. I know whereof I speak. Remember King's Deverill. Esmond Haddock brought the house down by enthusiasm and sheer volume. These things matter.'

'I remember it only too well, sir. But the two gentlemen seem set on the plan. I believe Lord Etringham is confident that a dose of the specific prescribed by Sir

Roderick, taken an hour beforehand, will calm his nerves sufficiently.'

I still didn't think much of the development. We amateur thespians have our defining roles, and this Athenian weaver was mine. A thin-voiced dotard was never going to cut the mustard.

'You seem to know a devil of a lot about what's going on, Jeeves.'

'After our successes on the Turf, Sir Henry is reluctant to dispense with my advice sir.'

'Sensible chap.'

'Thank you, sir. I took the liberty of pointing out that it might be possible for him to allow a part of Melbury Hall to be used for educational purposes while retaining ownership of the house and grounds.'

'So he wouldn't have to get rid of the whole building.'

'Indeed, sir.'

'But which part?'

'The home farm, sir, and the stable block, being contiguous, form a natural entity. They enjoy their own access to the high street and could be converted to boarding accommodation if necessary.'

'Where would the thoroughbreds go?'

'The horses would have to be sold, sir. This would raise some much-needed cash and would serve the further purpose of reconciling Lady Hackwood to the scheme.'

I nodded. I'd begun to catch his drift. 'And then the lads from the London youth clubs, from Walworth and Bethnal Green, come down in a charabanc to get a whiff of country air and learn about fossils at the same time.'

'Indeed, sir, with little or no inconvenience to the household. However, the success of the plan is dependent on Lord Etringham's performance this evening. He must be made to feel a welcome part of the village and the surrounding districts. I fear nothing less than a standing ovation will do.'

'Presumably you'll spend the day buying beer for the lads in the Red Lion.'

'Sir Henry has already despatched Hoad to start work on the more obdurate element.'

'Hoad? That's rather playing with fire, isn't it?'

'Alas, Sir Henry was unaware of Hoad's particular weakness. He pressed five pounds into his hand and told him to do his best.'

'Golly,' I said, not for the first time. 'And is that all?'

'No, sir, there is one other thing.'

'Go on.'

'Mr Venables was in need of a straight man or feed for his crosstalk act.'

I passed a hand across the fevered brow. 'Tell me it's not so, Jeeves.'

'There was only one player who was unexpectedly available, sir.'

'But what about Woody?'

'No, sir. Mr Beeching is to play Snout the tinker.'

'Well, what about Bicknell?'

'Mr Bicknell would consider it *infra dignitatem*, sir.'

'I see what you mean. But what about Hoad? It would serve him right. And after all he specialises in funny turns.'

'Most amusing, sir. But Hoad is already cast, as Flute the bellows-mender.'

'Was bellows-mending really a full-time occupation in Athens?'

'I am not in a position to say, sir. I fancy there may be a degree of poetic licence.'

There was a pause. I could see no way out of being the Collector's stooge, unless ... 'Jeeves, couldn't we persuade old Vishnu to take umbrage at all those things Sir Henry said to his son?'

'So Mrs Venables urged, I believe, sir. But Mr Venables is somewhat thick-skinned.'

'I've met elephants with thinner hides. Indian and African.'

'Indeed, sir. Mr Venables was most reluctant to miss a chance of impressing an audience. Mrs Venables left in high dudgeon after a substantial breakfast, taking the nine-thirty train, but her husband will not follow her until tomorrow. He was not to be deterred from having his moment in the spotlight.'

Rehearsals were well under way in the drawing room by the time I joined the company. Georgiana was directing operations, with old Venables sticking his oar in at every other line.

The scene she'd chosen was the one in which the rude mechanicals rehearse their play in the presence of the sleeping Titania, queen of the fairies. She awakes to see Bottom in an ass's head and, because Puck has done his stuff with the potion, at once falls in love with him; the scene ends as she leads him off hand in hand to the merriment of all. The good thing was that there was a line or two for everyone with only Bottom and Titania having much to learn.

It was clear that old Etringham had sat up all night swotting his lines and had done a pretty good job of it. His work, however, lacked snap. His Bottom sounded less like a workman on a beano than an archdeacon giving a Lenten address. You couldn't help wondering if he'd ever actually met a weaver.

Mrs Tilman made an admirable Puck, but Amelia lacked the ethereal quality that the part of Titania demands; her performance had a bit too much of the tennis girl about it: her court coverage was good, but there was little sense of gossamer wings.

Bed linen was to form the basic Athenian costume, with the addition of the odd jerkin or waistcoat, chisel and hammer; there was an outsize ass's head for Bottom and wings for Puck and Titania that had been fetched from a costumier in Dorchester the day before. This was all quite satisfactory; it was the acting that was a cause for concern.

'Sir Henry,' said Mrs Tilman. 'Could I make a suggestion?'

'Certainly, Mrs T,' said Sir Henry, who had landed the part of Quince the carpenter.

'Suppose Miss Georgiana and Miss Amelia was to swap parts? So Miss Amelia was Starveling the tailor and Miss Georgiana was the fairy queen?'

After a fair bit of 'No, I can't' and 'Yes, you must' between the girls, Sir Henry settled the matter by giving his blessing to the switch.

'All right, I'll learn the lines at lunchtime,' said Georgiana. 'Are you quite sure you don't mind, Ambo?'

'No, I've always wanted to play Starveling,' said Amelia – pretty sportingly, you'd have to say. Woody visibly swelled with pride.

'Bertie,' said Georgiana, 'I think it would be a good idea if you and Mr Venables rehearsed your crosstalk act now. Perhaps you could go into the library.'

'Right ho,' I said.

'I've got a script for you, young man,' said old Vishnu, holding out a piece of paper. 'But I warn you, I like to extemporise as we go along.'

As we walked down the hall I glanced down at the paper in my hand. I saw the following words. 'Feed: "I say, I say, what do you make of the Melbury Ladies'

Sewing Circle?" SV: "I found them most amusing. They had me in stitches.'"

It was going to be a long day.

The Melbury-cum-Kingston parish hall was ten minutes away in the two-seater. A red-brick, rectangular building designed by a chap who liked to keep things simple, it was set back from the road behind a blackthorn hedge. The date carved above the lintel was 1856 and one couldn't help wondering which village worthy had stumped up for it. Or perhaps there had been a subscription to mark the end of the Crimean War; I briefly wondered how many sons of Melbury-cum-Kingston had died at Sevastopol.

There were twenty minutes before kick-off, but the peasantry was already filing in by twos and threes. These sons of toil looked like men who knew what they liked, and I doubted whether bellows-menders or fairies came high on that list.

During a solitary luncheon in the sunken garden, I had more or less mastered the lines old Venables had thrust on me and I glanced down now at the papers in my sweating palm. I breathed in deeply.

'Very well, Jeeves. Let's get it over with. Into the valley of death . . .'

I pushed open the door and levered myself out of the car. Since I was not billed to go on until the second half, I decided to place myself at the rear of the hall, among the rougher element, to get a sense of what lay in store. From this vantage point I at once saw why so many of them had arrived early. It is normal practice for a village hall to have some sort of makeshift bar with cider and beer by the barrel, but this was an elaborate affair that took up half a side wall; its selection of beverages would not have disgraced a West End hotel, though the prices were such that any ploughman could keep plodding his weary way back for more. And plod they did.

The general whiff in the village hall, of damp plaster and dead chrysanthemums, was rapidly being replaced by the smell of warm yeomanry, pipe smoke and alcohol. In other circumstances I don't deny that I might have found it congenial. The two-bob seats filled rapidly with the local gentry, and I noted listlessly that Vishnu and I should be playing to a full house. A stiffish brandy and soda followed its twin down the hatch – and at that price, who could wonder that a third came close behind.

Sir Henry Hackwood appeared from the wings, in front of the curtain, to a decent reception. The stand-ees seemed pleased not to be subjected to a lecture from the vicar, as is often the case with such a bash, and were further cheered when Sir Henry told them he had paid for a barrel of beer from the Hare and Hounds for them to get stuck into during the interval. Sir Henry disappeared and the curtain rose on the Melbury Glee Club – six stout women in satin frocks and six sheepish-looking consorts wearing bowler hats. 'Glee' was not the word that first came to mind; 'dejection' might have been nearer the mark. The vicar's wife at the upright piano seemed under the impression that she was playing a dirge; the sopra-nos were obliged to hang on and warble for all they were worth until she caught up. 'The Ballad of Cranborne Chase', by contrast, turned into a straight six-furlong sprint between choir and vicar's wife, the latter appar-ently determined to make up for lost time. Either that, or she had remembered that she'd left dinner on the vicar-age stove. The piano got home by a short head, with half a length separating tenors and sopranos for the places.

Next on was one Susan Chandler, a ten-year-old schoolgirl with plaits and thick glasses who stood with her hands behind her back and her feet planted like a guardsman told to stand at ease. She eyed the audience in a threatening manner. '"By Last Duchess" by Robert Browdig,' she announced. It was not only the child's adenoids that made the next seven or eight minutes hard to endure; I hadn't the faintest clue what old Browning was on about, and I'm pretty sure that no one else did either. At the end I was relieved to see there was no sign of young Susan getting the bird; the applause was tepid, but the right side of polite. A small flame of hope flickered in the Wooster bosom.

The conjuring by Major Holloway's wife's brother would have gone down well in the Pink Owl in Brewer Street. The quick-fire patter seemed to have come from the paddock at some seaside racecourse, and the relish with which the conjuror withdrew the missing Queen of Hearts from the clothing of the saloon barmaid at the Hare and Hounds caused dismay in the two-bobbers. None of the above means the major's wife's brother was without his admirers; indeed, you could say that, so far as the standees were concerned, he was by some way the best thing yet. Just as well, because the Puddletown Barbershop Quartet, with which the first half closed, were a man short; and a barbershop quartet with only three barbers is bound to lack a certain something.

During the stampede for the free beer, I left the hall and went round to the stage door, or 'back entrance' as its homely architect might have termed it, there to join my fellow performers. Woody was coming the other way.

'All set, Bertie?'

'Yes, thanks. You?'

'Fine. Snout only has a couple of lines. We've all been trying to ginger up old Etringham.'

'Any luck?'

'Not much. He sounds like a speak-your-weight machine. How's your crosstalk script?'

'Pitiful.'

'There's a splendid bar in the hall. I'll send you through a zonker to put you in the mood.'

'It may take more than that, old friend.'

The backstage area doubled as a shed where various agricultural machines and implements were kept. Georgiana was already in costume as Titania, wearing a tutu, if that's the word I want – the sort of frilly thing you see in *Swan Lake*, anyway. There was a good deal of netting and feathery wings, and a tremendous amount of slender limb to boot; her hair was piled up and held by a fake-diamond tiara and her dark eyes were rimmed with some theatrical paint.

I became aware that I was unwittingly doing an impression of Monty Beresford's golden retriever on the Fourth of June and moved to push the lower mandible back into some sort of connection with the upper. Georgiana seemed oblivious of her appearance as she fussed over old Etringham, who was now wrapped in a sheet with a pair of knitting needles stuck in his belt. My own costume consisted of no more than the addition of a rhododendron flower in the buttonhole and a deerstalker borrowed from Sir Henry. Venables hadn't wanted the straight man to catch the eye too much; he himself wore a red beard and a top hat.

The second half got under way with the Melbury Tetchett string quartet. The best thing you could say about them was that, unlike the barbershop chaps, they were quorate. Whether the scraping sounded better out front than backstage I was in no position to say, but the re-refreshed audience was in generous mood. While they played in front of the curtain, the Ladies' Sewing Circle set the scene for their tableau vivant. A backdrop painted by the Sunday School showed a cloudy harbour with a couple of galleons. Stage left were two plasterboard pillars and a step. Centre stage was a rowing boat behind which a boy scout, concealed from the audience, lay flat on his face gently rocking the hull. The Ladies of the Sewing Circle disported themselves in set positions, representing King Solomon, the Queen of Sheba and sundry courtiers. The *coup de théâtre*, as we buffs call it, was the spotlight that shone through the backdrop towards the audience, bathing the whole scene in a twilight effect.

Sir Henry Hackwood announced: '"The Arrival of the Queen of Sheba" after Claude Lorrain.' On went the spotlight, up went the curtain and the sewing ladies were revealed in their positions.

The day I had won the Scripture-knowledge prize at Malvern House, Bramley-on-Sea was but a distant memory, but I was fairly sure King Solomon's court had not been all-female. And there was no mention in the Book of Kings that the visiting queen bore such a strong resemblance to Mrs Padgett, she of the pans and skillets.

However, there was something only too familiar about the voice that called out, 'I seen her move! The fat one!'

It was the slurred tenor that had lately sung 'The

Battle Hymn of the Republic' among the cold frames, and it belonged to footman Hoad.

There is a nice balance to be struck in watering the standees. The more the merrier is my general rule, but when he reaches a certain point of liquidity, your standee demands something with a bit of snap. He needs action. Static seamstresses are not enough.

Hoad's interruption seemed to open a floodgate. 'That one looks seasick!', 'All hands on deck!' were two clearly audible comments; they were followed by a burst of 'What shall we do with the drunken sailor?' It might have been worse had some unseen hand not rung down the curtain.

As a warm-up for my appearance with Venables, it was about as unpropitious as they go. I heard a female voice whisper 'good luck' as Venables and I pushed on from the wings to a rowdy welcome. The idea was that we should carry on for as long as it took them to get rid of King Solomon's court and set up a Wood near Athens behind the curtain. Two minutes ought to have been ample in my view.

'I say, I say,' said Venables, prodding me in the chest with a rolled-up newspaper, 'what did you make of the barbershop quartet?'

This opener was not in the script, but I'm nothing if not a trouper. 'I'm tone deaf,' I said. 'What did you make of the barbershop quartet?'

'I thought they hit the top notes pretty well. But it was a darn close shave.'

There are few silences more poignant than the one left for unforthcoming laughter. It was a sound – or absence – that was to become familiar over the next few minutes.

Old Venables, to give him his due, was a hard man to bring down. I suppose when you've 'entertained', to use the word at its loosest, the soldiery in the cantonments of Chanamasala after a hot day of polo and pig-sticking, the yokels of Melbury-cum-Kingston hold few fears.

We got through the Ladies' Sewing Circle having him in stitches, the old one about her ladyship's whereabouts ('they're still in the wash') and something about the Queen of Sheba and Mrs Holloway's conjuring brother that may have been indecent.

The ribs of the audience remained untickled. If the silence had been any stonier old Etringham could have taken out his little hammer and inspected it for the fossilised remains of B. Wooster. Somehow we got through it; eventually there was a cough from behind the curtain to let us know that the Wood near Athens was ready.

At the first sound of throat-clearing, I was off into the wings to hide my shame; Venables not only lingered but popped back for an uninvited encore. Eventually, even he had to concede that the game was up. All you could say was that the rotten eggs and tomatoes remained in their boxes at the feet of the standees. They were a patient lot – thus far; but no one likes to take home unthrown the market produce he has earmarked for other purposes.

I was watching from the wings as the curtain rose on the Wood near Athens. The Sunday School had provided another backdrop, this one of Greek temples and trees; the set consisted of a couple of potted birch saplings from Melbury Hall and a grassy bank made of papier mâché with an old green velvet curtain on which lay the slumbering form of Titania, queen of the fairies. A piercing whistle from the back of the hall greeted the sight.

On came the rude mechanicals, and with the words 'Are we all met?' Lord Etringham, as Bottom, got things under way. On the plus side, you could say that the writer of this scene was more gifted than the author of the crosstalk act that had gone before. On the debit side was the main actor, Bottom. His voice was not only that of a fellow well past his prime, it was that of an old gentleman looking forward to his bed. King Lear, perhaps, after long exposure on the blasted heath; but Bottom, no.

The audience was quiet at first, but then, for reasons not entirely clear from where I stood, began to laugh.

'If you think I am come hither as a lion, it were pity of my life,' said Bottom with about as much bravado as the curate announcing the hymn at evensong.

They liked it, though. And as I shifted to get a better view, I saw that Hoad, in the person of Flute the bellows-mender, was doing a bit of scene-stealing. It was simple stuff, hand motions to match the words of the other actors, but he had finally found the funny bone of the locals. When Bottom was instructing the actor playing the Wall to hold his fingers 'thus', Hoad's gesture was met by a gush of hilarity.

Bottom, meanwhile, had gone from the lifeless to the near-comatose. Mrs Tilman as Puck led him off stage, as per the script, but once in the wings, he sat down on a hard chair, shut his eyes and nodded off.

Back on stage, Flute had his first line. By happy chance it was, 'Must I speak now?'

The advice from the audience was pretty varied. 'If you think you still can' and 'You tell 'em, Les!' being two of the more repeatable. Hoad was swaying on his feet as he launched into some lines about 'brisky juvenal and eke most lovely Jew'. It may have been the fact that he clearly had no idea what he was talking about or it may have been the word 'eke' that touched the simple souls at the back, those who had known this Hoad as man and boy. They laughed, they roared, they stamped their feet: 'Eke, Les, eke!'

I was so wrapped up in the performance that I barely heard Titania in a stage whisper say, 'Quick, Bertie, wrap a sheet round you. You'll have to play Bottom.'

It was the hand of an assiduous gentleman's personal gentleman that effected the lightning-fast costume change and, with a murmured 'Forgive me, sir', lowered an ass's head over the occiput. It was the gentle shove of Mrs Tilman's Puck that ushered me on stage.

I have made a few entrances in my time, but I can honestly say that none of them has gone over as big as this one. It turned out that what the standees had been wanting all along was a man in a donkey's head. The sun had come out in their world. The string quartet was forgiven, the Queen of Sheba forgotten; the Collector of Chanamasala was as dust beneath their chariot wheel.

Now all eyes were on Wooster, B. This was the part that for more than a dozen years I had been reciting blindfold in my sleep, yet when I asked myself for the line, it was like looking into a huge and awful void. I heard my cue, but no words came. This rude mechanical and I were utter strangers. From the wings came a respectful throat-clearing, followed by a prompt. 'If I were, fair Thisby, I were only thine.'

It sounded familiar, so I said it. And I tried to give it a bit of weaver's oomph. So we staggered through the next bit, with Jeeves prompting. The audience seemed to think this was all part of the show; and even if not, they couldn't by now have cared less.

At last, Titania stirred. She spoke. 'What angel wakes me from my flowery bed?' There came a volley of whistles and catcalls as Georgiana unfolded the limbs and tiptoed over.

She came and stood by me with her hand lightly on my

sleeve. As she gazed up at me in her fairy-queen rapture, an odd thing happened. The words of the part came back to me, and I let rip with the full Monty Beresford West Riding accent echoing through the ass's head.

I thought Hoad's line 'Must I speak now?' had got the biggest laugh of the night, but it was as nothing to Titania's 'Thou art as wise as thou art beautiful.' The plaster was coming off the ceiling and the dust of decades was being beaten from the floorboards by the stamp of the standees' boots.

Georgiana had wisely cut the end of the scene, where various fairies hop about, so we were now in the home straight. 'And I do love thee: therefore go with me,' she was saying, squeezing my arm with most realistic grip; and even through the ass's headgear I was feeling the force of those brown, pleading eyes. '... And they shall fetch thee jewels from the deep ...'

Then something about the warmth of her low and throbbing voice seemed to calm the yokels at the back. 'And I will purge thy mortal grossness so That thou shalt like an airy spirit go,' she ended, and took me by the arm as the curtain fell.

The first thing we saw in the wings was Lord

Etringham, sitting up, drinking a glass of water, apparently restored.

'Quick, Bertie,' said Georgiana, 'give him back the ass's head. He must take the credit.'

It was a relief to get the wretched thing off. Lord Etringham was struggling to keep up with events, but no one minds going on stage to a hero's welcome, which is what he got. They cheered, they whistled, they clapped, and no one seemed to mind that Bottom had shrunk by almost a foot.

They came off stage at last, but the audience wanted them back for a curtain call.

'Come on, Bertie, you come this time, too,' said Georgiana.

I followed on, as in a dream. When we bowed again, Lord E removed the ass's head, to the delight of the crowd. Even the two-bob seats were up on their feet, and Georgiana pushed him forwards to take a solo bow.

As he did so, she picked up the head, and put it on me. 'Bless thee, Bottom,' she said. 'Bless thee! Thou art translated.'

Strictly speaking this was Quince's line, but no one seemed to mind. Then she took it off again, stood on tiptoe and, to the unbridled delight of those watching, planted a big kiss on my lips. I thought the ceiling might now cave in completely. Not knowing what else to do, I grabbed the dear girl round the waist and returned the kiss, with interest.

When eventually we managed to get off stage, things happened rather fast. The players went to change their clothes, but in a minute we were reunited backstage round some bottles of light ale and champagne.

Georgiana was standing beside me when the door opened and in came Lady Hackwood and Dame Judith Puxley, clearly the only two people in the hall who had not been amused. They stood there like Scylla and Charybdis, and the channel between them to the open sea was a narrow one.

'Well, young man,' said Lady Hackwood. 'Can you please explain yourself?'

'Explain what, Lady H?' I said.

'Explain what you mean by kissing my niece like that in front of two hundred people.'

I looked at Georgiana, who was back in her normal clothes, though still with the tiara and the fairy-queen make-up. I felt that I had compromised her in public, and the code of the Woosters allowed for only one way out.

'I kissed her, Lady Hackwood, because... Because ...we are engaged to be married.'

The pause that followed had a silence that felt bottomless, as it were.

'Is this true, Georgiana?' said Lady Hackwood eventually.

'I don't know. Is it true, Bertie?'

'It is if you want it to be, dear girl. Dashed odd proposal, I admit. But will you marry me? Could you bear it?'

'I want it more than anything on earth. Come on, you ass, let's go.'

'Where to?'

'I'll tell you when we're in the car.'

She grabbed me by the hand and led me from the room.

A couple of minutes later, the roof was down on the old two-seater as we purred between the fragrant hedgerows.

'Take the next right,' said Georgiana, her head resting on my shoulder.

'Where are we going?'

'We're going to have dinner at the Queen's Head in Bere Regis.'

'Then what?' I said.

'And then we're going to have the rest of our lives.'

CHAPTER
=ELEVEN=

I can remember little of what took place over dinner. There were in any event things said on both sides which might, if repeated, bring a blush to the reader's cheek. Georgiana was a passionate sort of girl and pretty good at expressing herself; I rather let her do the talking for both of us, restricting myself to the occasional 'You bet' or 'Absolutely, old thing'.

It was perplexing, to put it mildly, that this paragon of her sex should have formed such a high opinion of Wooster, B., but I felt it would be foolish to press her on this: I didn't want to be the cause of the scales falling from her eyes at this late stage. I've never really understood why girls fall for chaps at all, to be quite frank, but I suppose if a twenty-four-carat popsy like Pauline Stoker can declare undying love for an ass like Chuffy Chufnell then all things are possible. Women are, as my old house-master had remarked, queer cattle.

The gist – if I can convey this without breaking any confidences – was that Georgiana had fallen for me from day one on the Côte d'Azur on the grounds that I was 'different' from all the other chaps she knew (I thought it wiser not to press her on this 'difference'). She further felt there was a bond between us – some-thing about parents – and that although I obviously had lots of chums, only she could see and understand the 'real' Bertram. There was a good deal more in this vein – including a bit of hand-squeezing and eye-dabbing – that we can happily pass over.

In return, I told her that if hers was the face I saw on the pillow every day I should believe that some mix-up in the divine sweepstake had put my name where some other fellow's ought to be, but that I was delighted to carry on till rumbled.

There were then a few practical questions to con-sider. First among these was as follows: would Sir Henry

Hackwood consent to his ward's being married to a man who had spent several days under his roof impersonating a valet and then clambered over that same roof wrapped in a builder's dust sheet?

Georgiana thought it depended only on whether the old boy could be guaranteed continuing possession of his beloved Melbury Hall. Meanwhile, her mind seemed to have fastened on to the smaller details of the future.

'We can have the second floor, Bertie. Dame Judith's room is actually the best in the house, especially in summer. The views are wonderful.'

I repressed a shudder. 'No cold cream and curling papers.'

'Not until I'm at least seventy.'

'I rather like the room at the end, where I am now.'

'That can be the nursery.'

'And I suppose Amelia and Woody will have the first floor.'

'Absolutely. But I shall need to be in London during the week to carry on with my work.'

'Plenty of room in Berkeley Mansions,' I said.

'What about Jeeves?'

'He always said he'd hand in his notice if I got married.'

'I'll see if I can persuade him to change his mind,' said my fiancée.

We drove back slowly through the summer night, and when we arrived at the Hall there seemed to be some sort of party going on. There were cars parked outside and lights blazing within. We went up the steps to the front door.

'Let me go and speak to Uncle Henry first,' said Georgiana. 'I'll drag him off to the library.'

I was left to make my way to the drawing room, where a large portion of the two-bobbers and a few standees were continuing the midsummer festivities. Bicknell was pushing round the refreshments and someone was playing the grand piano. I saw the hawkish face of Beeching, P. and made a bee-line for him.

'What ho,' I said.

'What ho indeed, Bertie. This is another fine pickle you've got me into.'

'Not so fast, young Beeching. All is for the best though oft we doubt what the highest something tiddly-pom . . .'

'Are you blotto?'

'No. Not at all.'

'I thought perhaps that zonker had got to you. I

supervised the barman and it was a pretty hefty one. With a cherry on top. Must have tasted innocuous, but by golly . . .'

'It never reached me.' I had in fact completely forgotten about Woody's promised nerve-calmer.

'But I gave it to that fellow Hoad and said, "Give this to that ass, Wooster."'

We looked at one another for a bit.

I had a thought. 'I don't suppose Hoad even knows my real name is Wooster.'

A light came into the keen advocate's eye. He smiled. 'I think he gave it to the wrong ass.'

'Etringham?'

'Yes. That's why he dropped off.'

While we were mulling over this twist of fate, Georgiana materialised at my side. 'Darling,' she whispered in my ear, 'go and see Uncle Henry in the library now.'

'Wish me luck,' I said to them both.

The number of times I have been engaged to be married does not reflect well on me; even less flattering is the fact that none of the many proposed couplings got as far as the 'Tell me about your prospects, young man' stage with the intended's father.

The scene ahead, as I knocked at the library door, was therefore what Jeeves calls terra incognita.

Sir Henry Hackwood was standing with his foot up on the club fender. He had changed from his Quince costume into the green smoking jacket.

'Ah, Wooster. Sit down. Have a drink.'

I did as I was told, twice over, the ottoman yielding of its bounty.

'Pretty good do, that, wouldn't you say?' said Sir Henry.

'Rather. The paying public lapped it up.'

'Bobby Etringham was thrilled.'

'I'm not surprised,' I said. 'He went over big.'

'He doesn't remember much about it. It's important he just savours the triumph. No need to fill him in on the details.'

'None whatever.'

'Now, Wooster.'

'Yes, Sir Henry.'

'I've been talking to my niece.'

'Georgiana.'

He shot me a warning look, as if to let me know he was well aware of his niece's given name.

'I am going to be quite frank with you, young man. Do you play golf?'

'I ... er. Yes, occasionally. Not very well.'

'Are you familiar with a shot near the green known as a "son-in-law"?'

'No,' I said, wondering if my host had been attacking the ottoman a bit too freely.

'It's a slight mishit that's not a complete disaster. Calling it a "son-in-law" is a polite way of saying "Not quite what we were hoping for."'

There was a pause as I tried to work out what the old sportsman was getting at.

Sir Henry cleared his throat with a bark. 'Bobby Etringham's going to take the stable block and the home farm for his school scheme. His lawyer's going to send the papers next week. But it still won't meet all the requirements of the estate.'

There followed a delicate exchange on matters financial. Georgiana's inheritance, it transpired, was comparable in size to the Wooster war chest; so if I could foot the necessary bills until the Meadowes trust came into its own in a few years' time ... I quickly indicated a willingness to open up the pocket book to whatever extent would clinch the deal, starting with a cheque to S. Venables for the money he had lost with the Dorchester bookies.

Sir Henry did not exactly throw his bonnet over the windmill at this point, but he exhaled a big one and nodded a few times as it sank in.

'I've changed my will,' he said eventually. 'In the absence of any male heir, which is a great regret to me, I shall be leaving the Hall jointly to Amelia and Georgiana. This Beeching is clearly a clever fellow and will take silk in no time. I have no doubts of his sincerity where Amelia is concerned. She's too young to be married, really, but what can I do?'

'Indeed,' I said, rather feebly.

'That leaves Georgiana,' he said.

'She's a wonderful girl.'

'I know,' said the old baronet. 'I love her like a daughter. I swore a solemn oath to her late father, who loved her too . . .'

For the second time that evening there was a bit of handkerchief work, Sir Henry being less of a dabber than a dasher.

'She's made up her mind. God knows why she . . .'

He pulled himself up short. 'Anyway. She's a darn clever girl. She reads between the lines. She understands things I don't. I trust her. Do you love her, Wooster?'

'You bet I do, Sir Henry. And I always will.'

The old chap nodded once more, a trifle wistfully, it seemed to me. 'All right, then. Go on. Marry her.'

At this point I think I may have made it a straight hat-trick for the eye-dabbing tendency. I don't recall exactly; but if so, it was not for long, since there followed a manly handshake and a swift return to the drawing room where something about my expression must have given the game away, since, before I could even open my mouth, a pandemonium of cheering and clapping had broken out, while from the grand piano came the strains of 'The Wedding March'.

It was a few days before I found myself alone again with Jeeves. My time had been filled with back-slapping, telegrams and celebrations, culminating in a gruelling dinner at the Drones after which Freddie Widgeon was arrested on the way home for singing a Marie Lloyd song in Albemarle Street.

'Jeeves,' I said, 'may we speak frankly?'

'Of course, sir.'

It was another fine morning and I had little to do until twelve-thirty, at which time I had arranged to meet Georgiana for an early lunch.

'I've always understood that in the event of my getting hitched you'd be giving in your notice. Is that right?'

'Yes, sir. It has been my invariable custom to terminate my employment under such circumstances.'

'So it's the parting of the ways, is it?'

Jeeves glanced out of the window for a moment, then looked down at this shoes. There was something a little shifty in his manner. 'Not necessarily, sir. Perhaps I can explain.'

'Explain away, old friend.'

'In the event that a gentleman's personal gentleman were simultaneously to contemplate matrimony of his own accord, I feel that the propriety of the arrangement might be maintained.'

'You what?'

'I am also engaged to be married, sir.'

'Good heavens, Jeeves. Who to?'

'Mrs Tilman, sir.'

The power of speech had left me and I sat down heavily on the sofa.

'I knew Mrs Tilman when she was Miss Charlton, sir, in the employ of Sir Henry Dalgleish. I was unable to press my suit at the time as I had an understanding with another young lady. The unfortunate demise of Mr Tilman, however . . .'

'I see.'

'Mrs Tilman is a most excellent lady.'

'I know, Jeeves. My heartfelt congratulations.'

'Thank you, sir. She thinks highly of you, as well, sir, if I may say so. She was most helpful to me in the course of our stay at Melbury Hall.'

'Come again?'

'I informed her that you had played the part of Bottom, the weaver, while at school and it was she who suggested to Sir Henry that the scene from *A Midsummer Night's Dream* would make an apt conclusion to the evening. Sir Henry depends on her a good deal.'

'Yes, I noticed. But why did she want to see me tread the boards?'

Jeeves did not answer at once. 'When you planned

to flirt with Miss Hackwood, sir, whom did you consult about her tennis routine?'

'Mrs Tilman. At your suggestion, Jeeves. She told me she was meeting the pro. Then Georgiana turned up!'

'I fear Mrs Tilman may inadvertently have confused the days of the week, sir.'

'Or not so inadvertently, eh?'

'It was felt that if Miss Meadowes were to see you in such a light it would concentrate her feelings for you.'

'I see. And what about Plan B? Did Mrs Tilman fix for that to come a cropper, too?'

'No, sir. I regret to say that that was my doing. When Miss Hackwood was on her way to the bench I waylaid her and informed her that I had seen a Camberwell Beauty in the rose garden.'

'And had you?'

'I am not an expert lepidopterist, sir. It may well have turned out to be a Cabbage White. But Miss Hackwood was diverted.'

'And young Venables?'

'I told Mr Venables I had spotted an unsigned copy of *By Tramcar to Toledo* on the bench by the rhododendron.

He needed little urging to make his way there with all speed.'

'And what was the strategy there?'

'As with the first misunderstanding, sir. It was felt that when confronted with an unpalatable situation Mr Venables would be compelled to examine his own feelings.'

'Golly, Jeeves. You have been hard at work.'

'Mrs Tilman was a most willing aide-de-camp, sir. She wished to see a similar outcome.'

'So she played the role of Puck in more ways than one. And while we're at it, has young Venables got fixed up with this girl in Nottinghamshire?'

'I believe so, sir. Much to his parents' satisfaction. I understand they had some doubts about the suitability of the match with Miss Meadowes.'

A number of loose ends of which I had earlier been aware now seemed to be tied off.

'Mrs Tilman was very helpful with my alibi on the night of the rooftop incident,' I said. 'The next morning she said she'd seen me leave the library and go to bed ... And you were rather insistent on knowing where Plan B was going to take place.'

'I regret that a degree of dissimulation was necessary on occasion, sir. The reversal of our customary roles made it difficult for me to apprise you of my thinking at all material times.'

I hummed and hah-ed a bit. One or two other things were falling into place. The day that Jeeves had given me the morning off tea-duty, presumably so he could have another confab with his co-conspirator ... The way Mrs Tilman looked guilty when I mentioned how often in a day she seemed to bump into Lord Etringham ...

What was still not clear to me, however, was the nature of what you might call the Masterplan. I think I may have mentioned the odd sensation I had had of being the plaything of Unseen Forces, and I suppose I should really have guessed that the UFs were Jeeves and Mrs Tilman. But I still wasn't sure why they had gone to such lengths.

'Jeeves,' I said. 'Mrs Tilman seems an excellent woman who—'

'Most excellent, sir. Also a keen reader.'

'Yes, I saw her wading through a Venables travelogue. I hope you'll have many happy evenings swapping literary insights.'

'Thank you, sir.'

'And you somehow managed to get old Etringham on board. Did you realise that without his contribution the Hall would still have had to be sold? The deficit was beyond my means. Old Hackwood mentioned a figure. It was like the national debt of Bechuanaland.'

'I was aware that some additional capital was of the essence, sir.'

'But, Jeeves, what I don't understand is why you wanted all this to happen. Why were you prepared to go to such lengths? I suspect that there was something more than the feudal spirit involved.'

'Indeed, sir.' Jeeves looked uncomfortable. 'Before I enlighten you, sir, I should like to confess another minor subterfuge.'

'Go on.'

'It concerns Lady Worplesdon, sir. A colleague at the Junior Ganymede has a brother-in-law who works for a printer's in Clerkenwell. In return for a small consideration, he was prepared to make an imitation of a telegram such as Lady Worplesdon might have sent.'

'You mean there were no building works at Bumpleigh Hall?'

'None, sir. No visit was ever mooted.'

'But you offered to put me on the blower to her.'

'It was an invitation I felt confident you would decline, sir.'

'My goodness, Jeeves, you have surpassed yourself.'

'Thank you, sir. I felt it was essential for you to take up residence in Kingston St Giles. And I feared that a certain reluctance to interfere in the affairs of others might dissuade you from going.'

'So you rendered Berkeley Mansions unfit for human habitation. Your cunning is simply serpentine, Jeeves.'

'Alas not, sir. There were two developments that I failed to foresee. The first was that a copy of the local paper with a captioned photograph of the cricket team would make it into the real Lord Etringham's hands.'

'So his arrival was a surprise to you.'

'A complete surprise, sir. Though I did see how it might be turned to our advantage.'

'And the second one?'

'The strong alcoholic drink sent backstage by Mr Beeching.'

'It wasn't you who re-routed it so it would knock out the old boy?'

'No, sir. I saw the footman Hoad deliver it to Lord Etringham and was on the point of intervening when wiser counsels prevailed.'

'What were these counsels?'

'I found it hard to see how such a diffident gentleman as Lord Etringham could procure the approval of the audience. The part of Bottom, as you had rightly pointed out, demands a vigorous performance.'

'And no ovation, no fossil study centre.'

'So it appeared, sir. But at that moment the idea of an understudy or double, as it were, occurred to me. It was Mrs Tilman's belief from the start that if Miss Meadowes were to see you on stage in a part both heroic and vulnerable her protective instincts would overcome her, compelling her to make a demonstration of her feelings.'

'Which is why she suggested Georgiana to replace Amelia as Titania opposite me! Gosh, she's in your league as a strategist, Jeeves.'

'She is a keen student of the individual, sir. She has known Miss Meadowes for a long time and is aware that for all her literary education she is impulsively warm-hearted.'

'And then the zonker cleared the way for me to replace Etringham.'

'Indeed, sir. The drink seems to have had the desired effect. His lordship was unaware that it was alcoholic.'

'That's the joy of the zonker. Tastes like a fruit cock-tail, kicks like a mule.'

'I hope that Mr Beeching will in due course entrust me with the recipe, sir.'

'I should hope so, too. But just to be clear on this, Jeeves. When Georgiana and I are married we'll live here in the week and go down to Melbury Hall most weekends. Would you and Mrs Tilman be happy with that arrangement?'

'It is most gracious of you, sir. We should be delighted. I imagine Mrs Tilman – or Mrs Jeeves as she will then be – would still be based in Kingston St Giles, while I shall spend more time in London. But there is ample accom-modation for her in my quarters here and of course at Melbury Hall . . .'

'You can have your pick of the rooms, Jeeves. No shortage. Avoid the fakir's couch.'

'Indeed, sir.'

'I still want to know one thing, though.'

'Yes, sir?'

'Why did you go to such lengths – all this plotting and planning? These risks and impersonations? Surely this was beyond the call of duty.'

'The reason is a simple one, sir. From the day I first met Miss Meadowes I formed a high opinion of her. I believed that if matters could be brought to a satisfactory conclusion your personal happiness could be guaranteed.'

'You mean, you did all this for me?'

'Yes, sir. Your previous entanglements with the fair sex have seldom ended happily. I had begun to think of you as one of life's bachelors. However, there was something about Miss Meadowes that was quite different from ... From ...'

'All the others? Bobbie Wickham? Florence Craye?'

'Indeed, sir. I was naturally aware that in many instances – such as that of Miss Madeline Bassett – you were acting only from a sense of chivalry. Nevertheless, it was generally a relief to all concerned when the engagement was terminated.'

'You're telling me, Jeeves. But are you saying that with Georgiana, rather than try to bung a spanner in the works . . . You played the willing . . . Who was the chap?'

'The willing Pandarus, sir.'

'Yes. But why, Jeeves, why? What can it have mattered to you?'

It occurred to me at that moment that the answer was obvious.

I looked down at the floor. I had begun to feel a slight pressure behind the eyes and an odd thickening of the throat – a sensation that took me back to the day I mentioned earlier, in the sickbay at school when I received the letter from home. Yet this time there was no sadness – quite the opposite, in fact.

When I looked up for an answer, I found that Jeeves had vanished. From the pantry I heard the sound of a cork being expertly drawn from a bottle of champagne.

I pulled myself together and stood up. From the open window there came the sound of motor-car horns in the street below.

Jeeves wafted in with tray, bottle and glasses. 'I think Miss Meadowes may have arrived, sir.'

As I crossed the room, I said, 'Jeeves. The side-whiskers. If you insist . . .'

'It is entirely a matter for you, sir. It is not my place to make any such personal recommendation.'

I looked out of the window down to where Georgiana was attempting to park her open-topped car, to the considerable alarm and amusement of the local populace.

She looked up towards my flat and her eyes met mine. A sudden smile irradiated her face as she waved up at me. My heart was beating so hard inside my chest I feared it would burst the buttons from my shirt.

Hello, old girl!

From *Aunts Aren't Gentlemen* to *Young Men in Spats*, there are myriad opportunities to spend more time with the characters that Wodehouse created. But choosing between more than ninety novels and some three hundred short stories can be a little daunting. The following titles were chosen by the P.G. Wodehouse Society as being among their favourites, and can be guaranteed an excellent place to start.

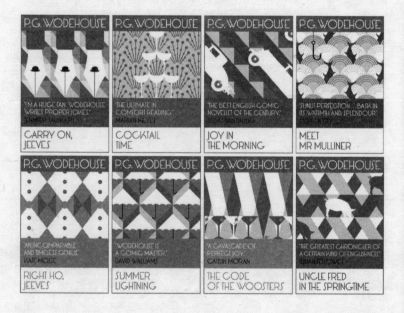

If you would like to become part of the Wodehouse community, please visit the official website: www.wodehouse.co.uk, become a fan on facebook: f/wodehousepage or join the P.G. Wodehouse Society: www.pgwodehousesociety.org.uk

Pip, pip,
Random House, proud publishers of Wodehouse

"I suppose we should get this over

Cumbria
County Council   cumbria.gov.uk/libraries

Library books and more......

C.L. 18F   24 hour Renewals 0303 333 1234

"I suppose we should get this over with so I might get a good night's sleep."

Without warning, Sebastian hoisted her up on the edge of the gate, causing her dress's hem to ride up her thighs. And while she made the appropriate adjustments, he climbed into the truck bed and had the nerve to position himself behind her, his long legs dangling on either side of hers. "Are you comfortable?" he asked as he circled his arms around her middle.

"No, I am not. I cannot have a decent conversation when I cannot see your face."

"You only have to listen to my voice."

Oh, that voice. That low, grainy bedroom voice that had enticed her on so many nights. And days. No matter how deep their conflicts had run, he had always been able to seduce her into submission.

Nasrin found herself leaning back against him, and turning her thoughts to the danger in succumbing to his power. "This is wrong, Sebastian," she said with little conviction.

"This is right, sweetheart. You're my wife."

* * *

In Pursuit of His Wife
is part of the Texas Cattleman's Club:
Lies and Lullabies series—Baby secrets and a
scheming sheik in Royal, Texas.